THE BLACKBIRD
& OTHER STORIES

THE BLACKBIRD
& OTHER STORIES

SALLY THOMAS

Wiseblood Books

WISEBLOOD BOOKS
P.O. Box 870
Menomonee Falls, Wisconsin 53052

Cover design by Amanda Brown
Cover art by Rachel Thomas
Typesetting by Louis Maltese

Printed in the United States of America
ISBN: 978-1-963319-95-8

CONTENTS

THE BLACKBIRD

A *set dance*, Miss Maggie said, meant that no matter who danced that dance, or where in the world, the steps were always the same. "If I walked into an Irish dance studio in Dublin," Miss Maggie said, "or in Mumbai, or in Cape Town, South Africa, or in Mexico City, and asked to see the Blackbird, I would see exactly the same thing everywhere I went."

At summer dance camp, they were dancing the Blackbird. The oldest girls, who knew it already, danced on the front row before the mirror, so that the younger girls behind them could watch their feet. The Blackbird, Miss Maggie told them, was a version of the hornpipe, which sailors were made to dance to strengthen their sea legs. That way they could walk the deck of a rocking ship and not fall down. When you danced the Blackbird, you crossed your ankles and rocked. It made sailors stronger; it would make you stronger, too. So Emlyn was learning.

In the mirror, the girls' upright bodies went up and down, piston-straight. Their feet in hard shoes clattered on the wood floor. Their stern faces looked back at them. Through the line of girls in front, Emlyn met her own reflected, uncertain hazel gaze. Catching herself looking at herself, she frowned harder. In Irish dance, Miss Maggie said, you never smiled. For the Irish, dance was a form of rebellion. Though the English had taken the people's religion away, even their very language, they couldn't stop the Irish from dancing. If you were Irish, Miss Maggie said, you could stand at a half-door, looking out at the street where English soldiers were passing by, and they would never know, from the stillness of your face and upper body, that your feet were dancing like mad behind the door. In this way, said Miss Maggie, you stuck it to The Man.

Every one of the Saint Patrick Dancers knew that this year Emlyn would dance the Blackbird in the Showcase, the number that closed each performance. Emlyn was only thirteen. Normally the set dance would belong to an older girl, the most senior dancer in the troupe. This year, however, there wouldn't be any truly senior dancers. Fiona, Kayleigh, and Carmen were going away to college. The twins, Sierra and Ashlynn, played on a traveling soccer team; they would be out till Christmas. That left a clutch of girls in the seventh, eighth, and ninth grades, who under ordinary circumstances would still be called intermediate dancers. Miss Maggie had had to move them up to senior positions.

In the meantime, still home, the college-bound dancers and the soccer players came to camp to help the younger girls. Emlyn and the others had to stand behind them, banging their hard shoes in unison, keeping time with the music and the flashing front-row feet in the mirror. If you blundered out of rhythm, you spoiled everything. Your feet weren't just feet; they were part of the music. If they went wrong, everything else went wrong, too. Emlyn frowned in concentration. Her feet kept time. Through a break in the line of front-row dancers, her own pale oval face scowled back at her. Stick it to The Man, she told herself.

Outside, the sun lay like a white weight over the parking lots. The dance studio occupied a storefront in a long shopping plaza that also contained a dollar store, a tag office, Chinese and pizza takeouts, and a barber shop where men sat all day, hiding from the heat. When Emlyn and her friend Lizzy passed the open door, they could hear the voices rise and fall, the barber's clippers sputtering to life. They passed the barber shop to get to the dollar store, where on camp break they were allowed to walk and buy snacks.

The littlest children, the ones still learning sevens and threes and the jig step, were not allowed to go out without Miss Maggie or a senior girl. Anyone in the group learning the Blackbird, however, could take a buddy to walk down the storefronts during these breaks. Emlyn and Lizzy were always buddies. It was Lizzy's mother who drove them to and from camp this summer, Lizzy's cheerful mother, whose silver Suburban smelled of leather seats and coffee, whose rosary swung from the rear-view mirror, who always asked Emlyn how her mother was feeling today.

"She's all right," Emlyn invariably said, the simplest reply.

Her mother did seem all right. Sick people, Emlyn had thought, lay in bed. You had to tiptoe around them and not disturb them, lest your noise startle them to death. Her mother was not in bed, at least not most of the time. Often, when Emlyn left for dance camp, her mother was outside, weeding her Mary garden in the sunny spot by the back door. In summer this garden bloomed with roses, lilies, rosemary, hot-pink rose campion with its velvety gray leaves. Marigolds grew like garish stars around the poured-concrete statue of Our Lady of Grace, who spread her hands out empty, as if to receive some offering. All Emlyn's life, her mother had spent summers weeding and tending that garden. Miss Maggie, her mother's friend, had given her the rose campion, a tiny sprig that had replicated itself even between the flagstones of the back walkway. Only when Emlyn's mother was in the hospital, through the long weeks of Lent, had she neglected her garden. The speedwell's frilled round leaves on their vining stems had grown up around the statue: tiny darling blue spring flowers, then a green obliteration. Now she was pulling weeds again. Her hair was growing in, shadowy, beneath her hat. When people asked, it seemed to Emlyn that to answer *she's all right* was to tell the truth.

Lizzy never mentioned Emlyn's mother. It was a relief to go with her from the studio, past the staring glass windows, under the overhang that shaded them from the sun, and into the dollar store. It was a relief to be greeted by the dollar store's ordinary, cheap smells: Pears Soap, floor wax, the sweat of the other hot people who came in to shop and, lately, the vague tang of stale pee not quite mopped up. An old man had wet himself and walked all around, up and down every aisle, not even knowing what he was looking for. The flabby-armed cashier in her green polo shirt told this story to everyone in the checkout line. It wasn't the first time he had wet those clothes, either. He had walked up and down, carrying his dried-pee stink with him and trailing new pee along the floor. Days later, the smell of his presence still lingered.

"Disgusting?" the cashier said, ringing up their box of knock-off Klondike Bars. "Honey, I'm telling you the truth. They ought not to let people like that out in public. That'll be one dollar and six cent." Her fat hands rustled their purchase into its plastic bag. Then she was talking to the person behind them in line. "Disgusting? Honey . . ."

Lizzy didn't mind that Emlyn was going to dance the Blackbird. She was a year older than Emlyn, but if she thought that Miss Maggie was being unfair, she never said so. Gaia, on the other hand, did say so. While they danced, Gaia's mother sat in the studio lobby in her blue batik harem pants and her long silky hair, scrolling through the internet on her phone. She didn't hear Gaia say, "It's just because your mother's Miss Maggie's friend. Everybody has to treat you like you're special. Your mother's sick, so we all have to feel sorry for you."

"Her mother is *not* sick," said Lizzy. "My mother asked Emlyn this morning, and Emlyn said she was fine."

"Then Emlyn's a liar," said Gaia.

This conversation took place on the back row, farthest from the mirror, in mutters beneath the music. All the while their feet flashed, their hard shoes rang out a treble reel.

"I don't tell lies," said Emlyn. "She's out right now weeding the garden." If not exactly truth, this was at least a plausibility.

"Whatever. You're behind the beat."

"No, you're ahead," said Lizzy.

Miss Maggie, broad and squat in her black jazz shoes and the big kelly-green camp t-shirt that covered her shorts, stood facing them at the front, like another reflection. The four-way medal at her throat shone silver as daylight. "Back row!" she called. "Keep up! Ba-da-bum ba-da-bum ba-da-ba--da-ba-da-bum!" She clapped as she spoke, and her auburn ponytail bobbed in the mirror. Gaia, keeping time, smirked at herself.

At home, Emlyn found her father reading in the living room. He had not turned on the lamp beside his chair. The light filtering through the drawn linen curtains gleamed in his glasses and hid his eyes. As the swinging door from the

5

kitchen creaked behind her, he glanced up, a quick white flash. "That you, Emmy? Enjoyed your Celtic endeavor?"

"It was all right," she said. "You know I'm dancing the Blackbird this year."

Her father turned a page in his book. "You might have mentioned that. Once or twice."

"You'll come see me, right?"

"I might." He turned another page.

After dancing all day, Emlyn was hungry, but nobody, it seemed, had given a thought to supper. Or to snacks, either. She had gone through the kitchen cabinets looking for crackers, potato chips, anything. "Where's Mama?" she asked.

"Mama's resting." Her father turned another page.

Emlyn tiptoed to the door of her parents' room. Ordinarily, when the door was shut, she would knock, or else just walk in. Today she didn't. She stood outside, holding her breath, listening. Could you hear someone breathing through a door? She couldn't hear anything. But then, before her mother got sick, had she breathed audibly through a closed door? Perhaps this was normal. It was hard to know anymore what was normal and what wasn't.

Theirs was an old house. Its two dormer windows, above the front porch, looked out like eyes into the crown of an oak tree. The backyard was all sun and marigolds and Our Lady of Grace. In the front yard, not much grew besides this tree. The grass beneath it threaded up thinly from the hard earth. Now, at the height of a dry summer, the oak's leathery leaves were curled in on themselves, the pale undersides showing. Still, they stirred and muttered outside the dormer in Emlyn's room. The tree was a living thing, a multitude.

Sometimes at night, after her parents had gone to sleep, Emlyn—who for some reason lately couldn't fall asleep— climbed out of her window to sit on the porch roof. Her parents thought that the window was painted shut, but she had worked at it, carefully and quietly, with a putty knife. Even at midnight, the porch shingles still held the day's heat, which soaked into her body as she sat with her knees drawn up, not thinking about anything in particular, not even really looking at the moon and stars, although of course they were there for her eyes to see. Before her, the tree stirred. On the ground below, its leaf-shadows, where the streetlight shone through, moved on the thin grass like a flock of feeding birds.

Now, though, in the hot afternoon, Emlyn lay on the floor beneath the ceiling fan and watched it turn above her. There were books on her shelf, but she didn't want to read them. She had a radio, but she didn't want music. She was hungry, still, but there was no point in going downstairs. She had already seen what wasn't in the refrigerator. Besides, she was strong. She was stronger than hunger. Lying on her back, she ran her hands down her torso, feeling her ribcage beneath her skin. She put her hands on her chest, where she was still flat. Beneath her sports bra, there were no fatty pads to scrunch in her fists, not yet. The sports bra was only to flatten out her nipples, those two rose-brown bites that dimpled up when she was cold or sweaty. Last year, Lizzy had been skinny like this: not hungry-skinny, but not-grown-up skinny. Now her thighs had fattened out. Her shorts fit more tightly across her behind. Beneath her dance t-shirt, her chest had two soft roundnesses that hadn't been there before. Her sports bra was to keep them from bouncing. Emlyn shuddered. Who wanted to *bounce*?

Through the floor she could hear her father walking around downstairs. The bathroom door shut, and the bolt clunked. A few minutes later, the toilet flushed. She heard his footsteps again, the creak of his chair as he sat back down.

Sometimes, listening, she found out things. She had found out recently, for instance, that her mother was anxious about her, Emlyn's, religion.

"I want you to take her to Mass," her mother had said.

Her father had said, "Of course I will."

"Will you really?"

"I take her now, don't I?"

It was true, he did take Emlyn to Mass. That was exactly what he did. He drove up to the church door, let Emlyn out, and said, "See you in an hour." Alone, she went into the cold foyer with the painting of the Sacred Heart, painted long ago by a girl of the parish who had entered a Carmelite monastery. When she was spoken of, it was only to remind the congregation that she was praying for them. Emlyn couldn't pass the painting without thinking of that girl, surely a woman by now, maybe even an old woman, shut away in silence, praying.

Emlyn tapped her fingers on the holy water in the font, crossed herself, and kissed her thumb, as she had seen all the Mexican girls do. She didn't know why they did it, that one extra little thing. But it seemed to add something to the act of crossing yourself, so she did it, too. Genuflecting at her pew, she repeated the action. Father. Son. Holy. Spirit. Thumb.

"I don't believe in it," Emlyn's father had told her, when asked why he didn't come to Mass himself.

"Then why do I have to go?"

"Because your mother wants you to, that's why. And it'll do you no harm. An hour of your young life, every week? You can manage that."

She turned on her side and put her ear to the floor. The wood was cool and satiny, its old finish worn in places to the bare boards. There were streaks and dashes of Sharpie marker where she had gone over the edge of the posterboard, making a school project. There were buttons of spilled oil paint from an art set her grandparents had given her for Christmas. There was dust gathered in slate-blue clouds along the baseboards, because nobody swept or vacuumed anymore. Through the floor, if she squeezed her eyes shut and listened with all her strength, she could hear the sigh of springs as her mother turned in bed.

"Miss Maggie feels sorry for you." Gaia was dancing furiously. "You're her little pet."

"Liar." Lizzy, between Gaia and Emlyn, danced harder.

"Bite me," said Gaia.

Lizzy brought out the next word daringly. "Bitch."

"Call me that again and I'll tell."

After that, Lizzy was silent, and frowned in concentration. Emlyn could see by her face in the mirror that she had decided to care about dancing.

Miss Maggie was clapping. "Keep up, girls! Listen to the music. Ba-da-ba-da-*bum*!"

Outside, the sun glared on the parking lot. Everything smelled of heat. The heat was a weight on their heads at break time, when they went outside, and the dollar store's air conditioning, damp and faintly musty, was a plunge into a pool. Emlyn and Lizzy walked side by side, their feet in flip-flops stepping over the cracks in the covered sidewalk. Their faces, arms, and legs shone with sweat.

"We're disgusting," Lizzy said. "I can't believe we go out in public like this."

After they had bought their ice cream, they stood outside to eat it and watch the cars pull in and out through the wavering heat. If you ran through those heat-shimmers, Emlyn wondered, would they scatter the way the water did when you ran through the sprinkler? If you looked at them from just the right angle, would you see a rainbow?

In the evening the nurse came, a guy named Scott, who looked as though he belonged in a fitness video, not in blue scrubs. Emlyn watched over the stair railing as he stood in the downstairs hallway talking to her father.

"She's sleeping more? How's her pain level? Has she used the morphine pump at all?"

Emlyn's father spoke in murmurs. Emlyn peered down at him. It was impossible, from upstairs, to hear his answers to any of these questions. After a moment he glanced up and saw her looking. "Excuse us, Emmy. We're having a grownup talk."

Scott said, "Hi, Emlyn. You okay?"

"Yeah."

"All right, then." He winked up at her. "If you weren't okay, you'd let me know, right?"

"I guess." Emlyn saw how the hall light prickled on Scott's dark hair. Then she went back to her room.

"Showcase!" Miss Maggie called. "Where's Emlyn? Front and center!"

"Break a leg." Gaia, who sat with her back against the wall, stretched out her own long legs so that Emlyn had to walk over them.

Sure enough, Emlyn stumbled over Gaia's feet as she went forward. Alone, she stood up before the great wall-sized mirror that showed the room behind her: bare wood floor, cinder-block walls, all the other girls sitting, waiting for their parts to begin. The fluorescent lights shone whitely down; one was flickering like distant sheet lightning. In the corner the big fan roared. She could feel it blowing at her back, stirring her hair.

The Showcase was called the Showcase because it demonstrated all the different steps an Irish dancer might do: jig, reel, hornpipe, the elegant slip-jig. But always the Showcase began with a set dance. This Showcase would begin with the Blackbird. Emlyn stood straight, chin up, shoulders back, fists clenched at her hips. In the mirror, her own face frowned back at her. *Stick it to The Man.* Miss Maggie started the music and counted her in. Emlyn began to dance.

Neatly her feet in the hard shoes tapped and shuffled and knocked on the hard floor. As long as she didn't think, she knew all the steps. Her feet crossed, and she rocked her ankles. Your ankles had to be strong to dance this dance. Like a sailor, you had to have sea legs. She held her own gaze in the mirror. Here and there, her feet danced on, intricate and tidy.

Then, as they crossed again, she thought about them. First her mind, then her feet, got tangled. She rocked too hard. Her ankle gave, and she was on the floor. The music went on without her.

"Ha ha," said Gaia behind her.

Miss Maggie had Emlyn by the hand. "It happens, girl. Don't sweat it. On your feet." Over her shoulder she added, "It could happen to anyone in this room. If you don't want to get laughed at when you fall down, don't laugh when it happens to somebody else." Her eyes found Gaia's. "Understood?"

Gaia nodded. She understood, all right. But when Miss Maggie looked away, she smirked at Emlyn in the mirror. The music began again. Frowning harder, Emlyn danced her way through the Blackbird. This time she didn't fall. When the music changed she turned and walked, chin high, to the wall where she had left her ghillies. As the littlest girls danced on to demonstrate sevens and threes, the basic reel steps, she sat down to change her shoes for the slip-jig.

Ear to her bedroom floor, she could hear Scott the nurse talking to her father. Then her mother's voice, querulous but muffled.

More loudly, so that Emlyn could hear, her father answered her mother. "Just use the goddamn morphine pump. Just for Christ's sake use it."

Then Scott's voice, low, soothing. Her mother crying, or coughing, or laughing. A yelping, hacking sound: it was hard to tell what it meant.

Emlyn went to the dormer window and looked out. The sun was going down, its molten light pouring through the oak leaves. Shadows moved on the grass like birds. Though it was early, and they were still awake downstairs, she raised the window and put her legs through, to sit on the sill with her feet on the hot porch roof. The heat seeping up through her tired legs felt good to her, like a bath. Between the trees and the steep roof of the house across the street, already bats were hurling themselves through the blue upper air. Their little twittering, the leaves' stirring, were part of the evening's great silence, which now Emlyn had entered. Sitting, she moved her feet softly in the steps to the Blackbird. Having done it over and over all day, if she could fall asleep she would dream it all night.

The previous Saturday, in line for Confession, she had stood behind a nun, a stranger, a tiny elderly lady in a knee-length skirt, her face a brown nut beneath her blue veil. Emlyn tried not to stare at her. Nuns didn't often turn up in their parish, but there she was, going to Confession like everyone else, leaning against the wall, eyes shut behind her black spectacles, praying a rosary. One by one, the beads slipped through her fingers. What would it be like, Emlyn wondered, to do nothing but pray? She thought of the girl who had painted the Sacred Heart picture in the foyer, who had gone in to pray and would never come out again.

Once, when she was younger, Emlyn had asked her mother whether heaven was like going to church, because if it was, she didn't think much of it. Her mother had laughed. Church was only a suggestion of what heaven was like, she had said. You would see God, but He wouldn't look like Communion wafers. He only looked like bread now, her mother had said, because if he showed himself as he really was, everyone who saw him would fall down dead at the sight.

As she waited in the Confession line, Emlyn considered the tabernacle, gleaming faintly gold behind the altar. God was in there, just as the priest was in the confessional. Over everything lay a dull, hushed Saturday-afternoon feeling. Even the little nun with her rosary had seemed not like a saint in heaven, almost, but only like any ordinary woman, tired, passing the time. She might have been waiting for a bus, not a sacrament. She hadn't looked as though she hoped that heaven would be better than church. When you were old, Emlyn thought, maybe the church experience started to grow on you, so that when it came to the heaven experience, you didn't expect much more than that. That nun had looked prepared to stand in line for the rest of her life, praying her rosary. Maybe eventually you stopped expecting anything at all.

At the end of dance camp, in the lobby with all the parents, Emlyn was gathering her shoes and her water bottle into her backpack when Miss Maggie called to her from inside the studio. When Emlyn came, Miss Maggie put her arms around her.

"Everything okay at home?" she asked.

Emlyn shrugged. "Yeah."

"I've got something to send your mother." Miss Maggie turned and rummaged in her big raffia tote bag. "Some Irish soda bread. And this little Saint Joseph medal. Look, it's vintage, really old. No telling how many hands have touched it. The stories it could tell." She pointed to the medal, newly polished and pinned to the blue ribbon tying up the big round raisin-studded loaf, shiny in Saran Wrap.

Emlyn took the loaf from her hands. Her mother had a

thousand Saint Joseph medals, almost as many as she had medals of Saint Peregrine, the patron saint of cancer. Ever since Emlyn's mother had gotten sick, people had been sending them to her. Saint Joseph, Emlyn knew, was the patron of families. He was also the patron of a holy death.

"Thanks," she said, though the gift wasn't meant for her. She ran to catch up with Lizzy. Together they went out into the late afternoon, the sinking white sun and the warm wet air. Outside, on the covered sidewalk, Gaia stood with her mother. She was crying.

Gaia's mother circled her in her arms. She stroked Gaia's fine light hair. "Sweetheart. Sweetheart."

"I hate her." Lizzy stood with her hand on the back door of her mother's car. "What a bitch. She thinks she's better than everybody else."

But as they pulled away, Emlyn watched Gaia's mother hold her and stroke her hair.

The sun was down now. The first star shone on the sky. It was a planet, really: Venus, white and steady. Or perhaps it was Jupiter, which came up with the moon at this time of year, like a child with its mother, near but apart. Where was the moon, though? Of course the moon went dark for part of each month; could Jupiter come up without it? With a pang, Emlyn remembered the big white Irish soda bread, tied up with ribbon, the medal pinned on. She had left it in Lizzy's mother's car.

Sitting in her window, she watched Scott emerge from the porch and descend the front steps, carrying what looked like a toolbox, with his medical things inside. His feet in running shoes went across the crisp thin summer grass.

Though she looked after him until it seemed that her gaze would burn the hair off the back of his head, he didn't turn around to see her sitting there. He didn't ask again if she was okay. If he had asked, she might have answered boldly this time, "What do you think?" Or she might have shrugged and said again, "I guess." But he didn't see her, and he didn't ask. Stowing his toolbox in the trunk of his little car, he got into it and drove away.

In the twilight, with the bats still swooping and the first fireflies blinking through the oak branches, Emlyn's feet moved again on the warm roof. Barefoot, she stood up and tried a little hornpipe step, brush and tap. Then, with the music in her head, she danced all the steps to the Blackbird. It was a set dance; you couldn't change the choreography. If you went into any Irish-dance studio in the world and asked to see the Blackbird, always, always, you would see the same steps. Now, though, Emlyn was dancing in a studio of her own making, an unseen roof studio, open to the sky. She could add steps. She could change the dance. Dancing faster, she began to improvise a little, breaking up the rhythm with a jig step, a bit of a reel, seven and three. Then back into the Blackbird, rocking her ankles, frowning, sticking it to The Man.

Above her, the sky rocked, too. Beyond, below: the tree, the thready grass, the hard earth. The roof was the deck of a ship, and she was a sailor, dancing to gain her sea-legs. Tap and shuffle. Cross and rock. Up and down went the vast sea of the sky. Up and down went the roof. Up and down went the ground below, shadowed and stirring now like the depths of the ocean. A little dry wind touched her face and hair. Tap and scuff, cross and rock. There was nothing now but the music in her mind, the enormity of the coming night, the very infinity of God who did not really look like bread, God who might at any moment toss you high on some swell, then let you fall. Up and down went the roof. Up and down went the ground. Up and down went the air, the sky, the tree. As long as Emlyn didn't think, her feet knew all the steps. Shuffle and tap, cross and rock. Through shifting leaves she met the sky's gaze and did not look away.

Somewhere in the gathering night, a door slammed. A voice was calling. *Sweetheart, sweetheart.* Emlyn kept dancing. In the little kicked-up breeze, oak leaves were scattering like startled wings. With them, Emlyn was dancing the Blackbird. She was a blackbird, flying. Her feet moved between roof and air, warm and liquid. Leaving the set dance behind, again she danced a step of her own invention. As long as she kept not thinking, her feet kept knowing what to do. She danced to the edge of the roof. Before her, all the open air wavered, full of light and shadow. In another instant she might step out onto it and go dancing among the leaves, a bird on the wing. Again, somewhere in the evening, the voice was calling. *Sweetheart!* Whose voice? Whose sweetheart? As she crossed her ankles again and rocked, she thought about her feet. First her mind, then her feet, got tangled. Out there, below her, beyond the edge of the roof, the shadowy yard stirred, light on water. For an instant, on that edge, Emlyn wavered. All the air opened before her: flashes of light, dark wings. *Sweetheart,* the distant voice called.

She staggered back and sat down hard on the hot shingles. The wind went on without her. Her sweaty legs were shaking, her whole mortal finite wingless body. This time there was no Miss Maggie to put out her hand. There was nobody to say, *It happens, girl.* There was nobody to still the laughter, nobody even to laugh. She was alone with her shaking legs, her salty lips, her knocking heart. Below, the shadows fed like blackbirds on the grass. The light's last bright medals glanced among the leaves. The voice in the evening called its sweetheart home.

DOING WITHOUT

Caroline awoke in the dark. Cash had unspooned himself and gotten out of bed. Her back was cold. Struggling up from the pillows, she saw him standing at the window, peering around the edge of the curtain.

"What?" she said.

Cash held up his hand. "Shush a minute."

"What time is it?"

"I said shush. I'm trying to listen."

Caroline rolled over and looked at the clock: just past four, on a morning in the week between Christmas and New Year's, dark as dark as dark. Lying back on her pillows, Caroline listened to the silence, straining to hear the little watch-ticking noise that meant sleet. Usually weather was what Cash got up to see.

After a moment she whispered, "I don't hear anything."

Cash glanced at her. "No? Listen. I keep thinking I hear footsteps."

"Inside?" Caroline's whisper was shrill with alarm.

"No, out there. On the driveway. Listen."

Obedient, she listened. Their bedroom, on the south side of the house, abutted a narrow plot of raised-bed gardens, tangled now in their winter neglect. If she closed her eyes, she could see the asparagus fronds coated in opaque frost, impossibly fragile. Beyond the garden beds lay the narrow gravel drive with its deep puddled ruts. Cash was always about to have it leveled and re-graveled. Now, as she strained to hear what he heard, she thought she did catch some sound, a crisping and scuffling, as of someone walking among fallen leaves.

She sat up. "Do you see anything?"

Cash shook his head.

"Well, it can't really *be* somebody. The dog would bark." As if in reply, her brindled dog Fisher, on his bed in the corner, whimpered in his sleep. His paws twitched.

Cash said, "That dog would bark *if* he felt like it."

He had not approved the acquisition of the dog. It had been Caroline who, never thinking to consult anyone, had gone impulsively to the shelter one day, chosen this large unhelpful animal, and brought him home.

"Well," she had said, "I need the company. The house is too empty."

"Why didn't you start a book club, then?" said Cash.

But Caroline had wanted something more constant and more devoted than a book club. Anyway, the company of women tired her. And she had never had a dog. She had felt that if she were ever going to have a dog, before it was too late, she had better act swiftly. Now the consequence of her swift action twitched his paws again and yelped, blowing out his lips. Cash grunted.

"Why don't you come back to bed?" said Caroline.

"I'm wide awake now. I think I'll go read in the den."

Caroline lay down again, but now she too was wide awake. She heard Cash switch on a lamp and settle himself into his leather recliner with a sigh not unlike the dog's. He coughed twice. His cough was a bark.

"Are you all right?" she called.

"It's just this tickle in my chest like I have sometimes." He coughed again.

The house was so quiet she could hear him turn a page in his book. She closed her eyes, but now that she wasn't trying, she kept hearing, too, that scuffle in the leaves she'd left unraked, back in the fall. A raccoon? A possum? The wind kicking up?

"Cash Mallory," she called.

"Yes ma'am?"

"I hear it."

"Told you."

"You don't think it's *somebody*, do you?"

"You said the dog would bark."

"Well, but." Again she sat up. This time she flung back the covers, gasping a little. The room was cold. Groping around, she found her thick woolly cardigan and thrust her arms into it, buttoning it over her nightgown. Feeling with her feet, she located her slippers. Then, as Cash had done, she went to the window and pulled aside the drawn linen curtains.

At first she saw only darkness. Then, as her eyes adjusted, the house next door appeared, a sloping blackness on the sky. She stared at the driveway until she could make out the sheen of puddles in the ruts, the stiff stalks of kale gone to bolt. Rustle rustle went the leaves. But she saw nothing more.

As she turned from the window, letting the curtains fall to, the dog jerked awake. Snorting, he raised his head. His tail whacked the wall. When she left the room, he rose and followed her, click click click. She went into the den and found Cash in his chair. He looked up impatiently from his book. "What are you doing out of bed?"

"I hear it now," she told him. "And it's kind of giving me the weeby-jeebies."

"I looked for a long time, and I didn't see a thing. Must just be the wind."

"I know. It's just, you know, I can't help thinking. What if—"

Cash looked at her hard, with what she privately called his *prosecution rests* expression, though he was a corporate lawyer who wrote contracts and never went to court. It was silly what she thought sometimes, silly and childish. Still, she thought it.

"Don't," Cash said now. "Don't even start."

Caroline stiffened. "Start what?"

"Whatever in your mind you're fixing to start." His gaze returned to his book. "Better just not even think about it."

For something to do, then, Caroline went to the kitchen, the dog at her heels. Her hands were shaking, and she had to take hold of the counter and breathe deeply, in on a count of four, out on a count of eight, before she could begin making coffee. So what that it wasn't yet five in the morning? They were up now. She wanted the business of coffeemaking, the warm smell, the wincing pleasure of the first black mouthful. She wanted to focus her whole mind on the measuring-out.

But even coffee was an ambush. It brought so many things back, a whole scene. John's roommate had made coffee, that girl, his law-school classmate. It was a kind enough thing to do. Here were John's parents, Cash and Caroline, summoned halfway across the country in the dark icy midwestern January. What could the roommate do about any of that? Nothing, except make coffee.

In spitting snow they had gone to his apartment, to see about his belongings: his duvet, his books, his ascetical clothing. In his bedroom, Caroline had picked things up, put them down. They might have been anyone's; she couldn't even tell that they smelled like him. What had he smelled like? Already she had forgotten.

Understandably, the roommate had felt intruded upon. "He always kept to himself," she told them, in a spirit of some defensiveness, as she handed them coffee in mugs that were none too clean. It was the thing people said about serial killers, not ordinary young men. Furthermore, she had used, without hesitation, the past tense, the tense for speaking of the indisputably dead. No, the roommate hadn't endeared herself. But then she hadn't wanted to. She had wanted them to go away.

"There's all this food," the girl had added, as Caroline and Cash prepared to take their leave. "It's his, not mine. There's like a year's supply of Ramen. What should I do with it?"

Caroline had stared at her. Did people who planned to jump off bridges buy a year's supply of food? She had turned to Cash then, some exclamation welling on her lips.

But Cash had only said, "Eat it. Or donate it to a food pantry." The police didn't need to see a cabinet full of boxes. Ramen wasn't *evidence*. It wasn't even a clue. And honestly, that girl had looked as if she could use it.

"I doubt she could cook much else," Cash had said later. "She didn't seem like the type."

That girl, Caroline thought now, sweeping spilled coffee grounds into her hand and casting them into the sink. The apartment had stunk of garbage not taken out, and of a cat's litter box. The good scent of fresh coffee had not been able to hide the other, more revelatory smells. The girl herself of course had been well-turned-out enough, considering that they had descended on her without warning, bearing their load of panic and despair. She had said, if not the right things, then the things a twenty-two-year-old girl in law school might reasonably be expected to say. To her, clearly, *loss* meant your rank in the class, failure to make the law review. Secondarily, it might mean breaking up with a boyfriend. There her personal comprehension petered out. But, Caroline supposed, she had tried.

Caroline had met girls like this before. During Cash's long career in the law, she had met them over and over. She had been chatted up by them at firm Christmas parties: junior associates in floppy bow ties and blazers, then later in sheath dresses. These days they even wore trousers. The costume changed, but the persona stayed the same, smiling a little pityingly at Caroline, who clutched her wine glass by its stem.

"You don't live in Charlotte?" the persona asked her. "You live out—where, now?"

Patiently, almost apologetically, Caroline would name her town.

The persona would regard her with polite disbelief. "But what is there to *do* out there?"

"Oh, well," Caroline would demur. "Not much, really. But it's a nice place to live. It's a good place to bring up children."

Again the bright, intelligent lipstick smile. The persona had seen the family photos in Mr. Mallory's office, the evolution of Caroline, Amelia, and John over many years. "And you didn't work? At *all*?"

"Well, no, not really." Caroline would study the toes of her pumps, which pinched her. To these affairs she was always fated to wear her least comfortable shoes. "The house and the children felt like a full-time job. I don't know how I would have had time for anything else."

"But," the persona might say, "did you do *without?*"

Without what, Caroline always wondered. What had she done without, that she would have missed in the slightest? It was true that they'd chosen a house in a small town, where the cost of living was cheaper. They could never have afforded a house that size in the city—not starting out, anyway. We bought it because we could, she had sometimes told people. But we stayed because we liked it.

"No," she would say in bewilderment, "We never did without anything we really *needed.*"

Through all those parties she had been looking forward to Christmas. The parties, dull and necessary as they were, had been the prelude to something lovely, the wave that lifted her toward it. Always, as she stood drinking wine, her mind had been ticking over her shopping list, organizing her menu. She never remembered the names of those young women who came to talk to her. She hardly knew what she said to them. It didn't matter. There were children in her house. Later, there were grown children coming home. In imagination, wherever she happened to be, she dwelt on the gifts she had chosen for Amelia and John, the meals she planned to cook. Every year she brooded with care over the joy to come.

And then, before the joy had time to take root in her, it was over. In January she would come to, in the dreary infancy of another year, and think, *What happened to all that?* Always, always, the beautiful moments had evaporated in shopping, cooking, worrying. She had meant to treasure her children. She had meant not to let them slip through her fingers. But they had gone from her.

That year, Amelia had left the day after Christmas, with a wave of her hand and a crunch of gears. She had had a graduate-school paper to write, a party to go to, somebody she was maybe sort of seeing who wanted to see her, or something. Caroline never did get the story straight. But John had stayed on with them through New Year's Day, long enough to help Caroline take down the tree and carry the decorations back to the attic. That was what she remembered: standing on a chair, handing ornaments down to him, while the dry needles shook loose and rustled to the floor. Had that been a beautiful moment? Well, she had often reproved herself, it's a moment I had. I should have thought it was beautiful.

"I remember this," John had kept saying as he put the fragile things into their tissue wrappings. This angel. This star. This paper Santa Claus I made in kindergarten. Of this last item he had said, "I can't believe you still put that thing on your tree."

"Well." She had smiled. "You made it for me, remember? It's a keepsake. I look at it and think of little old you."

"That's good."

She had noticed nothing unusual in his voice. There had been no sign to read in his tousled hair as he bent over the boxes, no subtext to anything he had said or done. Not that she'd been looking for it. Putting the boxes away, with their rustling tissue and their piney, cinnamony Christmas-candle smells, she had thought, See you all next year. She had felt only the usual pang, nothing more.

"See you soon," she had said to him, standing in the cold beside his packed car. What else would she have said? Along the drive, she remembered, the hollies had bent, dark and glossy, beneath the weight of their berries, brilliant in the gray day, unexpected as the sight of your own blood. But why unexpected? You knew what was inside you. You knew that a cut would bleed. Still, that sudden crimson, welling up, could make your knees wobble. John had put his arms around her, squeezed her so hard she'd thought her ribs would crack. Then he had gotten into his car and driven away. She had stood waving in front of the house. Then she had gone back inside.

All that Christmas, Caroline had been worrying about Amelia, not John. Amelia, always bristling, sparking with energy and the promise of outrage, had seemed tuned up just then into a different key altogether. Maybe it was graduate school, Caroline had thought, or else it was this person she was maybe, possibly seeing. Something had altered her vision, anyway, like a filter on a camera, to render everything about her home in a gloomy one-note sepia.

On Christmas Day, after Caroline had set the table for dinner, Amelia had come along and reset it, changing out the Spode Christmas Tree dishes for the everyday white ironstone, laying these on a black tablecloth she had produced from someplace. Had she bought it especially to bring home? Had she kept it hidden in her suitcase, to whip out at this moment? Or was it something she used every day, in that unseen life she led, and couldn't bear to be without, even now? Caroline certainly had never owned a black tablecloth.

"There," Amelia had said, strewing handfuls of glitter

down the table. "Don't you like that better?"

Caroline had hesitated. Clearly there was a right answer here, and a wrong one. "It's very *striking*," she had said at last. She knew better than to mention what cleaning up glitter was like.

Amelia had lit the plain white tapers, and in their wavering light, the table had shimmered starkly, black ice in headlights. "I don't think we should be sentimental about Christmas."

"Well, no."

Yet Caroline had wondered. If you couldn't be sentimental about Christmas, what could you be sentimental about? And if you weren't sentimental, how else were you supposed to feel? To her Christmas had seemed the one time of the year when you could reliably let your guard down, your foolish feelings show. If Amelia wanted to take away even that, what would be left? Already she had searched out her own paper Santas and stars from the ornament box and had burned them in the charcoal grill on the patio. Nothing left of those little inconsequential memories but ash.

Watching her from the kitchen window, Caroline had wanted to weep, and had steeled herself against the feeling. People talked of the *terrible twos,* but Caroline would have given her very soul to be back there again, watching a child throw herself to the floor screaming because she'd been handed the wrong color cup. What nobody talked about were the *terrible twenties.*

All through the holiday, Caroline had observed Amelia minutely at every opportunity. There was Amelia's hair, cut short as a boy's in a way that seemed to flaunt her angular face, a defiance presenting itself to you every time she turned around. There were Amelia's skinny legs in leggings—well, *I* would feel naked in pants like that, Caroline thought, but I guess she can carry them off. There was Amelia on her laptop, emailing someone continually and secretively, with a look on her face that said, Oh, my God, get what my mother is doing *now*. There was Amelia, who did study psychology, after all, taking every word anybody uttered and turning it around: *What I hear you saying is.* What Amelia heard Caroline saying was, somehow, never what Caroline had meant to say.

Only afterward, when it was too late, had Caroline preoccupied herself with John. She had examined all her memories of him for signs of trouble. He had looked thin, but surely that was a function of studying hard. He had seemed quiet, but when had John not been quiet? He hadn't called anyone to go for a beer, but John had never been a bon vivant. Anyway, the holidays always passed so quickly. You never had as much time as you expected, or needed, to do all the things that you wanted. And then it was over. You could never call it back again. All you could do, in the wake of what you'd lost, was to resolve to notice, better, what was already gone.

"Yes, I *have* gone to grief counseling, thank you very much," she had been able to tell Amelia on the phone. *So there.* Because she had been to grief counseling, she understood that when you felt whatever it was, the terrible feeling, rising like a tide around you, you could save yourself by noticing something real. You trained your mind on your hand, for example, or the couch, or a flower, any material thing in the world outside you. *Mindfulness*: that was the word the grief counselor had taught her. Caroline, however, looking at her hand, asked herself, *Is* that there? What if I am a dream? What if I'm nothing but somebody's thought?

In the dark kitchen, the coffeemaker hawked, spat, and beeped three times. Pouring out into two mugs, Caroline savored the crisp hot splash. Outside, the wind had risen. The overgrown holly scratched at the window, making her jump. Again she heard the sound that had awakened Cash: the scuffling in the leaves, as of footsteps.

Dog at her heels, she carried Cash's coffee into the den. "I heard it again."

"Heard what?" He accepted the coffee without thanks.

"That noise."

"What? Oh, *that* noise."

She waited while he slurped at his coffee. He loved the first sip, too. He was the one who had taught her to love it. When they married, she hadn't been a coffee drinker. Now she couldn't imagine the day without it.

He set his mug down. "It's the wind. And the leaves. It's what we get for not raking up *all* those leaves last fall." He coughed again wetly. "Boy, I tell you. This tickle in my chest. It just *will* not go away. *Aggravating?*"

"You could go to the doctor," she said.

"For a little tickle in my chest? Come on. It's just the cold. And the weather coming in, like the news said."

Just the cold. That's what you told me last fall, when you had the same cough and couldn't rake the leaves, she thought but did not say. Christmas Day, calling home, Amelia had been worried. Amelia was married now, to Michael, whoever he was exactly. Though of course there had been a wedding, with photographs, Michael remained a mystery. All Caroline knew was that Amelia didn't come home for the holidays. "We both have to work, Mother," Amelia had told her. "We get today off, that's all. It's not worth it." Caroline might have bridled at *not worth it*, but before she could work up her indignation, the conversation had shifted.

"I don't like that cough Daddy has," Amelia had said. "Make him see a doctor, Mother."

"Well, darling." You try making Cash Mallory see a doctor, Caroline had thought, but she was careful not to say it aloud.

"That's not my job," Amelia would have said, and Caroline would have heard her *boundaries* clanging into place. Amelia put great stock in *boundaries* these days. There was much you couldn't say to her, nothing you could expect.

"How is Michael?" Caroline had asked perfunctorily.

"He's fine."

"Well," said Caroline, "that's good." After that the conversation had petered out, and Caroline had hung up feeling like an empty house, all its windows dark. That had been Christmas this year, a phone call, come and gone with a click and a silence.

The dog shoved his nose against her hand and moaned, deep in his chest. When Caroline glanced down, there he was, gazing up at her with ardent eyes.

"It's not breakfast yet," Caroline said. "Can't you tell time?"

He moaned again, with greater urgency. No, he couldn't tell time. The people were up, that was all. The coffee ritual triggered his own morning routine. Sighing, Caroline went to the back door to let him out.

In the doorway, he hesitated, sniffing the air.

"I know it's cold," said Caroline. "But it's too late to

change your mind. Just *go.*"

With reluctance, still sniffing, he ventured onto the back porch. After another moment's hesitation, he descended the steps, turned into the back-door flower bed, and, hugging the side of the house, peed copiously onto a camellia. Then, with haste and bustle, he trotted back up the steps and into the kitchen, taking up his position over his food bowl.

Caroline crossed her arms. "It's five in the morning, you loopy dog. You really want to eat now?"

He bulged his eyes at her and wagged his tail. Dutifully Caroline fetched his scoop of kibble.

As she crossed the hall again to the den, she paused to listen. Outside, the leaves shuffled. The metal gate to the side yard groaned.

"*Cash Mallory.*"

"What?"

"Don't you hear it?"

"I hear it. It's some front coming in."

"Is somebody out there? Or not?"

"You let the dog out, didn't you? Did he act like there was anybody out there?"

"Well, no. But. He's acting kind of, you know. What if it's not a *person*, Cash? What if it's—I don't know—" She looked to him for help. Please understand what I'm talking about. Please help me say it.

Resting his book on his knee, Cash regarded her as from the opposite edge of some vast chasm. Even across that distance, she could read his mind. He didn't understand and wasn't about to help her say it. She made no sense. How could she?

"Look, Caroline," he said at last. "I thought I heard something, but I didn't. What I mean is, I heard the wind. For a minute it sounded like somebody walking, but it wasn't."

"You thought it was. It got you out of bed."

"I was wrong."

"Cash," she began, but he held up his hand to silence her.

"Listen to me. I'm sorry I got you up. I'm sorry I got you all *worked* up. But I'm here to tell you the truth. Whatever you're thinking: don't. It's just not possible."

She folded her arms on her chest. "*What's* not possible? And how do you know?"

"I just know. You need to for goodness sake let *go*."

"You sound like Amelia. And can't either one of you make me." Caroline turned on her heel and went back into the bedroom, followed by the dog. He couldn't make her, either. All he could do was not let her out of his sight.

Now he circled and collapsed onto his bed with a grunt. Setting her coffee on the nightstand, Caroline went to the curtained window. This time she didn't pull the curtain aside. She knew what was out there, and what wasn't. So she told herself. On the driveway with its frozen puddles and its scurf of leaves: that was where they had first heard it, whatever it was. Cash had said it was footsteps. He had thought so. But she was the crazy one who couldn't let go. Even if it was nothing, only the wind, still it was out there. She felt it. It watched them, maybe, when they weren't paying attention. Even if it was nothing, the thought made her shiver.

She put her eye to the crack in the curtain and peered out. Above the trees and roofs, the sky was starting to flush rose and gold, the colors brilliant with the clarity of winter. If a storm had been brewing, it had blown itself out in the dark. Likely, she thought, the weatherman had been wrong. If he told you it was going to snow, you made your dutiful trip to the grocery store for milk, bread, and toilet paper, but you also prepared yourself for nothing to happen. There was something cheerful in the frenetic rush to be ready for a storm, a letdown when it didn't happen, and life went on just the same, unvaried by emergency. In a way, it was a relief. In another way, you were sorry.

Clearly now she could see the gray gravel drive, the brick wall beyond it that divided their property from the neighbors'. The wind was stirring. She could hear it rattle the stalks of banana pepper and tomato that she hadn't bothered to pull at the first frost, all the way last fall. It was an empty sound. Out there, the drive was empty. The new day cresting over the empty treetops: empty. What she had hoped, or feared, or both, had melted away into the morning.

What if I'm left with this, she asked herself. What if this is it, for the rest of my life? But what did she mean by *this?* Was *this* simply a matter of waking every day to absence, and steeling herself to keep doing it? Turning her mind to things of this world, insisting to herself that they were real and she could trust them? Not believing a word of it?

What do you *do* out there, all those young women had asked at all those law-firm parties. And the answer, the real one, which Caroline had not vouchsafed to any living soul, was this: I love my children. It was real, an occupation and a satisfaction. It was *not* nothing. So she had thought at the time. She had taken pleasure, even pride, in the thought, in its very secretness, like a baby growing inside her, unknown to anyone but her. All those years, it had been her joy and hope. Now what did she have to cherish? A taciturn man, a dog. Her daughter hanging up the phone. The wind outside.

Until Cash put his hands on her shoulders, she didn't know that she was crying. She had thought she was out of tears forever, but apparently the supply was inexhaustible. Apparently, too, they came so naturally to her that she could taste them on her lips and not know what it was that she tasted.

"It'll be all right," Cash said. Through her cardigan and nightgown she felt his fingers tighten on her clavicle. "It'll be all right."

"If you say so."

"It really did sound like footsteps. It's not just you. I thought so, too."

"That's not what I'm crying about."

"Well," said Cash, "I didn't think it was." After a moment he turned her around and pressed her to him, rubbing his chin in her hair.

Her body resisted. Though he pulled her close, she held back, stiffening, maintaining a span of air between them. "You know it won't be all right," she said.

In the silence, she could feel him breathing into her hair. A warmth, then nothing. Then warmth again.

"That's what we thought," he told her. "In the beginning, that's what we thought."

"It's what we *know*."

"That we'll never be happy again? But *aren't* we still happy, just a little bit? Sometimes? In spite of ourselves?"

"I don't know," she sobbed. "How can we be?"

He sighed, a long, sad warmth. "I think we just have to be. I don't know how. Maybe we just have to let it sneak up on us, and not worry about how to make it happen. Just be surprised by it."

"I don't like surprises."

"I know you don't."

"I don't have to like them. I don't have to smile and say, *Isn't this wonderful?* When it's not."

Caroline pushed Cash from her and ran her hands through her hair. The vehemence of her own voice, and of the hatred which welled up in her now in place of tears, made her gasp—hatred for Cash himself, hatred hard and black and implacable. Hatred because Cash *was*, here and now, incarnate.

"*Don't* you, whatever you do," she said, "tell me how I'm supposed to think and feel. Do you hear me? *Don't.*"

Cash stepped back as if she had struck at him. "I won't. I don't."

"Good." She scrubbed at her eyes with the heel of her hand. "Don't."

"I love you, Caroline." His voice shook. "That's something. Isn't it?"

"Yes. It's something." Not enough, she did not say. Still, her anger fell from her. Suddenly she was exhausted. She leaned on Cash again and felt his warmth.

For a while they stood together, watching, for lack of something better, the blank drawn curtains through which the rising light was steadily filtered. Just outside the window, a cardinal called: *chip chip chip chip chip*, a pebble of sound striking the clear window of the air. In the cold, would anyone answer him? Did he mind that the spell he wove, of love, longing, and desire, would not so much be broken, there in the small of the year, as simply run down, peter out, give up its sweet red ghost?

Listening, too, Cash smiled. "Hear him, now. What is it about a bird in winter?"

"They're here all year. They'll eat up the holly berries." Caroline wiped her eyes again. Not for the last time. Just maybe the last time for now. "Let me make you some breakfast," she said to Cash.

THE COOL OF THE EVENING

They went away in the old blue Plymouth. Wren's grandfather peered angrily over the dashboard as he drove. Every day he and Wren's grandmother drove into town for the
noon Mass, which was almost the only place they went any
more. Mass, the grocery store, the beauty parlor. If Wren's
grandmother wanted to go somewhere, Wren's grandfather
had to carry her there in the car. Nobody in Memphis knew
how to drive, her grandfather said. They didn't tell you they
were going to turn. They didn't signal with their arm out
the window. You had to look for some little blinking light,
and by the time you saw it, it was almost too late. The Plymouth had manual steering, and her grandfather dragged the
wheel this way and that as though he meant to wrestle the
car to the ground.

They passed the Esso filling station, the last outpost of
Wren's neighborhood, and bumped over railroad tracks.
Fleetingly Wren saw the leafy corridor the track ran through,
May-green, gold-lit, full of stirring shadows in the spring
daylight, not a place in itself but a secret going-away to
some other, more real place. Always, no matter how many
times she crossed those tracks, this flash of secretness made
the hair stand up on her arms. From your car at the crossing,
if you looked fast enough, you glimpsed that green tunnel
curving into mystery. Then you left it behind.

Today the secret feeling seemed to go with her. Right
now, as she rode in that car, her fourth-grade class was taking their Monday-afternoon spelling test. She was not tak-

ing the test. She was not wearing her blue-and-green plaid gym jumper over her peter-pan-collared gym shirt and black stretch shorts. She was wearing regular shorts, with yellow smiley faces printed all over them, and a matching smiley t-shirt, as if this were a vacation. She had not brushed her hair. Her mother had not thought to tell her to brush it, and now it hung down her back in rough waves, with tangles underneath that would hurt to comb out. She might have dreamed school; it felt that unreal. When she was at school, all she wanted was to be not at school. But now that she was not at school, something in her longed, just a little, for the vanilla smell of the ditto sheet on which the week's test would be printed out in purple. Meanwhile, the familiar streets of East Memphis were sliding by, strange to her all over again because she did not usually see them at this time on a weekday.

Wren's father liked blues music, songs about trains. Often he played them for Wren while she ate her breakfast or did her homework, sometimes when she didn't want to hear a song. He was like that, singing to you, urging his gift on you so you couldn't refuse it. This was one of the things Wren's mother couldn't stand. She liked to say no. There was a song Wren's father liked to sing, about catching a train to Vicksburg. Where was Vicksburg? Wren imagined that it lay at the end of that May-green tunnel the trains she knew ran through. *Going to Vicksburg,* the song said. *Going to Vicksburg in the cool of the evening.* Her father liked to whisper that phrase, under the voice of the guitar that went on and on like a train's wheels, carrying him someplace in his mind, until her mother told him to knock it off.

"A few days," Wren's mother had said, tapping her cigarette into the red metal ashtray. They had had a whole set of these ashtrays, red, yellow, green, and blue, metal trays with beanbag bottoms that kept them anchored to a tabletop. Suddenly, though, this red one was the only ashtray left in the world. "Maybe a week. Just till I get things figured out."

Wren had looked about her at boxes, empty bookshelves, the cabinet that had housed her father's stereo, a glowing entity of knobs and dials, bearing the mystical name *MARANTZ*. The piano was gone. Her mother had said that it was cheaper to buy another one than to move the one she had.

"Why can't I help figure things out?" Wren had said.

Her mother had turned on her then, the way she did sometimes. "Because you can't, that's why."

She had seemed animated just then, alight with something that might have been anger or might have been joy. She was *ferocious,* Wren had thought. That was it. She had been dumping books into boxes as if she meant the books harm. She shook back her long hair, so straight it sliced the air as it swung.

"I know, Grandaddy," Wren's grandmother said. "Let's us stop at the TG&Y."

"What on earth do you need at the Tee, Gee, And Why, Virginia?" That was her grandfather's way of talking, to turn single letters into whole words.

"Well, you know, we can find us some kind of little teen-einsy something."

Wren bounced on the back seat. "Last time I was in there with Mama, they had a monkey on the pet aisle."

"I'm not buying a monkey," said her grandfather.

"Maybe they'll have a little *stuffed-animal* monkey," said her grandmother.

In the makeup aisle, Wren fingered the eyeshadow cray-ons with longing. Blue, her mother wore, and some of her cousins. She wondered what it would feel like to draw that shimmering color on her own skin.

"Darling, that's not for little girls," her grandmother called. "Looky, I found this thing." Peeping around the end of the aisle, she held up a troll doll with a hard plastic dent for a navel, a gush of green hair. "Don't you think he's right cute? Or ugly, I'm not sure which," she added, holding him at arm's length and squinting through her cat-eye glasses.

"Come *on,* Virginia." Wren's grandfather stood at the checkout counter consulting his pocket watch: gold, with a thin lid that sprang open at some secret touch of his thumb-nail.

There was nothing Wren really wanted in all the TG&Y. Eyeshadow was not for little girls. The monkey was sold, or dead. She accepted the troll doll, watched it be paid for, and carried it dutifully out to the parking lot in the palm of her hand.

"I declare, the toys get funnier and funnier-looking," her grandmother said. "*Car,* Grandaddy!"

"I see it, doll baby."

They drove south, out Getwell road, going away from town toward Mississippi. Gradually the neighborhoods gave way to fields, with here and there a little house held up, it looked like, by the tar paper tacked to its outside. If she lay back and shut her eyes, Wren could feel when they turned into their own road: an easing down, a sigh beneath the wheels, the darknesses that were trees passing over. As the tires ground on gravel, she heard Sad Sack, the old dog, baying close to the house. She opened her eyes and saw the pond, scummy in the early heat, where she couldn't play because of snakes. She saw where the drive forked toward the barn lot. One last mule still stood in the fringed shade of a mimosa. Who fed the mule? She didn't know. It just stood there, always. In the loop the driveway made in front of the house, a black Chevrolet like an overgrown beetle sat parked, as it had been Wren's whole life. Now, wagging and whining, Sad Sack emerged from his dusty spot beneath the forsythia. Climbing from the car, Wren patted his bony head. He rolled his bloodshot eyes at her, and his houndy smell stayed on her hand.

"Where are the baby wrens?" she asked her grandmother. Every year a pair of wrens nested in the grille of the black Chevrolet. Wren believed that this was why nobody drove it. On her last visit, three weeks earlier, her grandmother had taken her out on tiptoe to see the pocket of sticks, grass, and moss, the tiny heads peeping out.

"Oh, darling, they've flown, flown away," her grandmother said, singsong. Everything she said was a lullaby. She took Wren's hand. "Your daddy *loved* those wrens, when he was a little boy."

"And he named me Wren." Of all the cousins, she was the only one not named after a saint. The family was full of Anns, Michaels, Catherines, Stephens, Margarets, Cecilias, Lawrences, Dominics. There was a Mary Elizabeth as well, and a John Francis, though nobody called him that. He answered to *Bud.* Even she, come to think of it, was Wren Marie. The priest would not have baptized a plain Wren, so her mother said, with the hard look on her face. If her grandfather had to say her name, that was what he said, *Wren Marie.* Otherwise she was just *she* and *her.*

Stepping down the long front porch, fitting her feet exactly to the herringbone pattern of the bricks, she imagined her father not as a grown-up man whose hair hung too long and curly over his forehead, but as a child coming home. He would slam the heavy front door behind him. He would hear the punch bowl jingle among its glasses on the dining-room sideboard, the golden murmur of the clock chimes, though the clock never told the time. He would smell the old-house smell. "Damp," her mother said. "That basement floods."

He would see the olive-wood crucifix over the living-room door. Mimi, his grandmother, Wren's great-grandmother, who though she was dead now had been an avid traveler, had brought that crucifix back from a trip to the Holy Land, before her father was born. Now he was thirty. "A thirty-year-old *child,*" her mother said. Wren had studied the world map on the wall at school, but she had never found the place named *Holy Land.*

She ran now into the dark paneled den and marched her hand down the keys of the upright piano, to hear it rumble. This was another of her mother's irritations, that piano. "*Why* they can't get that thing tuned," she said. Her sentence dangled meaningly. "It's not a bad piano. Why let it go to rot like that?" She couldn't bear to hear Wren play "Chopsticks" on it, or "Heart and Soul," the two songs anybody could play without thinking. Wren's mother could play many other things besides "Chopsticks" and "Heart and Soul." Wren's mother said that playing those two songs did not mean you could play the piano. It meant only that you could play "Chopsticks" and "Heart and Soul."

Wren's grandfather had carried her blue suitcase into the back room. She heard the toilet flush, water running. After

44

a moment he re-emerged into the den, an unlit cigar in his hand. Across the dim room the two of them regarded each other. Soon Wren would be as tall as her grandfather; he was a short man. He parted his thick white hair neatly in the middle and flattened it down with hair tonic. When he combed it, the comb's marks stayed there, like plowed furrows. He wore his baggy trousers high on his torso, his crisp plaid shirt tucked firmly in.

"Well, now," he said to her.

She smiled at him a little uncertainly. What exactly the right answer to *Well, now,* might be, she had never discerned.

"It's about that time," he said. "Do you want a Co-Cola? Grandmama's in the kitchen."

"I'll go see what she's doing," said Wren. Her mother had told her to be helpful. Anyway, helpfulness eased her out of conversation with her grandfather. She went through the spidery unlit pantry, stacked with newspapers and Jim Beam boxes, and into the kitchen where her grandmother stood before the refrigerator, holding open its door as if it were her dance partner.

"Grandaddy wants his drink," her grandmother said. "Can I fix you something? Some juice?"

"Grandaddy said I could have Coke. I can get it myself," Wren told her. "I can help cook supper, too."

"Can you, now? That stove is *hot*. Does your mother let you touch the stove at home?"

"I can make a grilled cheese. I can make hotdogs. I can make Jello and boil the water."

"Don't you go spilling that hot water on you, darling. It would burn, *burn,* if it touched you. It would *hurt.*"

"I *know,*" said Wren. "One time I picked up a sparkler on

the wrong end. It was all finished, but I guess I wanted to hold it again. I was *six*," she added contemptuously.

"Well, just so you don't get burned any *more*."

With her glass of Coke crisping and popping in its ice, Wren followed her grandmother back to the den. She watched how her grandmother walked, stiff-legged and hustling, though she moved slowly, carrying the drink. Her grandmother's knees did not bend much. Everything about her was straight up-and-down, all but the two little points above the high-waisted belt of her flowered dress. Though she was no taller than Wren's grandfather, her body didn't sink into itself the way his did, head and shoulders riding a cushion of stomach, but instead rose from her waist like a plant trying to unfurl a new shoot. If Wren were to turn on the pantry light, she would see her grandmother's scalp glow pink through her frosting of white hair.

Compared with her friends' grandparents, who were old, Wren's grandparents were old-old. Her father was their youngest child, their seventh, the baby and the only boy. His closest sister was nine years older than he was. Wren had cousins older than her parents. At Christmas when they were all together, the teenaged and college cousins went upstairs—*to play,* they said. Wren could have told on them. They snuck bottles from the pantry up to the haunted room, with its bronze door knocker like a woman's hand. They smoked cigarettes with their heads out the dormer windows. The haunted room was called *haunted* because Mimi, their great-grandmother, had died in one of the matched twin beds, each one kept neat and straight now beneath its scrolled headboard. If Wren sat on one of the beds, the older cousins cried, "That's the one, Wren! That's the bed where

Mimi died. You think her ghost likes you sitting on top of her?" But if she moved to the other bed, someone was sure to say, "Nope, it was that one."

"Do you want to go upstairs and play?" Wren's grandmother asked now.

Wren shook her head: not this time. Not alone.

In his brown wing chair, her grandfather was drinking his drink and reading the paper. The cigar, still unlit, peeped from his breast pocket. Later he would go outside to talk to the dog and smoke it. Now he looked up from the paper. "Say *no ma'am* to your grandmother."

"No ma'am," Wren whispered. Tears pricked her eyes. To hide them she lay on her stomach on the oval rag rug, so walked-on nobody could tell that it hadn't always been dust-colored. Dust was what it smelled like, too, when she bent her face to it.

"Get up out of that dirt," her grandfather said, "and sit on the sofa."

"Grandaddy," said her grandmother.

"Virginia, she's got to mind."

To show that she could mind as well as anybody, Wren leaped up from the floor, upsetting her drink.

"Oh, oh, oh," said her grandmother, like an excitable little dog. "Oh, let me just get a rag."

"Wren Marie can get a rag." Her grandfather returned to his paper. Wren, minding or helpful, or maybe both at once, went into the kitchen and ran water on a sponge.

At five o'clock the news came on. After the old Latin grace they sat down at a card table in the den to eat and watch. Supper was cube steak with gravy, tater tots, macaroni and cheese, green jello salad with cottage cheese and crushed pineapple mixed in. Wren's grandparents drank iced coffee with their meal, and Wren drank more Coca-Cola. The news bored her; it was full of something the President had done. With a sigh she went on eating tater tots and watching a reporter in a trench coat stand in front of the White House.

After supper, to show how helpful she was, Wren carried their plates to the kitchen. She stood beside her grandmother at the long white porcelain sink, drying as the clean wet dishes were handed her.

"You should get a dishwasher," she told her grandmother.

"I have one." Her grandmother poked her.

"Well, but a *real* one."

"I don't think I could get used to one of those machines."

In this way too her grandparents were unlike other people. They disliked things they didn't already know about. Her grandmother could work any crossword puzzle, could write a poem that rhymed, could correct your grammar and say, "*Quelle heure est-il?*" in French. But she could not, for example, run a washing machine. She had tried once. "Granddaddy and I went to one of those *washeterias*," she habitually told the grandchildren as a funny story. "In we went with all our dirty clothes, our towels and things, and there was this *wall* of machines all going around and around, and not a soul to help you." The punchline of the story was that they had turned around and walked back out again, and now sent everything, even their underwear, to the dry cleaner's. Of course she never said the word *underwear*. It was Wren's mother who said that, with a shake of her head.

"How did the clothes get clean before?" Wren always wanted to know, but nobody had ever been able to tell her.

So there was no washing machine at her grandparents',

and no dishwasher either, that didn't have two hands and a mind of its own. They continued to drive their old car with its heavy manual steering and the gear shift on the column, instead of something new. "*Hatchback*, or some such nonsense," her grandfather said darkly. They did not go to McDonald's, where you had to approach a counter and order from a wall-mounted menu. They avoided many complications by staying home.

Also, in the evenings, they insisted on saying the rosary, all five decades, out loud, beneath the picture of the Blessed Mother that Mimi had painted long ago, when she was a girl in Mobile, at school with the nuns. This image of a romantic young lady in blue, one pale hand patting her pinkly Immaculate Heart, had hung above the den fireplace as long as anyone now living could remember. The aunts and uncles groaned when they forgot and overstayed their visits and were stuck at rosary time. The cousins, those that could, escaped upstairs. Sometimes Wren went with them, joining their silent creep away from the edges of the room and out into the safety of the pantry or the entrance hall. The punch bowl or the clock might protest, but you could tiptoe, holding in your laughter, up the stairs and past the linen closet, to make a show of knocking on the haunted room's door with the brass knocker like a woman's hand. Of course you had to knock quietly, to be admitted with gusts of suppressed hilarity by whichever cousins had gotten there first.

When the cousins were there, Wren, the youngest, was borne along on their currents. But when she was alone with her grandparents, she liked to sit in the den, all dark except for the candle on the mantel, mysterious. She liked to hold a rosary from the tangled collection her grandmother kept in a bowl beneath the Mary picture, and to say the prayers as they ticked over, miles on an odometer. Though she knew the prayers by heart, they always felt novel, like visiting itself. At home they never prayed, not out loud for other people to hear.

But it wasn't time for the rosary yet. The light still hung in the sky. Just now she was finishing the dishes and hearing her grandmother call her to come outside. A mockingbird sang in the rambling rose. She went out the kitchen door, patting Sad Sack who rose from the porch, whining and wagging as always, and into the back yard. She took her grandmother's hand to hear the bird, but after a moment, pulling free, she ran away barefoot across the damp grass.

"Darling? Where are your shoes?" her grandmother called after her. "You'll get hookworm, running around this old country yard."

But Wren didn't listen. She ran past the clothesline and the smokehouse to the gate. Beyond the gate were the woods, full now of crickets tuning up, birds tuning down. They were full too of snakes and poison ivy. She could not go into them. But she could hang on the gate and look into the trees, where the first darkness was gathering.

Her grandfather stood on the back porch, smoking his cigar and patting Sad Sack. In the twilight, with the house light behind him and his head wreathed in smoke, he looked a figure of mystery, a short fat fairy king. Doubling back, Wren cannoned into her grandmother, who said, "Oof," and put her arms around her.

Before prayers, Wren played alone in the back bedroom. She hated to admit that she still played with toys, but these toys, in their big baskets on the deep windowsills, were her

Wiseblood Books
Joshua Hren, Louis Maltese
P.O. Box 870
MENOMONEE FALLS, WI   53051
United States
5038607953

Order Date	Phone #	Customer PO	Order
8/12/2024	**15032449720**	**SPK-11932646-1**	**SPK-119**

Quantity	SKU	Title
1	9781963319958	The Blackbird and Other Stories SPK-11932646-1 1

Total Quantity: 1

Ship To:

Susan Davis
7885 SW 69th Ave
Portland, OR 97223

r	Ref#	Ship Via: USPS Media Basic		
-1			CTN Type	CTN Qty
			2B	NA

oldest friends. They had belonged to her aunts, her father, all the cousins before her. For now nobody else wanted them, and they were hers. She played with the little hard-rubber farm animals, pigs, sheep, and chickens. All their feet ended in pedestals as if they were toy statues, not toy versions of actual animals. The chickens were as tall as the sheep.

When she tired of the animals, she played paper dolls. Betsy McCall and her friends, plus various mismatched others, made a kind of family. It was mostly a girl and lady family, but there was a father, a heavy, glossy cardboard gentleman with pomaded hair, a tight-fitting white undershirt, and polka-dotted boxers. Different ladies took turns being the mother and dressing the little girls.

The night was settling down like a bird on its nest. Looking up from the bed where she knelt with her paper dolls, Wren could see straight through the window to the sky's clear blue underside. The peeper frogs in the trees raised their whistling song. The light from the hall made a yellow slice on the floor, and her grandfather was calling her for the rosary. "Wren Marie! *Prayahs!*"

On quiet bare feet she came through her grandparents' pass-through room with the spindle bed, through another little hall where a broken radio in a mahogany case had stood in silence all her life, and into the den. They had turned off the lamps. Her grandmother was lighting the candle in its etched-glass globe on the mantel. Wren slipped onto the footstool by the fireless hearth, and her grandmother put a plastic rosary into her hand. In the dark the beads glowed green-white, a foxfire light she shaded by curling her palm around it.

"Monday," her grandfather said. "The Joyful Mysteries.

For a special intention." He cleared his throat and raised his rosary's heavy crucifix to his forehead. "In the name of the Father, the Son, the Holy Ghost. I believe in God . . ."

Wren sat, hardly listening. *Special intention* meant a prayer you didn't want to name aloud. She thought of all the things she too didn't want to name aloud, or couldn't. There was her mother, alone in the house where they all three had lived, slamming things into boxes with that fierce set to her mouth as if she *wanted* their life to be broken. There was her father, who yesterday morning had hugged her hard and long, then had not been home for supper. There was the corner of the living room where his guitar had stood. There was that feeling she had, of a railroad track vanishing into its tunnel of leaves, taking its secrets with it. She imagined the train on its unseen way, *going to Vicksburg,* with green all around it and shadows breathing out softness.

Glancing up out of her thoughts, she saw that her grandmother was crying. In the shivering candlelight the tears made shiny tracks down her powdered cheeks and dropped onto her hands, lumpy with blue veins, and onto the tarnished silver rosary that had been her wedding present.

Her grandfather saw, too. "Oh, *God,* Virginia," he said.

After a silence, he went on without pausing, "Our Father who art in Heaven hallowed be Thy name Thy kingdom come thy will be done on earth as it is in Heaven . . ."

Her grandmother did not answer, "Give us this day our daily bread." Wren said it for her. She heard her own voice as something separate from herself, hard and dry as her mother's face, saying the words about trespass, forgiveness, temptation, evil.

"Well," her grandfather said when at last the prayers

were over, "I guess we'll watch the news. Virginia, put Wren Marie to bed."

"I'm *nine,*" Wren wanted to say. "Nobody *puts* me to bed." But she let her grandmother, more silent than usual, take her hand and lead her to the back bedroom.

Her grandmother said, "We didn't measure you, darling, yet, did we?"

"You measured me last time I was here," said Wren. "That was three weeks ago. Do you think I've grown since then?"

"You never can tell." Her grandmother opened the closet door where everyone's height was recorded: Wren's father's, the aunts', all the cousins', written on the edge of the door, on its inside, in black pencil. By now the door was a confusion of names, dates, and numbers, but if she looked carefully, Wren could find herself, her own name ascending among the others as she grew.

"Jump up and stand against the door, now," her grandmother said. Wren stood straight while the mark was made by her head. She stepped aside, and her grandmother unrolled the measuring tape. "Four feet, ten and a *half* inches," she proclaimed. "You were only four feet ten and a *quarter* last time." She wrote Wren's name, the date, and the new height on the door.

"You *are* growing, just fine. A *tall* girl." She hugged Wren tight and saw her into bed. Then she went out, leaving the door open. In another moment the television boomed from the den. Wren wriggled a little between the sheets. Then, remembering, she reached up for her troll doll, which she had stood on the windowsill beside the plastic farm animals. She didn't like him all that much, he hadn't been really what she wanted, but now that the lights were out she feared that in his plastic nakedness he might be cold. She settled him beneath her pillow and was instantly asleep.

It was a thin sleep, filled with shards of dream. In one fragment she came to her own house, to find it empty and dark, all its belongings taken away. In the haste of their moving, they had forgotten her. She was left behind, alone. Moonlight shone through the naked windows. From room to empty room she went, calling out some name. A closed door kept appearing before her, a light showing beneath it. Was someone at home after all? Someone she knew, or a stranger? Try as she might, she could never reach that room. There was always another dark room, a hallway, something she had to go through to get to it. Somehow she never did get through. No matter what she did, the lighted room retreated, always a little farther away.

She dreamed, too, other smaller things. She dreamed of morning sun on the kitchen floor, her father singing "Hello Dolly," accompanying himself on a ukulele. Her mother at the piano, gathering music like water in her hands. Evening on the backyard grass, fireflies hanging in the shadow of the apple tree. Herself in bed, her own bed. Voices in the hall outside.

She strained so hard to hear those voices that she woke up. For a moment she wondered where she was. Then, smelling the country night and the musty old house, she knew. Everything had fallen silent. Only the spring frogs, outside, unseen, spoke a language she didn't know. Somewhere in the woods an owl called, rasping and querulous. Another owl answered it. The hall light was gone from the floor. In their own room, door ajar, her grandparents snored decorously in their spindle bed. Darkness lay like a weight on her heart.

Then, from far away, she heard the rain begin. It came like a slow train, bumping, starting, its wheels whispering on a weedy track, its wind blowing the tall grasses.

"Going to Vicksburg," she whispered to herself. "Going to Vicksburg in the cool of the evening."

The rushing, rustling, bumping noise came nearer. Suddenly it was all around her. From inside it she could hear all its drippings, spatterings, clicks, murmurs, a thousand feet pattering past, a thousand voices. Each voice cried out in a different tongue. Each said one word: *Peace.* A green coolness sighed at the open window. In bed, Wren sighed, too. The world was turning, taking her with it. Outside it was raining, raining, raining. Soon the night would be washed away. She pulled the covers to her chin and slept again without dreams.

A NOISE LIKE A FREIGHT TRAIN

Caroline stood, cereal bowl unwashed in her hand, watching the brown thrush in the laurels outside. It was spring, a green day, heavy with threatened rain. Overnight the ferns in the shadow of the house, there on that north side, had poked up their furred gold fiddleheads and were unrolling. If she went out and knelt down, she might catch them at it.

As she'd bent to the sink, she had heard the thrush call sweetly and fluidly, a rainfall of song. Glancing up into a window full of trees, she'd seen the brown flash, the commotion of wings among the dark leaves. A nest, she thought. Or about to be one. She had already seen wrens fussing around the glazed earthenware birdhouse bottle she'd hung long ago on the peeling gray clapboard of the garden shed. Every spring these wrens made over the bottle as if they had never seen it before. Or maybe these were new wrens, who hadn't. She preferred, though, to think of them as the same ones year after year, always surprised by what they'd forgotten they knew.

The thrush flew out of the laurels again, and away. Caroline turned on the water, squirted pink dish liquid a little wastefully into her bowl, and sloshed it out. Who was there to see her waste dish liquid? She dried the bowl and put it away in the glass-fronted butler's-pantry cabinet. Then she stood at the open door, in her old chambray workshirt and loose drawstring pants, looking out onto the back yard.

The early sun had gone; rainclouds seemed caught in the top branches of the pecan tree, with its little tentative leaves. Somewhere in the neighborhood someone was hurrying to get grass cut before the rain. She could hear the growl of the mower, could smell the cut grass, a smell as green as the air itself.

Well, she was not in a hurry. Shutting the door. She moved about the downstairs doing her morning chores: a little dusting here, a little sweeping there. Fisher, her old brindled dog, got up groaning from the worn leatherette couch in the back room, where she had spread a blanket for him. As he pressed against her legs, she sidestepped him and went on sweeping up his hair along the hall baseboards.

"I could make another one of you," she told him. He moaned and pressed closer. "Is it *weathering?*" she said. "Do you feel *weather* in the air?"

Fisher's dark runny eyes bulged in his white face. He hated storms, even when they hadn't happened yet. But she loved them. She loved to be inside her house in a storm, drinking English Breakfast tea in the lamplight while rain ran like tears down the windows.

In the room at the top of the stairs—Amelia's bedroom until Cash took it over—there was not much to do. She had cleaned it thoroughly six weeks ago, after the home health service had come to take away the oxygen machine and the miles of clear plastic tubing that had brought Cash's breath to him. Now, in defiance, she flicked her duster at the bookshelves. Always, before, she had marveled at how the dust mounted up. As soon as you turned your back, there it was again, lapped softly over everything, dulling the wood surfaces. But today there was hardly any.

Maybe, returning to dust, Cash had taken it all with him.

He had *been* the dust in that room. And now he wasn't. It was strange to her already, to think that he ever *had* been, that she hadn't simply dreamed all those years of marriage. The blue blanket lay in a precise rectangle at the foot of the bed, just as she had folded it. On the bare nightstand she had set a fresh box of tissues. She had pulled the first one up through the cellophane slit, where it continued to bloom, a deathless white flower. Goodness knows, she thought, when somebody is ever going to blow their nose again in this room. It lay clean and orderly in the cloudy light through the bare window. Outside, the back yard needed cutting. She would do it herself later, if the rain held off.

When they'd bought the house, early in their marriage, the downstairs master bedroom had been a selling point. "We can get old in this house," Cash had said. He and Caroline had looked at each other and laughed at the idea. They had put the children upstairs, themselves down in the sunny room overlooking the vegetable garden and the driveway. They'd had their own adjoining bathroom, and beyond it, the little back den where the dog slept now. A suite of rooms to themselves, a whole house around it: after law-school apartments, all this had seemed a paradise. At night they had lain in bed, holding each other in the moonlight that washed in through the sheers. They had been happy, Caroline had thought: so happy they hardly noticed.

Then, without warning, in their fifties, both the children—*gone,* was how Caroline generally put it—Cash had withdrawn to the upstairs room. Already, then, his cough was beginning to nag at him. He came home from his Charlotte office at night white and wrung out.

"I like the view up here," he had told her, wheezing a little. "It's quiet. I can work from home some days. Nobody bothers me."

Who's even here to bother you but me, she had thought. At first, two days a week, he had gone to work by commuting upstairs, instead of to Charlotte. Then two days became three days, then four. At last he was not going in at all. At the big table Caroline had bought him, he wrote contracts and wills, did research on the mystifying computer, anything the junior partners knocked his way. More and more it was make-work. He had come downstairs to join her for meals and bed.

Then, as his lungs deteriorated, he had not done even that. There was less make-work, and less, and finally none. He'd simply stayed upstairs, sitting in the rocking chair with a book, sleeping alone, propped upright on many pillows, in Amelia's white iron bed. It was easier than going up and down, he said. Besides, he liked the view. He didn't want to be trapped down below. One hospice nurse had complained loudly about the stairs—what kind of crazy puts a sick man in a room like that?—but Cash had been adamant. He'd wanted to die with a view of the sky, and so he had.

From that room Caroline moved to the other upstairs bedroom, dim and enclosed, its tan linen roller shades pulled down. She had dusted in here only last week: chess trophies, high school and college diplomas, honor-society cords and Phi Beta Kappa hood still dangling from the closet door. And yes, on this nightstand, too, she had set fresh tissues—when? Years ago. Every now and again she had to pull a tissue out and throw it away, seeing that it had grayed. This is just a little ridiculous, she had told herself the last time. I don't know why I bother. I'm turning into my mother. Next thing, I'll have plastic covers on all the furniture, and a plastic runner across the living-room floor. Well, John, her son, had been meticulous. He would have been a good lawyer, she thought. The least she could do now was to keep his room the way he liked it, as if—though she didn't—she expected him to return.

In the kitchen again she took up the red enameled kettle, ran cold water into it, and set it on the stovetop to chortle, huff, cluck to a boil. It was an old kettle; the noises it made were all its own. When John had been at home, he had made tea in it—unlike the rest of them, John would never learn to drink coffee. It was his hard-headedness. That was what Cash had called him: hard-headed. Caroline could not taste the musky Lapsang Souchong John had loved without thinking of the phrase *hard-headed.*

Methodically, as John had done—he had been so particular, for a boy—she shook the loose black tea into the blue-and-white transferware pot. Oh, wait, she should have run hot water into the pot first, to warm it. John would have scolded her. He liked things done right. Well, the tea would taste fine, even if she hadn't warmed the pot first, even if she'd skimped just a little on the ritual.

It did taste fine, she thought, settling back on the living-room sofa. She had turned all the lamps on, so that the room with its soft stone-colored walls would glow against the green outside, green pressing against the windows so intensely that she thought it might crush the house. No, the house would push back with its light and warmth, its paler greens. The Chippendale sofa was a worn gray-green damask; the cotton rug at her feet had a dull green stripe. She had paired spring-green candles on the mantel at Easter, beneath the slubby oil portrait of her and the children, done long long ago. In the painting Amelia, four and freckled, her amber hair cut straight across her forehead, stood at Caroline's shoulder. She glowered at the camera—the painting had been done from a photograph, to save them all hours of posing—with pouting brown eyes that said, If I do stand here like a good girl, what will you give me?

She still had that look. Caroline had only to glance at the painting to remember exactly who Amelia was: Amelia, all grown up now and living in Texas, with a husband and a child whom Caroline had hardly seen. Of course they had come for the funeral, she reminded herself. In that general atmosphere of unreality, they had swum about her like fish in an aquarium, strangers sharing the same murky water. Only Amelia had appeared in high relief, all-too-angularly corporeal. *Miss Hat Rack,* Cash had liked to call her.

Caroline's gaze returned to the painting. John, the baby, was nothing more than a vagueness in a long lacy christening gown. Young Caroline's young ringed hands held the gown upright as if there were no body inside it, only a bobbling downy head, its face a collection of features seen through mist, affixed balloon-like to its yoked collar. Well, it was hard to paint babies, she imagined. By the time you finished sketching one set of features, the face had changed entirely. She possessed many photographs of John, but even those seemed inexact. You pointed your camera, you caught some fleet moment, or so you thought. You never really caught it, only its shadow.

Even pictures, though of course she clung to them,

seemed not much good to her. The day Cash died, as she waited for the undertaker to collect him from the bed upstairs, she had come down alone and dusted their wedding photograph in its oval silver frame. Those people smiling back at her: who were they? Had the bride noticed the skinniness of the groom's neck that day, or only later? What had possessed her to put on that fluttering fairy-princess dress with its butterfly sleeves? She had certainly never been tempted to wear anything in that style again, or to apply makeup with such a heavy hand, or to sleep with her hair rolled up on orange-juice cans. Whatever it was that she had just lost, it wasn't those people, or that day. You could never save anything, not really, she had thought. In the end it hardly mattered what you meant to do: what happened happened. *Que sera sera*, like the song that was silly already, a cliché, the first time she heard it on the radio.

Back in the present, Fisher prodded her hand with his cold nose to make her pat him. "If a tornado came and swept the house away, Fisher, and us in it, we wouldn't be any worse off than we are now." She scritched his head; he stood with his eyes shut, perfectly still, not to waste a drop of her attention. "Except that I *would* like to finish this cup of tea," she added.

She was putting the kettle on again when the phone rang.

"Hey, Mama," said Amelia, a thousand miles away.

"Well, hey, darling. Are you not at work yet?"

An expressive exhalation. "*No.* I was on my way. I had dropped Mallory off at day care. Then just as I got back on the freeway, they called and said she'd bitten somebody again, and to come get her now."

"Oh, dear," said Caroline. A thought struck her. "You're not driving and talking on a cell phone, are you?"

"I'm sitting in standstill traffic and talking on a cell phone. I have to get up to an exit where I can turn around and start back the other way. Fortunately my first appointment canceled, but still."

"Can't Michael—"

"Ha," said Amelia. "Ha ha hardy ha."

"What does that mean?"

"It means ha ha ha hardy ha."

"Well," said Caroline.

"It is what it is, Mother." Another exhalation, which meant something, Caroline was sure. "Oops, we're moving again. I'll call you back later." Like that, Caroline was left alone, holding her end of the line, a frayed anchor rope.

Which end, she wondered, held the anchor? Did Amelia call her mother to offer comfort, or to receive it, or to take Caroline's temperature and diagnose her? So often it was hard to say. After the funeral, Amelia had ordered Caroline to seek grief therapy, again, which was only natural, since Amelia was a psychologist and used to this kind of thing.

"Well, darling," Caroline had said. They had just shut the front door on the last mourner, and were standing in the kitchen amid the shambles of the reception food, quiches and vegetable trays and half a spiral ham. She had still been wearing the black dress that she hated, and the shoes that hurt her feet. "Are you worried that I'm going to *grieve wrong?*"

Amelia had been standing at the window, tapping her foot, watching her husband Michael push their daughter Mallory on the little swing Caroline had hung from the pecan tree. Probably, Caroline had thought wickedly in her exhaustion, Amelia thought that Michael was *swinging wrong.*

After a moment, Amelia had turned from the window. "I just want you to *process* things, Mother. Not pretend that everything's just the same. La la la, nothing's wrong, look at me, I'm fine. *That's* what I'm afraid you're going to do."

"Would that be so bad?" Caroline had said.

"It would be a lie." Amelia had been tapping her foot again in impatience. Her eyes had strayed once more to the window.

"Not if I really was all grieved out."

"Well, that's a lie, too," Amelia had snapped. "Nobody is ever *all grieved out.*"

Outside the birds had fallen silent. A sudden gust of rain struck like pebbles against the south-facing windows. The trees along the property line—two maples and a holly—bowed and bucked like ponies. Beneath Caroline's patting hand, Fisher shivered. After a moment he slunk away to hide under the dining-room table.

"That's right," she called after him. "Be safe."

But she didn't want to be safe, all of a sudden. She wanted to be outside to see it. Setting down her teacup she went onto the screened front porch. The rain misted in through the screen; after a moment the peach fuzz of her face was jeweled with it. The wind, turned chilly, smelled of wet asphalt. Her short silver hair lifted like Fisher's hackles.

"Goodness," said Caroline to the shining-wet porch. "This *is* a storm."

Overnight, it seemed, the hostas on either side of the porch steps had poked up like scrolls from the black mulched ground and unfurled themselves to be read. In the glowering light they glowed golden, and the rain tickled on their ribbed elliptical leaves. The front-yard dogwoods had let go their last white tatters, but Caroline's azaleas, light and dark pink, some almost fiercely red, held their own against the rain's lashings. The iris, too: had they been this tall last year?

As she stood considering the growing things, as once upon a time she might have observed her children when they thought themselves unwatched, old Jackie Link came walking up the street.

Jackie Link! Caroline turned to go inside, but it was too late: he had seen her.

"Hey," he called from the curb, storm water rushing over his feet in their torn black sneakers. "How you been?"

"What are you doing out in the rain?" she called back.

"Out *looking* for something to do. Just got through cutting uh, cutting uh, cutting uh—*Jim's* grass. How come you ain't called me to work?"

Because, thought Caroline, when I call you to work, pretty soon it's you calling me for money when you don't want to work. Because it is not my Christian duty to keep you in Budweiser. Immediately she regretted that thought. Did she think, criminally, that she owed him *no* Christian duty? Surely she did. It was so hard sometimes to know what exactly your Christian duty ought to be, or how to go about it.

Shoulders bent against the rain, Jackie studied her last-autumn's planting of evening primrose and black-eyed Susan—leaves emerging from clay—in a strip along the curb. "What you been doing to my yard *now?*" he said.

This was the other reason Caroline didn't like calling him. With Jackie Link, it was his yard or nobody's. Who moved my garden cart? Where my snips? What you been doing with my rake? I waited *years* to have my own yard, she always thought. I didn't wait all that time to have somebody else give my nandinas flat-tops behind my back.

"Those are flowers," she answered him. "I wanted some summer color along the edge there, by the street."

"Weeds. Be taking over your grass. What you ought to plant you is some of that uh, that uh, that—you know what I'm talking about. That candytuft, you know. Nice and low. Spread, but not too much."

"Maybe I will," she said.

Spray, Jackie Link always said. Kill them weeds dead. Cash would let Jackie spray. Cash would tell Jackie to edge Caroline's beds, where the flowers sprawled out into the lawn. She gets mad if you mow 'em, Jackie. Just bring some of those bricks from the back and build something, I don't care what. Make it look decent, that's all I care about. I just want it decent.

Well, thought Caroline, so do I, but somehow her caring was different, or her idea of *decent*. She never could explain it to the two of them, and confronted with them both, their combined knowledge and experience, she had generally surrendered. Cash, in the room upstairs, his window facing the back yard, had not seen her putting in black-eyed Susans, those un-meek inheritors of the earth. She had done it in a spirit of haste and secrecy, lest she be found out. Under cover of darkness, so to speak, except that she had done it in full daylight and in view of all the neighborhood. And now she had been discovered.

Jackie studied the black-eyed Susans as they came up, the felted dark-green leaves, soft as his rib-knit cap, in their tidy pairs. Liars: there was nothing soft or tidy about them. Jackie glanced up at Caroline. From the screen porch, she met his look. Though his eyes were filming over with cataracts, something snapped in them, a little blue spark.

"You got fifty dollars you could advance me right now to pay my light bill? I'll come back and edge this bed for you. Make it look *good.*"

"I'm sorry," she said. It was true: she didn't have fifty dollars. She never carried money—cash money, as they said— only the credit card that let her earn reward points for plane tickets to go see Amelia and the baby, which maybe now she meant to do.

"Huh." Jackie studied her for a moment with his frosted eyes. He shrugged at the yard. "You *sure* you ain't got fifty dollars right now?"

"Sorry."

"Twenty?"

"Sorry."

"Ten."

"I don't have any cash on me this minute, Jackie. I'm sorry."

"Well, I guess I'll go on down, see if Bobbie need any work today."

"Good luck," said Caroline. "Don't catch cold in this rain."

"*I* won't catch cold. I *like* to work. Rain or shine. I'm all about the pennies. *All* about the pennies."

Caroline watched him slosh away down the street. I should have made him come in, she thought with a pang, though she knew he wouldn't have come. The old proprieties, the most obvious of them, anyway, were long gone— and good riddance to them, she thought with sudden vehemence, remembering her mother's maid, Lorraine, climbing heavily into the back seat of the Oldsmobile. She, Caroline, a mere child, had ridden in front with her mother to drive Lorraine home. Nobody did that anymore.

Well, nobody had a maid anymore, not to speak of. *Help,* her mother had said. Nobody had *help,* not in the way they used to, as part of the normal fabric of daily life. Once a year, for Caroline's birthday, until he had gotten too sick to think about it, Cash had paid a service to come in and do a *deep clean.* What was so deep about it, that it cost so much, Caroline had always wondered. She could dust her own light fixtures, in her own good time. Funny, she reflected, that her mother, who had never thought once, let alone twice, about relegating a grown woman to the back seat of her car, would have been as ashamed of Caroline's dust as if it had been her own. Well, her house was clean enough. She kept it that way. She had dusted with her own hands and never asked anyone else to do the work for her.

Still, she could invite Jackie Link in until she was blue in the face; he would never accept. His place, he clearly believed, was in her yard. She planted. He beat back what she planted, edged and arranged and ordered it, whether that was what she wanted or not. So they would go on forever, she imagined, as long as they both stood upright. It was progress of a sort. But it never seemed to go anywhere.

Her thoughts trailed off as she stepped back into the house. All this time, the light had been turning greener and greener. The new leaves outside were electric in their greenness, incandescent with life. There was a flicker in the air, a shudder of thunder, and Fisher shivered against her.

"It's out there," she told him. "It can't come in here and get you." But of course it could. This was tornado weather. They were in it now. That it hadn't come inside and gotten them before didn't mean that it *couldn't,* or *wouldn't.* That the house had been standing for ninety-three years did not in any way guarantee that it would stand for ninety-four.

Through the propped-open door she heard the cry of the coal train at the foot of the street. The birds had battened down—this wind now would have blown them out of the sky—but the train came on, creeping inside the city limits, making its sharp remarks as, unseen by her but still known, it rounded the bend under the Poplar Street viaduct and bore down on the crossing. Through the rain's noise she heard the crossing bell ding-danging, the train's horn flowing out like a pennon on a battlefield, wide at first, but tapering to thinness before it melted away. A noise like a freight train. That was what the weather people told you to listen for. What if, she wondered, you were so busy listening to a real freight train, harmless, a block away, that you never heard your own destruction bearing down on you? Even in your own house—safe as houses, people said—you were never safe.

Hard, hard, the rain clattered in the laurels. The dark shining leaves bent their rigid backs against it. Caroline jumped: the lights had blinked. Warm light, then nothing, only the green-black enormity of rain and wind. She was alone in it, her heart skipping. Alone, in the eye of some power. It looked at her, and in that instant she was afraid.

Then, before she had time to think, the warm light returned, normal and consoling. In an instant the army of the rain had passed over and away; only a few camp followers pattered apathetically behind. The noise of the coal train dwindled to nothing. In the kitchen, on the gas burner, in the sudden silence, the last water in the kettle frizzled away.

"Good heavens," Caroline said to the dog. "Look at me, forgetting my tea. I might have burned the house down."

In the kitchen she picked up the kettle and examined its blackened bottom. If she kept this up, soon enough it would burn right through. Today she'd been lucky. With some effort the black would scrub off. The kettle would survive. Nobody would ever have to know.

IN THE DARK

Anne moved through the house in her bathrobe, snapping on lights. In the living room she opened the heavy rubber-backed curtains. At almost nine o'clock, the July sky still looked transparent, like a glass of blue food coloring. The house stood at the top of the street; from the living room window Anne could just see the Great Salt Lake, a silver skin on the bright western horizon. Somewhere in the neighborhood someone was grilling out. The smell of lighter fluid was strong and vaguely aphrodisiac, reminding Anne of her childhood summers back east, her crushes on one boy cousin or another, the long bright evenings, the sparklers she'd wave to write her beloved's name on the air.

Across the street, silhouetted against the pale rainfall of a sprinkler, Mrs. Sorensen was walking her dog. One evening last fall, when Anne had first moved in, Mrs. Sorensen had accosted her as she'd stepped outside for the mail.

"What do you do in there?" Mrs. Sorensen's gray permanent had bristled against the streetlight. Her caterpillarish terrier snuffed at Anne's bare feet. "That house looks shut up like a tomb all day long."

Anne had run her tongue over her unbrushed teeth. After so many years, it still felt odd to be caught at her waking routine. "We're just kind of nocturnal," she'd finally said.

"Well." Mrs. Sorensen had smiled her disapproval. "That's a rental house, and they've had all kinds of people, but we're a nice neighborhood here."

"Time to get up," Anne called to Katherine now from

the bedroom doorway. The lump under the covers stirred and moaned.

When Anne said, "We're skipping school tonight," however, Katherine sat up, her short dyed-black hair on end, like cat fur.

She wrinkled her face at Anne. "What? I did my math."

"Good for you. I'll check it over later. But first we're going on a field trip."

"Oh, no." Katherine flopped back on the bed.

"Oh, yes. I want you out of that bed and into your clothes. You've got twenty minutes."

In his room, Gareth had stripped to his Clone Wars briefs and was slathering sunblock across his stomach. Anne had drilled it into him: This is your second skin. Even at night, she couldn't be sure he was safe without it.

He turned to her and held out the tube. "Do the parts I can't reach?"

Warming the lotion in her hand, she worked it into his back. Then she put her arms around his chest and hugged him. He tipped his cheek back against hers. They looked at themselves in the closet-door mirror.

As always, Anne noticed her own weatherbeatenness, the contrast with her son's milky skin. "Look at me. I'm such a haint."

"You should have stayed out of the sun." Gareth nodded sagely.

"Yep. See what it does to you?"

She would never forget what it had done to him. He'd been one week old, in his car seat under the plum tree. That day, she had taken him outside to nap in the shade while she staked the tomatoes. A summer baby: she'd thought that was lucky. The others had screamed and fought while she stuffed their jerky newborn bodies into snowsuits. Gareth she could snap into a onesie, cover with a cotton blanket, and leave napping in the soft June air. She'd bent to the bristly vines, sun warming the back of her head. Though it was Saturday, Byron had gone to his office on campus. In the house, she had left five-year-old Katherine reading *Blueberries for Sal*, whispering the memorized words as she gazed at the pictures. Thomas, aged seven, had been kicking a soccer ball against the fence. Anne's postpartum body had felt heavy, strange, and sore inside her clothes, but summer was unrolling before her its expanse of quiet outdoor days. She had hummed to herself as she knelt in the damp earth.

The soccer ball's obsessive thunk-thunk against the fence had begun to rasp at her nerves. "Give it a rest, Thomas," she'd said. But he had already caught the ball and was staring toward the plum tree, where the baby had begun to cry in a particularly piercing way.

"Mom. Look. What's wrong with Gareth?"

His lips were swollen, his eyes; blisters were blooming and breaking all over his face, his scalp, his torso beneath the thin cotton shirt. He looked as if he'd been dipped in acid. She snatched him up in the car seat, shouted for Thomas to get Katherine out of the house, and somehow they'd driven up the hill to the hospital. One minute she had been standing in her back yard with dirt on her hands; the very next, she was plunging through the automatic doors into the emergency room, bearing her screaming baby like some live flaming dessert on a platter. The older children were crying, too, hanging onto her shorts.

"He was in the shade," Anne sobbed to the ER doctor,

who had looked as if he wanted to book her for child abuse right there. While the hospital ran a background check, Anne had sat in the cold waiting room, her children staring at the TV above the reception desk, where videotaped episodes of *My Little Pony* were playing, the same music, the same plotline, the same pastel colors over and over. Somewhere behind the double automatic doors lay her baby in agony. She couldn't leave the others to go to him; she couldn't take them with her into the burn unit. Every half hour, she punched B Office in her speed dial. He didn't answer.

Thus had begun life as they now knew it: blackout curtains, Gareth confined inside until the sun went down. As he grew up, Anne had shifted her schedule so that she could be up for hours in the dark, watching his dim form as he splashed in a baby pool on the deck, played on the monkey bars in the moonlit park. At first Thomas and Katherine had continued to go to school. Thomas played soccer, had friends. In the afternoons he went to their houses, so that Gareth and Anne could sleep. Katherine, who sat by herself with a book at recess, began begging to stay up with her mother.

"I'm lonely," she had moaned. "You only love Gareth any more."

Whether Gareth had an allergy to sunlight or some malfunction in the way his skin produced melanin, the one certainty was that his time mattered. There wasn't going to be enough of it to waste. The doctor thought that with care they might get him to sixteen. Melanoma was the usual development. The average life expectancy was twelve.

"Look," Anne had said to Byron, "we could keep him cooped up inside all the time, let him live through TV. Or we can make the night his day."

"How can we do that, Annie? What's that going to do to Tom and Kath? You can't just turn their lives around. What about school?" Byron, leaning his elbows on the kitchen table, had run his fingers through his hair until it stood on end. With his bent wire glasses, his crazy hair, his bony arms, he'd looked like a candidate for the loony bin.

Not Anne. In the face of their lives being over, she had remained reasonable and resolute. It was then that she'd pulled out the home-school curriculum guide she'd sent off for. Byron had picked it up, glanced through it, tossed it aside. "What do I do if you all go on this graveyard schedule?"

"Teach night classes. Or—we can at least have dinner together, spend the evenings. You don't go to bed that early." But Byron had always been a morning person, up with the sun. He loved the desert. He loved hiking and climbing. He liked to come home from campus and sit on the deck photosynthesizing. As Anne talked, she could see plainly what he envisioned: the whole family turning sickly yellow, like houseplants in a science experiment, consigned to survive in a closet.

That they'd held it together for five years—Byron working all day, Anne and the children eating dinner food for their breakfast in the evenings, Byron falling asleep on the family room floor while the kids tried to romp with him— was a dubious miracle. Anne had been almost glad when, three years ago, he'd finally walked out for good. Except for Thomas—except for losing Thomas—the divorce would have been unqualifiedly a relief.

Now she brushed Gareth's hair out of his eyes. "We're

going on a hike," she told him.

"Oh, wow. Where?"

Katherine, in the bathroom, shouted, "I'm not going."

"You are going," Anne called back. "This is your dad's arrangement."

"Dad?" Gareth said. Since the divorce, he'd seen Byron once a week, always in Anne's house with the blackout curtains pulled tight. Too often he was staggering with sleepiness in the morning or evening, when Byron chose to come by.

Byron had asked to have Gareth visit him when Katherine did, but Anne had refused. "I'll keep him inside, Annie." Over the phone, she'd heard his voice crack with frustration. He was trying to keep things amicable, she knew, but he had his limits.

"He can get sunburned standing by a window. Those plastic blinds aren't enough."

"You're being unreasonable." Byron's philosophy was that a short, adventurous life was better than a fastidious one, however much longer. Anne's take was that if Byron could afford to have a lawyer write to her, inviting her to discuss these matters further at her convenience, he could also afford to buy blackout curtains.

"Where is this hike?" Katherine asked when they were all in the car. She slouched in the front seat, fiddling with the radio dial. In her saggy black jeans and her giant t-shirt, she looked larger and lumpier than she had to, Anne thought. Her face was spotted with acne cream, a paler flesh-tone than her actual skin.

Anne cranked down her window. The wind was powdery-dry and cool. "Antelope Island. Again, your dad's idea."

"Are you staying?" Gareth said. "Or just dropping us off?"

"He says I'm supposed to stay. For some reason." She couldn't imagine what that reason was. On the phone, though, Byron had been cordial. He wanted them all to be together. Thomas would be there. He was sure Anne would want to see Thomas.

Yes, Anne wanted to see Thomas. At the thought of seeing Thomas, her knuckles tightened on the wheel. He was fifteen, an almost-grown stranger. The last time she'd seen him on a daily basis, he'd been twelve, Katherine ten, Gareth five. Thomas was Byron's collateral: as long as Anne withheld Gareth, Byron would not encourage Thomas to see Anne.

After his visits with her, Thomas would report to Byron that being at his mother's was like living in a cave. "He says he's still growing stalactites," Byron would tell Anne with obvious satisfaction.

They drove north on I-15. To the east and south, the mountains hunkered black against the clear, dark sky. The moon, just rising, was nearly full. The air rushing in on them smelled of the Great Salt Lake: briny, urinous.

"Pee-yew," Katherine said, pinching her nose. "I can't believe we're getting closer to this on purpose."

Anne said, "Cheer up. It's not supposed to be so bad out in the middle. It only stinks from here because the brine shrimp wash up on the shore after they die."

"Beautiful." Katherine rolled her eyes.

In the back seat, Gareth bounced, straining against his seatbelt. "I bet we'll see tons of stars. I wish I'd brought my telescope. Don't you wish I'd brought my telescope, Mom? I wish you'd reminded me."

"Sorry."

They took the Syracuse exit and drove west on the two-lane highway through flat farmland. Here and there were banks of lit houses, subdivisions with names like "Canterbury," which made Anne smile. Other people's wishful thinking amused her.

"How can people stand to live here, smelling the lake all the time?" Gareth said.

"Probably they're used to it," Anne replied. "After a while you just wouldn't smell it. The air in other places would smell weird."

At the entrance to the causeway, the ranger's small booth was dark and locked up. Anne leaned out to peer at a note taped to the door.

"Is that for us?" Gareth shouted from the back seat.

"Can't you shut up for five seconds?" Katherine turned the radio up. The announcer's voice—*We're gonna rock your socks off*—boomed against the windy silence.

Anne turned the radio down, ignoring Katherine's yelp. "Okay. He says to meet them out at Buffalo Point, where there's a deck of some kind. He says the gate's open at the other end of the causeway."

"How did Dad get us in?" Gareth said. "That sign back there said the island closes at ten."

Katherine said, "You're so stupid. How can an island close?"

"No name-calling, Katherine. You know the rules. Wow, look, waves!"

Anne pointed out the window. To their right, the water, glinting in the moonlight, smacked the rocks along the shoulder of the causeway. White spume flew up. "Pretty wimpy waves, actually," she admitted. "Not like the ocean. But still. Look at the gulls resting on the water."

The birds rode the dark ruffling surface like white sailboats calmly at anchor. Gareth gazed out wonderingly. He would never see an ocean, Anne thought. "I wonder if we'll see falling stars," she said aloud.

"That's in August, Mom. The Perseids." Gareth loved stars. Once, just after they'd moved, when Anne wasn't looking, he'd gone up to the attic and climbed out of the one grimy window to the steep-pitched roof, where she'd found him scanning the sky with a pirate's spyglass from the dollar store. When she'd realized where he was, her heart had stopped. For Christmas he'd gotten a real telescope on a tripod from Santa, with a note attached that read, *For back yard use only.*

"*The Pertheids*," Katherine mimicked him in a mincing voice.

"Mom."

"Give me a break, both of you. I can hardly see where I'm going." Swarms of tiny bugs rose in the headlights like fog. Anne could feel bugs in her hair, but the car had no air conditioning. Beside her, Katherine made snorting noises; the bugs were going up her nose.

The causeway curved away from the shore like a question mark. To their left, in sheltered Farmington Bay, the lake lay flat. Before them, the island loomed massive and dark. They passed the Armed Forces memorial, the marina, a double-wide trailer with a sign that said, *Drinks. Gifts. Sunset Lake Cruises.* They followed the road to the left, over what felt like the island's spine.

In a hollow, Anne saw the dim outline of a shed, with

pickup trucks parked around it. "That must be where they keep the buffalo."

"There's buffalo here?" She could feel Gareth bouncing again.

"No buffalo," Katherine said. "We are not stopping to see buffalo."

"But I've never seen a buffalo."

"Yeah, well, it's dark. They're all sleeping. What's there to see?"

"But," Gareth said.

"Just one more thing you'll never see: a buffalo awake."

Anne pulled the car to the side of the road and turned on Katherine. "I have heard enough." Her voice shook. "You don't have to like this little excursion, but you may not be cruel. Understand?"

Katherine ducked her head and muttered something.

"I said, do you understand?"

"Yes, I understand," Katherine said fiercely. "I understand just fine." She pulled her spiky bangs, the only long part of her hair, down over her eyes. Closed for business.

Want her? Anne imagined herself asking Byron. He'd been the one to let Katherine get that punky haircut. For her own part, she was exhausted from fighting. Lately she'd found herself striking up conversations with the clerk at the twenty-four-hour pharmacy, just to talk to somebody polite. Katherine could be ugly about anything: Anne's history lesson was boring, Anne's dress made her look fat—*No offense, Mom*—Anne put too much cumin in the chili. It was Anne's fault that Katherine had no friends.

"But you've never had friends," Anne had actually snapped once, in the heat of an argument, before she could stop herself. When Katherine didn't speak to her for three days afterward, she'd considered it her just desserts.

Buffalo Point was a hill, a gravel parking lot, a shuttered snack bar, a wide wooden deck with picnic tables. Gareth tumbled out of the car, his sneakers skidding on the gravel, and ran toward the deck shouting, "Dad! Dad! We're here!"

"Run away while you still can." Katherine heaved herself out of the car.

Three people were leaning on the deck rail, looking out at the lake. Anne felt the back of her neck prickle. She hadn't been considering just how much she did not want to go hiking with Byron. Her one thought, accepting the invitation, had been Thomas. It had been three weeks since she'd seen him. Her hunger for him was like the hunger of late pregnancy, when she'd had to eat right then or pass out.

In the months just after the separation, she had tried taking Thomas out to dinner once a week, but that had been a failure. She had chattered too much, like a girl on a bad first date, while Thomas clenched his jaw, looked out the window, and refused to answer any of her questions. Finally she'd surrendered, and now he mostly expended his Mom-time in watching television and doing homework, as if to maintain his connection to a more real world. In recent months, unpacking from her last move, she'd spent hours poring over his baby pictures, trying to remember his milky smell, the curve of his skull under his fine hair. She remembered how, after the divorce, his things had lain in ambush: one soccer cleat behind the back door, a much-chewed red toothbrush in the bathroom cabinet, a CD case under the front seat of the car, a collage he'd made out of acorns and pine needles the summer he was five, taped to the back wall of his closet. Even now she kept these things, though she had long since given up meaning to return them to him.

"Dad! Tom!" Gareth ran across the deck, his feet clomping in their heavy basketball shoes.

Byron's silhouette turned. "Hi, Gare." The shadow beside him turned, too. The shadow that was Thomas looked steadfastly out at the lake.

Anne let herself be pulled along in Gareth's wake. Behind her, Katherine moped and muttered to herself, hanging back, Anne knew, because what she wanted was to throw herself at Byron the way Gareth did.

Byron came forward with his familiar, gawky ease. Despite everything, his touch on her shoulder was gentle. "Annie, I'm glad you came."

"Thank you," she said stiffly. Face to face with Byron, confronted with the physical reality of him—overlong sun-bleached hair, ropy muscular legs in worn khaki shorts, glasses glinting in the gnat-ridden glow of the one street lamp by the deck—she felt wooden and tongue-tied. "This was a good idea. Nice of you."

"Hey, Kath," Byron said, moving around Anne to take Katherine in his arms. Katherine mumbled something unintelligible, and Byron stepped back.

"We're going to hike out to the point, guys, but first I want you to meet someone. Annie, Gareth, Kath, this is Bree. My fiancée. We're getting married at Christmas. Bree, the family."

"Hi!" said Bree, a shade too brightly. Anne was aware of her appraising glance. *So this is the ex-wife.* Well, the ex-wife could look appraisingly back. In the dark, Bree was a flash of pale hair, a litheness. How old are you, Anne wondered. She herself felt three times as gray and doughy as she normally did. She wanted to bolt for the car, floor it all the way home. Instead, speechless, she put out her hand to shake Bree's and managed a grotesque approximation of a smile. Bree's hand felt cool and damp, the kind of hand a person would like to be touched with. Too quickly Anne withdrew her own clumsy paw and put it in her pocket.

"So," Byron began, "I thought we'd all hike to the—"

Katherine's wail cut him short.

"Spiders!" She pointed to an enormous web swaying between two posts of the deck railing. Fine as a bridal veil, it gleamed faintly at the edge of the lamplight. At its center, something massive and dark crouched, waiting.

"Good hunting." Anne, fanning gnats away from her face, found that she could speak again.

"That's so gross," Katherine moaned.

"I think it's beautiful." Bree stepped closer to inspect the web. Even in that vague light, Anne could see now that she was not quite as young as her voice or her hair. Still, she radiated an impression of muscular, sun-warmed health. "Spiders are such miraculous creatures."

"We usually smash them," Gareth volunteered.

"Oh, you shouldn't do that." Bree's voice was earnest. "You can trap them with a glass, and slide a sheet of paper or something under it, and take them outside."

"Where they promptly freeze to death, which is the humane way," said Katherine. Anne smiled at her.

"Bree's a ranger here," Byron was explaining proudly, in what sounded to Anne like a carefully edited paragraph. "She's also an adjunct in our writing program, which is actually how we met. Creative nonfiction is her thing, environmental writing, eco-microfictions. It's because of her that we're able to come out here after hours. This is the best time, she keeps telling me. She loves all the nocturnal animal drama."

For the first time, Thomas turned to acknowledge them. "So you people are right up her alley."

"Thomas." Anne moved to hug him.

Deftly he shifted himself out of reach. "Hi, Mom."

I've missed you, wept her insatiable inner mother. Aloud she merely said, "How's things?"

He shrugged. "Okay."

"School?"

"It's summer, Mom."

"Oh, right."

"We have to do school in the summer." Katherine cut in on them—cut in, thought Anne, like an unwelcome partner at a ballroom dance.

"Sucks for you," said Thomas. "Dad and I have been climbing a lot."

"Well, we went to the drive-in movies last week."

In a burst of inspiration and claustrophobia, Anne had searched the paper for the least unlikely-looking double feature: a James Bond and something about cops. They could go to the movies any time, but she was dying to be outside. She had ended up luring Gareth to the video arcade, while Katherine sat on the station wagon's tailgate, swinging her legs, chewing the gum Anne had let her buy, gazing abstractedly at explosions, derailments, and women spies in ripped cocktail dresses.

"That's lame," said Thomas.

"It was totally lame. But it beat doing math all night."

"Sucks for you," Thomas said again.

"Okay, troops," said Byron. He spoke self-consciously, as one accustomed to employing terms such as *intertextual* and *discourse community* in addressing groups of people. "Let's not stand here flapping our jaws. Let's move it on out."

He strode energetically to the end of the deck. Bree roused herself from her scrutiny of the spider's web and sprinted to catch him up. He held out a hand to her, and she took it.

Out of habit Anne hung back, counting the children as they fell in behind their father. One, two, three. Everyone accounted for. She would bring up the rear of the hike, to make sure nobody got left behind. That was how they'd always done it, back in the day when night hikes had seemed a novelty: Byron the head, Anne the tail, children in the middle, the family animal's living, leaping body.

Now the two younger children caught up with Byron and Bree, clustering on them. Thomas lagged behind, though not far enough behind to let Anne think he was waiting for her. She was glad enough, for the moment, that he was leaving the others alone. When he was with them, he and Katherine fought as though they'd never been apart. He couldn't be in the same room with Gareth at all. Gareth harassed him—"Play Monopoly with me, Tom, play Minecraft, come watch Star Wars, see me walk on my hands"—and Thomas, who had made the wrestling squad, responded by pinning him to the floor until he cried.

"You bully your brother," she had accused Thomas once. "You play too hard, and you enjoy it."

Naturally, Thomas had protested. "This is how boys play, Mom. He thinks he doesn't like it, but he does."

"If he's crying, he doesn't like it. You need to learn when to stop."

Thomas had looked down at her from the remoteness of his new height. His eyes had narrowed. "Maybe he needs to be a kid, Mom. You need to let go a little, let him get roughed up."

"That's your father talking." If everyone listened to Byron, she had refrained from saying, Gareth would be dead by now.

She could remember the exact moment when she had known, in her bones, that the marriage was over. They had been in the car, she and Byron, driving home after yet another doctor's appointment, Gareth in his car seat fast asleep, in the protective space suit he wore for rare daylight forays out of the house. In angry whispers they were rehearsing again the same argument.

"You heard what he said, Byron." Again. What the doctor said again. "We've got to be more careful. Even light through a window counts as exposure."

Byron, driving, said, "I heard."

"Well?"

"Look, Annie," Byron said. "We already put blackout curtains on every window in the house. We already keep him inside while everybody else in the world is out there living. We already put that damn astronaut suit on him. We make him look like a freak. We make him live like a freak, in the dark. I guess I just don't see the point anymore."

"Well, no. You don't." She'd glowered, squinting a little from the brightness, at the daylight scene: ordinary buildings, houses, cars. The world, awake, carrying on its normal round, had made her so angry she couldn't say any more.

The world didn't understand. Byron, who should have understood, didn't understand, either. Years of arguing, explaining, pleading, reframing the argument—none of it had worked, and he would never understand. In the sunlight, she had seen this as clearly as she saw the sharp white mountains against the sky.

It was no wonder, Anne often thought, that the demographic of her support group for parents of children *on the spectrum*, as they said, of Gareth's condition, stood at a ratio of two single parents to one married couple. I'm not alone, she liked to remind herself. If there were a consistent theme to their monthly meetings, held at Bill and Nada's All-Night Café, it was that flailing around in wreckage was the single defining activity of the human race.

Of course, the support group had its limits. In Utah there were only two other children on Gareth's particular *spectrum*, and neither of those children had siblings. Whenever Anne tried to talk about Katherine, her sulks and glowers, her refusals to do this or that, the others looked at her as if she'd started to pick her nose at the table.

"You've got to make her empathize," Nedra always said. Nedra, the other divorced parent, was always more than ready with empathy whenever the topic of ex-husbands arose. Her daughter Pauline was five. Whenever Pauline came over to play, Gareth treated her with exaggerated deference, pushing her on the swings and letting her boss him. He liked playing with Pauline; he was young for eight and didn't mind being railroaded into games like "wedding," which Pauline wanted to play over and over. Nedra couldn't watch this game without crying.

Georgie and Dan, the couple, had a one-year-old son,

whom they brought to meetings. While his parents tried to talk, Micah climbed over them, messed with the tabletop jukebox, ate packets of sugar, and poured his juice on the floor. Georgie and Dan were always saying things like, "I admire your curiosity, Micah."

On the subject of Katherine, when Anne ventured it, they waxed earnestly sage in a way that made her want to throw the salt and pepper shakers at them. "Excuse me," Dan would say. "Excuse me, but don't you think you're sweating the small stuff here? I think that if you look at the big picture . . ." Dan was fond of the big picture. Anne thought that probably, in some small corner of the big picture, there would be a detail of her breaking Katherine's neck, tiny and trivial as Icarus' legs waving from the sea. Meanwhile, she knew better than to bring up Thomas in the group. Doubtless they would feel that whatever she had paid for Gareth's life, he was worth that cost and more.

Well. In her mind she took up her conversation with Dan as she plodded up the stony trail. He is worth it. But of course Dan knew that. Dan and Georgie thought Micah was worth great sacrifice, too. At last month's meeting, in fact, Dan's vasectomy had dominated the discussion. From the corner of her eye, Anne had watched Georgie nodding and crying simultaneously as Dan talked, while Micah slept for once on her shoulder.

In the dark Anne watched her feet in white sneakers—Byron, Thomas, and Bree all wore hiking boots—pick themselves up and set themselves down. Laughter floated down from the ridge above her. Byron and Bree must be farther ahead than she'd thought. She increased her pace. Alone, everyone else invisible before her, she was walking along the island's knobbly backbone, among boulders higher than her head. Branches of the trail led away among the boulders and disappeared. She couldn't imagine where else they could lead. There was nowhere to go, except to the end of the land. Somewhere ahead, the trails must converge as a family tree, after generations of spreading, dwindled at last to one child. On either side of the ridge, the lake lay still and black. At the horizon, a seam of light was all that remained of the day. Somewhere, hidden in a fold of the land, a coyote pack set up a chorus of cries, high thin strands of sound curling into the clear sky.

"Wow," she could hear Byron saying, ahead of her. "Of course, that's probably what Thoreau said, the first time he saw Walden Pond. You know? 'Wow.' Only later he wrote it down better, after he'd had time to think."

"Or Shakespeare." That was Bree, a little breathless for a woman in such good shape. "The first time he sees this woman with wiry hair and bad breath, he goes, 'Hubba hubba.' Later he writes the sonnet."

"Exactly. Hey: hubba hubba."

"Oh, Byron, stop." Bree laughed again.

Anne tried to shrug off the chill that crept over her again. She made herself listen instead for the other voices, other footsteps. Somewhere in the night Thomas was walking with the silent tread of a wildcat. She concentrated on picking up some signal from him.

Wildcat. The thought made her shiver. Last winter, a mountain lion had come down out of the foothills into her neighborhood, following the deer that infiltrated the city, looking for forage, when the snow foreclosed on their high-country grazing. Mrs. Sorenson had found a dead deer stashed under her pyracanthus and, in annoyance, had seized it by one leg and dragged it, with more determination than strength, to the curb for the city to pick up. On her way to bed in the early morning, Anne had seen this extraordinary scene through her dining-room window as she'd stopped to pull the blackout curtains. More extraordinarily, the same scene was repeated several mornings in a row: Mrs. Sorenson, in curlers, quilted bathrobe, parka, and snow boots, hauling a deer carcass up her driveway and muttering to herself. At last, overcome by curiosity, Anne had put on her own coat and boots and had gone out to intercept her.

"Somebody's bright idea of a joke," Mrs. Sorenson had said sharply. "It's not one of your kids, is it?"

"I don't think so," Anne had replied.

"Not sneaking out at night to pull some funny stuff?"

"Not that I know of."

That night she and Gareth had gone out walking. Snow was falling again, and the darkness was magical with it, a white whirling that turned dark wherever the streetlights struck it. Muffled in their hooded coats and snow pants, they had strolled hand in hand, sometimes running and sliding on the dry powder, sometimes kicking it, sometimes lying down in a yard to make snow angels, then jumping up laughing, running and sliding away before anyone saw them. Anne still remembered the happiness that had flooded into her, filling her as the sharp dry cold filled her lungs when she breathed.

"What's that?" Gareth had said suddenly, as they neared Mrs. Sorenson's house. He had pointed to the street.

She had looked where he pointed. The street, newly

white, was marked with prints, large and obviously fresh. Quietly she had reached for his hand.

"Walk with me. Walk very slowly. If I tell you to put your hands over your head and yell, don't even look at me. Just do it. Make yourself look big and scary."

Step, step, step, they went through the snow. Crisp crunch, crisp crunch. Anne had pushed back her hood, so that she could see all around her. A flight animal, a deer, had eyes far back in its head, round bulging eyes that could see almost behind it. This was why. Step, step, step. Crisp crunch, crisp crunch. They were crossing Mrs. Sorenson's driveway. The deer, which Mrs. Sorenson had deposited by the curb that morning, was gone. Had the city come in the daytime, while they slept, to haul it away?

"Why are we being so quiet?" asked Gareth.

"Good question. Why are we being so quiet?" She raised her voice so that it echoed among the snowy houses. "Let's sing something. Let's sing 'Winter Wonderland.' *Sleigh bells ring, are you listening?*" she sang.

"Mom." For the moment, he sounded like Thomas or Katherine, an ordinary child embarrassed by his mother.

"*In the lane, snow is glistening—*"

They were past Mrs. Sorenson's house, approaching their own front walk.

"*A beautiful sight, we're happy tonight.*"

"Mom, really. You're going to wake up the whole world."

"Good. They need waking up. *Walking in a winter wonderland!*"

Up the walk. Only the steps to go.

"Hang on a sec." Gareth had pulled his mittened hand out of hers, swerved off the shoveled walk, and floundered, through the waist-high drifts in the yard, back to the street.

"Gareth!" she'd shouted. As she plunged after him, he had slipped and gone sprawling. "Yah, Gareth!" She was making as much noise as she could as she struggled through the snow. "Yaaaaaah!" She waved her hands wildly over her head.

As she reached him, panting and waving, he was clambering to his feet, something clutched in his fist. Grabbing his arm, she half-dragged him back up the yard, slipping and staggering, still waving her free arm and yelling. Up the steps again, open the front door, into the hall, slam the door. Lock it, even. Why not be sure?

"What in the ever-loving hell was all that noise?" Katherine called from the kitchen.

"Oh, nothing. Just being silly." Anne was shrugging her coat off, trying to breathe normally. She ruffled Gareth's hair. "What's in your hand?"

Gareth grinned and held up a Lego figure. "The Mandalorian. I thought I'd lost him in the snow."

Now, pausing on the trail, Anne called into the darkness, "Gareth? Katherine?" Nobody answered.

She raised her voice. "Byron?"

"Yup?"

"Where are the children?"

"They went ahead a little way. Don't worry. The trail ends at the point. They can't get lost. There's nothing between here and there but rocks. Trust me." Anne heard a murmur of Bree's voice, both their soft laughter.

Laughing at me, Anne thought. Ridiculous Mom Overreacts, Again. Infuriatingly her eyes filled with tears.

She rounded a bend and found herself among more boulders, so close on either side of the trail that she had to turn sideways to slide between them. "Erf," she said aloud. "I'm too fat for this." Was that why Byron had asked her to come along on this outing? To watch her get stuck between rocks, so that everyone could laugh? So that Bree could feel smug about her own body, so that Byron could feel smug about Bree's body, which undoubtedly—That thought she bit off and cauterized before it could finish bleeding from her mind.

At the next bend, where the boulders gave way to a clearing stubbled with rocks and brown grass, Thomas was waiting for her. Shamefacedly—she thought, though of course it was too dark to tell—he held out his hand to her.

"Footing's kind of rough through here. I thought I'd better make sure you got over it okay."

"Thanks."

She took his hand, trying to seem nonchalant. It was a warm, dry, hard hand, with strong fingers accustomed to finding the tiniest hold on a rock face. She resisted the urge to raise it to her lips and kiss it.

"So, things are okay with you?" She made herself ask as if she didn't really care.

He shrugged. "Yeah. Mostly. I have to take algebra two and chem in the fall, and I'm not looking forward to that, but otherwise . . ."

"I thought those were eleventh-grade classes. I haven't missed a year, have I?" She laughed self-consciously. It was entirely possible that she had missed a year of his life. Just mislaid it. Or slept through it.

"Nope. I'm accelerated." It was his turn to laugh self-consciously. "Like a plane taking off. Shooom." He mimed take-off with his free hand. "That's me."

They walked in silence, Thomas holding her hand loosely, guiding her.

"About Bree," he said after a moment.

"What about Bree?"

"You know she's living with us, right?"

"No," Anne said, "I didn't know that. It's not really my business, is it?"

"Well, she does live with us. She moved in last week. That's why I couldn't come see you Saturday. I was helping move her books."

"I see. And—" She hesitated, feeling her way forward. "Are you happy about that?"

Thomas sighed. "I mean, she's a nice person. She's fun. She likes to backpack, and climb, and camp, all the good stuff. I like her fine, I guess. She's better than some of the others. But—"

"It's one thing to like a person," Anne said carefully, ignoring *some of the others*. "It's another thing to have that person living in your house with you all the time."

"She's a vegan. That's kind of—well, tofu. You know."

"I see," said Anne.

"But I was wondering." Thomas paused.

"Yes?"

"Well, I was wondering—I was wondering—if this would—have any effect on the custody thing."

Anne tensed. "Do you mean could I sue your father for sole custody because he has a woman living with him?"

"That's—pretty much. Yeah. I mean, he said something about that, and I just wondered. Could you?"

"Well, yes, I guess I could."

They walked in silence again. Anne was thinking: I'm going straight home to wake up Carolyn. Carolyn was her lawyer, from the pro bono legal center. All the times Byron had tacitly threatened her with a dispute over Gareth, and now she had him. She could have Thomas back, as fast as she could say cohabitation. But surely Byron knew this. What was his game, she wondered. It wasn't like him to have a game. Straightforwardness was far less work. Now, though, something was up.

She looked up at Thomas, prowling beside her in the dark. His jaw in silhouette was not the soft line of a child's, but lean, sharp, a man's.

"What would you want me to do?" she said at last.

He swallowed. "Well, I—I don't know. I mean, no offense, Mom, really, I don't want you to take this the wrong way, but—"

"I know." Of course she knew. Of course Byron knew. He was perfectly safe. "You want to stay with Dad."

"I just need him." There was a note of desperation in his voice.

"I know you do."

They came out onto the point, with the lake spread on three sides around them. Against the dark-blue sky, four figures stood with their backs to Anne and Thomas, looking out over the water. The two adult figures stood apart from the children, their shoulders touching, their arms looped about each other. As Anne watched, the taller figure bent its face to the other's.

Quietly she moved away from Thomas. "You go on out to them," she whispered. "I think I'll head back down."

"Mom—"

"No, it's okay. Go look at the view. I'm tired. Tell Gareth and Katherine I'll be waiting at the car." She gave him a little push, and he stepped forward. Then he looked back, worried.

"I'll be fine," she said.

She walked down quickly, blinking back tears, stepping and sliding on loose stones, almost falling twice before she reached the trailhead again. She crossed the parking lot, unlocked her car, and got into it. Switching on the headlights, she saw gnats swimming in the twin cones of brightness. She flicked the lights off again and let darkness engulf the car: a whole universe of darkness, and there she sat at its center, in the driver's seat, alone. Somewhere in the salt-scented night, the coyotes were wailing again.

She had nodded off, almost, when a shadow materialized at the driver's side window. Anne snapped awake with a little cry of alarm.

A dry laugh in the dark. "Gotcha. My side's locked." Anne leaned over the passenger's seat to let Katherine in.

She collapsed into the car. "Well."

"Well?" said Anne.

"Well."

"Well?"

"Did you hear the one about the three holes in the ground?" said Katherine. "Well, well, well."

"Did you have a nice walk?"

"Oh, yeah. It was tons of fun. Dad and Park Ranger Barbie sucking each other's faces behind every rock they came to. Sorry," Katherine said, awkward and embarrassed. "I guess I shouldn't have said that. I'm really sorry."

Katherine was staring straight ahead, as if she were still at the drive-in movie. Anne put a tentative hand on her arm. "Well, I never expected Dad to live like a monk."

"Anyway. Ugh." Katherine hesitated an instant. Then a dam seemed to burst. "Anyway. So at the point he told us they want us all to be in the wedding, and weren't we happy to have Bree for a stepmother, and maybe we'd all come and spend weeks with them, maybe even live with them, they're going to buy this fabulous house in the canyon, and even Gareth can live there, and la-da-la-da-la, so I said, fine, whatever, and started walking back here so if I had to puke they wouldn't see me do it." Her voice was rough with threatened tears.

"Oh, honey." Anne hesitated. "Would you—like—to live with them? Have a more normal life?" Even as she spoke, she could hear what an idiotic question it was. No, Mom, I would freely choose to live like a bat. Are you kidding me? She braced herself for the caustic response.

But all Katherine said was, "I don't know." She had covered her face with her hands; her voice through her fingers was muffled. "I mean—I don't know. I just don't even want to think about it right now."

Anne folded her arms on the steering wheel and let her head drop onto them, her eyes close. Byron and Bree. There was something inevitable even in the ring of their joined names. They would buy the fabulous house in the canyon. Even Gareth would live there. So they said. Could she fight them, if they wanted to fight about Gareth? If it came to that, would she have the energy? Would it matter so much, after all? A stray gnat sang in her ear. She breathed the saline air, exhaled. This was the air at the end of the world, and it was bitter in her mouth.

Across the parking lot she heard Gareth's laugh ring out. They were back. Straightening, she pushed her hair out of her eyes, got out of the car, and went to meet them. Their four dark forms approached her, crunching across the gravel: Gareth running and skipping, Thomas loping diffidently behind him. Farther back, Byron and Bree walked slowly, shoulder to shoulder.

Anne raised one hand in greeting. The night was huge around her, dry and windy, dizzying with stars. Beyond the curved shore, far out on the water, beneath that enormous sky, white gulls rode the dark swells in their sleep.

THE BEACH HOUSE

The rooms smelled of damp, but that was to be expected. When Caroline opened the sliding doors, the breeze came over the wrinkling sound to ruffle the yellowed newspapers on the coffee table. Far across the open water, the pier lights at the foot of the bridge showed like a cluster of grounded stars in the dusk.

Up and down the stairs she labored, carrying things from the car. I used to think the beach was relaxing, she thought as she bumped her green Coleman cooler from one step to the next, pausing to rest between bumps. Surely I'm not that much more tired than I used to be. Of course the drive had taken it out of her: ten hours. Early that morning, braking at the stop sign at the top of her own street, she had thought of the long road and been almost afraid to go on. But she had gone on, and now here she was, exhausted but all in one piece.

Before leaving home, she had given her daughter, who lived in Texas, only the vaguest suggestion that she might be hard to reach by phone this weekend. She carried a cell phone, but it intimidated her, all those things you touched on the glowing little screen. Now as she rested she imagined what Amelia would say. *What do you think you're doing, Mother? By yourself? Are you out of your mind?* Defiant, she bumped the cooler up one more step. The half-melted ice inside sloshed and rattled.

In the galley kitchen, she transferred the cooler's contents into the refrigerator's staring white depths: hotdogs, pimiento cheese, some turkey breast from the deli, eggs, cooked shrimp she had bought from a seafood place on the mainland, a bottle of the sweet German wine Amelia laughed at. Well. This time next week she'd be fasting before surgery. No more wine, no more fun. She meant to enjoy herself now.

Up and down the inlet, this May Wednesday night, most of the houses stood dark, but across the water music was playing, some song she didn't recognize. A man stood silhouetted with his fishing pole against light through a glass door. The man was nobody she knew. These days she wasn't likely to recognize any of the people who would come and go. It was years since the Emersons, for example, had come down. Richard had left Paula for a girl named Toy, and young Rick had gotten into drugs. That was the last Caroline had heard of them. Their house, more exposed than her own, had blown away in one of the hurricanes, and a new one stood in its place, a whole self-conscious Victorian-looking edifice on stilts. Often enough through the years, and especially here, in her own old modest cypress house, Caroline had thought on Paula with pity.

Amelia, meanwhile, had grown up, moved away, been married, had a child, gotten divorced. She called home almost daily now, to be sure that Caroline was taking her vitamins and exercising. *You should lift weights, Mother. Resistance exercise is what you need. That old-lady walking won't do anything for your osteoporosis.* Next Tuesday Amelia would appear at Caroline's house in the flesh, *to see you through it, Mother.* Though naturally she loved Amelia, Caroline found herself dreading this prospect.

To be sick was bad enough. To be sick and managed by

Amelia was intolerable to contemplate, though of course she would have to tolerate it. Better not to contemplate it, then. While she was at it, she would not contemplate John, either. She would remain here, in the present, in her empty house, with her shrimp, her hotdogs, and her bottle of sweet wine. She meant to please herself this one time, and so she would. Children playing under the house, their brown arms and legs breaded with sand, the sun in their hair: it was all such a long time ago.

When she had brought her supplies in, she poured a glass of the sweet wine and, determined to savor everything, took it onto the high porch. She stood at the rail, looking over the darkening water. The tide was coming in; the wind urged it along in stiff blue rollers that sloped in to smack the sea wall. Far out beyond the bridge she could just see a gas rig lit up like Christmas, wavering in the restless air. Except for the growl of the air conditioner in the house across the way, all she could hear were the night-breathing sounds of water and wind. She finished her wine, washed the glass, and went to bed with the windows open.

Seagull laughter woke her before the light did. Dragging on an old t-shirt dress—*Mother, you're not wearing that thing in public*—she poured cereal into one of the old blue Bakelite bowls and ate it on the porch. Spread before her, last night's cast-iron water rumpled now like mercury under a milky sky. A pelican came rowing across her vision, making her laugh: he looked like an old man riding a bicycle, upright and satisfied.

Across the inlet the man was out again, fishing: a small man, slight in his cargo shorts and blue sport shirt, which even from that distance she could see had been meticulously ironed and starched, so that it fit him like a shirt-shaped box. His hands handling the fishing rod were slight as a child's. He wore a pointed straw hat and, on his very small feet, white ankle socks and a pair of black men's flip-flops.

Caroline smiled to herself. The idea of Chinese people going to the Alabama beach had never occurred to her before. It wasn't that she thought they couldn't, or shouldn't. It was just that she hadn't thought of their wanting to, even if they did live as close as Mobile, not far away in China. As she watched him, the man looked up. His hat tilted back, and he saw her. She gave him a tentative wave. Did people you didn't know, who might not even speak your language, want you watching them while they fished? He waved back, a stiff little gesture like a phrase in translation. The hat tilted down again, hiding his face.

After breakfast she inspected the house. People at home in North Carolina had thought she and Cash were crazy to have a house so far away, instead of at Wrightsville or Carolina Beach or the Outer Banks. When they weren't there, which in recent years had been most of the time, the house was rented out. Everywhere now she found evidence of renters' carelessness: scratches in the wood floor, coffee stains on the butcher-block counter. In the utility closet under the house, the old fishing poles were a hopeless tangle of line and rusted hooks. She didn't want to fish, but it was a pity, she thought, remembering how carefully Cash had kept things.

The dock was still good. They had had it rebuilt after the last hurricane, and now the little ridgelets of water hurried past it on their way out to sea. As Caroline watched from under the house, a blue heron came stepping along the seawall and onto the dock, where it stood like a plastic replica of itself, staring out with blank gold eyes. The fishing man across the way jerked his pole up; something small flapped on his line. With stately unconcern the heron opened its wings, dangled its legs, and flew over the water to stand on the dock opposite.

By the time she had looked into all the closets and cabinets, scrubbed out the bathtub, run the dishwasher and washing machine with a cupful of vinegar each, and lain down for a very little rest, the pale sun had crawled up the sky, rinsing it a thin midday blue. In the bedroom Caroline pulled on her black-and-white camellia-printed skirted swimsuit. *You aren't that old, Mother. Why do you have to wear that awful old-lady bathing suit?* Back on with the t-shirt dress and a hat, and she was ready for her decorous walk to the Gulf side of the island.

This early in the year the heat didn't beat up hard from the pavement, and she could cross the main road without having to wait for traffic. Walking in the bright day she felt well, as if the sun had bleached away the faint stain of illness that hung cloudlike in her mind's peripheral vision most of the time. As she came over the dunes with their rattling grasses, the wind freshened. Dry sand blew against her legs. The tide was out; before her the beach stretched long and shining, with a dark fringe of seaweed at its hem. Far out the brown waves rose, rolled over, fell with a muffled clash. On the horizon, a white fishing boat nodded in the swells, trailing lines like strands of Rapunzel hair. A cloud of birds followed it, a wake in the air.

Along the scalloped edge of the water sandpipers ran

on twinkling legs, advancing, retreating, picking at unseen things on the wet sand. She remembered a nature notebook she had urged John to keep, the summer he was six or seven or eight. He had filled exactly one page—or, not filled it but marked it, with a tiny, cramped line drawing of a sandpiper whose legs were an upside-down vee. *Sadpipper*, he had written beneath the drawing in his equally cramped left-hand print. And beneath that, *I hate nachr*. Somewhere at home she still had the notebook, empty save for that one page. And here were the *sadpippers*, pipping along the sand as they had always done, not caring in the least what anyone thought of them.

Caroline walked up the beach into the wind, water frothing around her ankles. On her right hand the houses stood in their washed colors, yellow, blue, mint green, like candy houses, the sun in their eyes. In front of one house someone had set up a cabana in the sand, with metal poles. Overnight the wind had peeled back the plastic tarpaulin cover; it flapped loose like a broken wing. Here and there on the sand, white jellyfish glistened. In a clot of seaweed Caroline saw a whole sand dollar and picked it up. She felt she had found a real dollar, tucked there by some generous hand.

All day she was alone, which she minded less than she'd feared. Time didn't exactly stand still, or cease to exist, as people often said time did at the beach. But it didn't matter to the birds, plying their own trades across the sky and water, or to the little quick anoles. On the porch, reading, she watched one anole change from green to brown as he skittered from the weathered floorboards to the raw unpainted railing, spreading his dewlap until the cold red blood showed through it like a second heart made visible.

"Who do you think's going to see that?" she asked him. "You think I'm going to lose my head and run away with you?"

When he paused to spread his dewlap, she could see him breathing, the dry thin skin inflating and collapsing over the frail, frail spine and ribs. She could step on him, she thought, crush him like a cockroach. It would be that easy. Fragile as they were, how did the race of anoles persevere? This one seemed unlikely to repeat himself any time soon. On the other hand, he was quick and canny. Even as she watched, he flicked away out of sight.

At sundown she had her glass of wine and ate the cooked shrimp, peeling back the crackling translucent skins. Though she felt hungry, having skipped lunch, her puny hunger seemed hardly worth the effort of cooking or going alone to a restaurant. Across the inlet, the lights of the one inhabited house spilled onto the water. Again she heard music. By now she knew that it wasn't just an unfamiliar song; it was a woman singing in a whole language she didn't know, an alien mewing voice. Still, it was beautiful.

The fishing man had taken off his pointed hat and been joined by more people: another man, two women, several children of various sizes who were running up and down on the dock and in the patchy grass around the house. There was a smell of lighter fluid and charcoal, but the food smells that followed were different somehow, not the expected burgers and hotdogs. The people talked and laughed. The low, dry clouds flamed suddenly like the swelling dewlaps of a thousand anoles. A boat coming in drew a widening greater-than sign across the russet sound. The next minute, the sun was gone, the boat had vanished around the point, and the water looked cold. Still the talk and laughter, the singing woman's undulant voice, carried over to where Caroline sat with her empty glass in her hand.

In the morning, drinking her coffee on the dock, she saw a man emerge from the house next door and walk down to the sea wall, frightening the heron away. He was a short, thickset man with a bare grizzled chest and a stomach that hung over the waistband of his khaki shorts. In the morning sun his naked scalp glowed pink. He carried a crab net with, she suspected, a chicken neck in it, or something of that sort. She watched him lower himself, groaning, onto his fat knees and hand the net down its chain into the slopping water. With more groaning he stood up again, turned, and saw her.

"Morning." A Yankee voice, her mother would have said.

"Good morning." Her own voice came out as stiff as the Chinese man's wave, from disuse. The only person she had spoken to in two days was a lizard; that conversation had necessarily been brief.

"Did that noise bother you last night?" He stood up, a shadow against the morning light, flexing his thick hands as if they hurt him. "I thought it was gonna be Murder on the Orient Express if they didn't shut the hell up."

"Oh, they were just having fun," she said. "We used to have some noisy nights here ourselves, when our children were growing up."

"That's your house? Not a rental? You own it?"

"My father built it. Of course we do rent it out now."

He cast an appraising eye at her house. "I'm looking for a place down here to buy. Rochester, New York is not where

I want to spend my old age. I've shoveled enough damn snow."

"Do you have family down here?" she asked.

"Do I sound like I have family down here?" He laughed a hoarse bronchial laugh, half-cough. "I don't have family anywhere. Not that speak to me. Eh, but I make friends. No worries."

"Well." She looked into her empty cup. "I think I'm ready for a refill. Good luck with your house hunting."

"This is a nice spot. If you ever decided to sell, you'd let me know, right? Joe. Joe Keough. I gotta card in the house."

"I'll keep that in mind." She smiled at him, rose, and went up to her own house, leaving the porch door open to the breeze.

In the heat of the day she went out in the car to run errands. At the seafood shop she bought a half-gallon of frozen gumbo; in the Ship-and-Shore she picked up instant rice, a pair of ninety-eight-cent flip-flops, and a new straw hat, wide as a sombrero. As she was checking out, she saw some of the Chinese group—the two women and a collection of children—puzzling over a bottle of something in the pharmacy section. The women's voices rose in what sounded to her like argument, though perhaps it was just that they were speaking Chinese.

"We get all kinds these days," said the woman at the register. "People come here from ever where now."

"Well, I think that's *nice*." Caroline spoke firmly.

"Oh, it's intristing, that's for sure." The woman slipped Caroline's groceries into a paper bag and handed it, crackling, over the scarred formica counter.

By the time she got home, the light had changed. Over the Gulf, towers of cloud had risen, white on top, blue-gray at their roots. She went upstairs to put her groceries away, then came down again and sat on the swing beneath the house. The water in the inlet darkened and hardened into ridges. Far out beyond the bridge, clouds fringed like jellyfish were dropping rain over the bay and onto the mainland. The wind stiffened. The next minute it was raining on the inlet, a rain like a heavy beaded curtain rattling as someone passed through. Dimly across the water she saw figures scurrying under the Chinese house, saw grownups gesticulate to children. Her own children would have been out in the rain, she thought, getting soaked and courting the lightning. She recalled Cash roaring at Amelia and John to get out of that water: NOW, he said. Or was it her own father she remembered, shouting at her? These children stood docilely under their house, looking out, looked at by Caroline, like children in a picture book.

While her gumbo heated, she stood at the window watching the rain blow over the Sound and away. The bridge reappeared from behind its hedge of cloud. Next door, the man she had spoken to in the morning came down his steps and onto the sea wall, carrying a fishing rod. Across the way, the two Chinese men were also fishing. There's not much in this inlet, she could have told them. Only croakers, eels, and the inedible sea catfish whose spines cut you when you tried to back the hooks out of their jaws.

Not that she had done much fishing herself. Her primary function as a grownup, when she wasn't cooking, cleaning, or putting lotion on people's sunburns, had been to sit on the swing, drink wine, and talk to Cash and John while they fished. As a girl, she had not been forbidden to fish, exactly, but she hadn't been invited to fish, either. That had been something her father and brother did, hours on end, not speaking except to say pass me another piece of squid.

Well, you could learn a lot by watching. For example, she was learning right now that the man next door had a reel that stuck when he tried to cast. The next minute she learned that he had a temper—he had thrown the whole rig into the water and stormed heavily back up his stairs. Both the Chinese men looked on in interest. They too learned by watching. She saw them confer with each other and gesture at the water. Americans, she imagined them saying. Waste, waste.

She went back to the stove to stir the gumbo, scraping the scorched skin off the bottom of the cast-iron Dutch oven. Standing there with her old metal spatula in her hand, her elbows bonily awkward, her short silver hair on end in the humidity, she might have been her own mother, fifty years ago. The gumbo smell was the smell of every summer. Was she hungry for it? Surely she was. It wasn't time yet to be losing her appetite.

A knock at the sliding glass door startled her from her thoughts. Behind the drawn blinds, a broad shadow raised its arm to knock again. For a moment she thought she wouldn't answer. Perhaps he hadn't seen her watching him. *Don't open the door to a stranger, Mother*—she could hear Amelia lecturing. But there she was anyway, as if she couldn't help it, pulling the blind cord, putting on her smile, opening the door.

"Good evening," she said.

"Looks like it's gonna be an okay night after all. I was

going to fish, but my reel—"

"Yes," said Caroline, wondering how much he would mind if he thought she was laughing at him.

He shrugged. "Cheap piece of crap. Made in China. Makes me wonder what those guys on the other side are using. They must know something the rest of us don't."

"I imagine they do," she said, carefully neutral.

"I came to see if you and your husband wanted to have a drink with me."

"Oh," said Caroline in confusion. Had she led him to believe that she had a husband, living and present? Would it be better, safer, to let him go on believing that? A stranger, a man who threw fishing rods in anger? Amelia would have advised her to lie, which perhaps was why she heard herself telling the truth.

"I'm a widow. I never can get used to saying I instead of we." She hesitated, then plunged. "I was about to have a glass of wine. Will you join me?"

There: she had done it. She had opened the door and invited him in. Now she was pouring the wine into the blue plastic dollar-store goblets, then wincing a little as she watched him taste it.

"Whew, that's sweet stuff."

"Well, it's what I like," she said in apology.

"I got gin at my place. Sure you wouldn't rather have gin and tonic?"

"Oh, well." Again Caroline hesitated.

"I can bring the stuff over here. Your porch is nicer than mine."

"Oh, well . . ." Once the treatment started, there would go all her chances to drink gin and tonic. She had never been a gin drinker, but surely that was different, and subtly better, than having never drunk gin until it was too late.

While she dithered, he was gone and back again with the blue gin bottle and a plastic liter of tonic. "You got ice, I guess. I put the lime in my pocket. Now, look. I can make yours mild or strong. What'll it be?"

"Oh, mild, please," said Caroline.

Stiffly she sat in her adirondack chair and sipped at her drink. To her surprise, its faint bitterness, edged with lime, was pleasant on her tongue.

"You like that?" In the chair beside hers, her companion rattled his ice.

"It's very nice."

"You sound surprised."

"Well, I'm set in my ways."

Her companion said, "I introduced myself, lady. Now it's your turn."

"Sorry." She flushed, embarrassed to be caught in absent-mindedness and poor manners. Here he was in her house. Perhaps, not waiting to learn her name, he was the one with no manners. "I'm Caroline Mallory," she said, apologizing again.

"And do you come from around here, Mrs. Mallory? Your accent says you do."

"Well, I grew up in Tennessee, but I've lived most of my married life in North Carolina, outside Charlotte. I don't *think* I sound like Alabama."

"I meant Southern. *Yawl.*"

Classed as a foreigner, Caroline sighed. Cash had grown up two streets over from her in Palmyra, Tennessee. They had been on the same Methodist youth retreat at Edgar

Evins State Park, when she was in ninth grade and he was a junior. Of course he hadn't known who she was then, but it was something, to have shared an experience before they could know that they shared it. Meanwhile she wondered whether the people across the way were in fact Chinese as she'd assumed, or something else entirely. No, she reprimanded herself, they do not all look alike. It was simply that she had assumed without asking.

"You said you had children. Grown and gone, I guess."

Caroline smiled. "Oh, yes. Long ago."

"I never had any kids. Dodged that bullet."

From the corner of her eye Caroline studied him as she sipped her drink: blunt profile, baggy cheeks, eyes sunk far back in their fleshy pouches. In his company—these days she didn't often find herself in the company of men—she was pierced anew with longing for Cash, who if not perfect had at least been familiar, in his terse, sinewy way. At the end he had been almost fleshless, his body no more than a whisper. Dying, she thought, had been another kind of love-making, more intimate than physical intimacy, though you didn't lose yourself in the same way. Instead you felt yourself becoming more present, more weighed down in your body, as the other person ebbed away, until at last it was only you in the room, breathing the air that was left to you.

Till death do us part, you said so glibly on your wedding day, not thinking of death at all, certainly not thinking that each of you had chosen a person to die with, and that that, more even than living together, more even than suffering together, would define what bound you. The loophole, of course, and the great problem, was what to do if you were the survivor. When your own end came, who would be with you? Once, on a plane in turbulence, while Caroline sat white-knuckled, the lady beside her had said, "Well, we're all here together." But I don't want to go down in flames with you, Caroline had thought in despair. I don't even know your name.

"I can smell your food cooking," her companion said. "Otherwise I'd invite you to dinner."

"It's just gumbo I picked up at Skinner's. I don't know how I thought I was going to eat a half-gallon. Will you have some with me?"

If she had been a third person, observing herself now, she would have gaped at such recklessness. Picking up strange old men at the beach—she could imagine what Amelia would say.

The strange old man she had picked up heaved himself with a groan from his chair. "I'll make us another drink."

Later, when he had gone home with his bottles, leaving his card on her kitchen island, Caroline washed the dishes and put them away. Then she stood looking at the room. In her childhood, the walls had been bare weathered cypress, real cabin walls. On the wall over the old sofa had hung the mounted tarpon her father had caught, the summer he went out on the Duke to deep-sea fish. The fish was long gone. After her father's death, her mother had taken it back to Palmyra and sold it in a yard sale. That old thing, her mother had said. Can you believe somebody in Palmyra, Tennessee, paid twenty dollars for it? Still, as if she read it in the blank space on the wall, Caroline remembered her father cleaning fish on the dock, her brother Lant squatting beside, running his finger down a tarpon's long exposed backbone and licking the blood.

Lant was in California now, retired from running a chain of health clubs. He and his wife had no use for this house. It was Caroline who had kept it. She and Cash had had it drywalled and painted cream inside, the ground-down linoleum pulled up, the wood subfloor refinished with polyurethane. She had chosen the pair of blue-denim-slipcovered chairs, the brown twill sofa. With a sense of surrender, because she had never liked consciously "beachy" decor, she had filled a glass-column vase with shells and set it on the kitchen island they had made by knocking out a wall between the cramped old kitchen and the living room. It was an old house, as beach houses went. It had managed not to be blown or swept away in storms, not yet. But you'd never know that, she thought. Its inside was blank and new, anonymous, so that anyone might feel at home there.

"I like this place," Mr. Keough had repeated over his fourth gin and tonic. "You've kept it up good."

"It's a responsibility," she'd demurred. "We've changed a lot over the years. You have to, to keep it in good shape. Sometimes it's hard to believe it's the same house."

She had brought out, from the wicker ottoman, an album of photographs she'd put together one rainy summer some years back, when Amelia's marriage was coming apart, and— at any rate, Caroline had needed something to do. Now too it was something to do, to show someone the house's history. There were photographs of her mother and father after the war, when they'd just built the house, the two of them standing on some precursor of the current dock, her father with his hands in his suit pockets, her mother in spectator pumps and a wide skirt. There were she and Lant in black-and-white, flanking their father as he held up his catch, a cigarette affixed to his smiling lips.

The next few pages revealed her high-school self in a crocheted bikini—"Whoa," Mr. Keough said—drinking what was probably rum-and-coke, though her mother had thought it was only Coca-Cola.

More pages. Her and Cash. Her and Cash and Amelia. Her and Cash and Amelia and John. Sand castles. People fishing. Fish people caught. Amelia and John with Cash and some enormous fish. Cash with Richard Emerson, who later left his wife for a girl named Toy. The two little boys, John and Rick, riding their fathers' bare brown shoulders. Herself at the stove. Herself and her mother, whom they'd brought with them until she couldn't climb the stairs any more.

High-school Amelia and some boy she'd met on the beach. College Amelia and some other boy. John, a teenager, grimacing at the camera. John in the driveway the week after college graduation, washing the salt from his new car. John the summer between his two years of law school, fishing with his shirt off, the merciless sun casting his ribcage into sharp relief. She had turned the page quickly.

There were Amelia and baby Mallory. More baby Mallory. Toddler Mallory. Preschool Mallory. Second-grade Mallory with no front teeth. More Mallory, including some recent snapshots Amelia had sent from Texas, which had nothing to do with the beach but which Caroline had had in her purse. She brought them out and stuck them in the album as she turned its pages, so as not to lose them. When she left, she thought, she would take the album with her. She had copies of most of the pictures at home, but it was stupid to leave family artifacts in a rental house in a hurricane zone. Stupid of her to have trusted the weather all this time: the weather and the soundness of her house.

Sitting there with this strange man in the lamplight, knee to knee, turning the pages of the album, she was as surprised at herself as if she had just walked in on someone *in flagrante.* But she wasn't doing anything flagrant, she protested inwardly. She was merely sitting on a twill sofa with a neighbor—not a terribly attractive neighbor, either, not a neighbor to tempt her—passing the evening in a way that was marginally more pleasant, maybe, than passing it alone. Looking at photographs together was not a binding interaction. She might wake up tomorrow to find that he had gone away while she slept, and this would not affect her. It would not be any kind of loss. In fact, the reverse might happen: she might decide, in the small hours, to pack up her car and leave. He would wake up, walk outside, glance over at her house, and be met with its emptiness, and that would not change his life, either. This was like any meeting at the beach. People came and went. You took up with them while your visits coincided, and then you returned to your real life, seamlessly, leaving behind whatever you had picked up on the sand. The vase of shells was all right here. In her real house it would never have done.

By Saturday the island had filled up. Up and down Caroline's narrow inlet the houses were occupied. Far out on the Sound, jet skis inscribed the silver water with their broad circling wakes. When she hadn't seen Mr. Keough on Friday, she had thought, perhaps even hoped, that his week was over and he had gone home. But early Saturday morning, there he was, standing on the sea wall with a new and, she presumed, better fishing rod, casting into the inlet, reeling in whenever a boat came laboring past. She stood carefully out of sight to watch him. The Chinese families, too, appeared to be staying. As she drank her second cup of coffee, she saw the women come out together to their dock and sit side by side in lounge chairs, drawing their skirts up to sun their knees. Two little boys in pillowy orange life jackets climbed down the ladder into the lapping water and bobbed about like corks.

Late Saturday afternoon, after her walk on the beach and her nap, tall thunderheads rose again from the Gulf. Boats puttered into their docks and were lifted hydraulically out of the water. The Chinese women, who surely hadn't sat there all that time, folded their chairs and put them under the house. The sky flickered; rain came down like nails. Caroline opened her fridge and contemplated the remains of the gumbo. Even after Thursday night's supper—Mr. Keough had drunk more than he had eaten—and her frugal Friday meals, there was still a lot of the half-gallon left. How much gumbo could you eat?

She was just taking hotdogs from the freezer when the sliding glass door opened behind her. "Pardon me walking in, but it's wet as all hell out there. I thought you might have dinner with me someplace."

"Well," she said, wondering how exactly she felt about his walking into her house. They were on friendly terms, beach-neighbor terms, but was this quite—? Again she imagined what Amelia would say.

This evening he wore an expansive flowered shirt with a narrow, pointed, open collar, through whose gap a tuft of gray hair showed. Had he polished his bald head, or was it rain that shone on it? On his feet, small and narrow for a large man's feet, he wore leather loafers of a sort Cash would have dismissed as feminine. Somehow those shoes made her feel safer. He seemed less like a man who would throw things in anger, more like a man anxious to make a good impression, even if he did walk in without knocking.

"There's this country club place at the other end of the island. I went over and looked at the menu. It seems all right. You ever eat there?"

"Not in years," said Caroline. Why eat out when you can cook fresh fish right here? That was what Cash had always said. Of course as property owners they belonged to the country club. Her mother had prevailed on them to take her there sometimes.

"You ready now?" he asked. Caroline looked down at herself in confusion. She was wearing, again, the old t-shirt dress, and her feet were bare. At that moment she could not remember even whether she had brushed her teeth that day.

"Let me just—" she gestured helplessly at herself.

He shrugged. Did it matter to him how she looked? "I'll meet you downstairs."

They sat in the bar, looking out of the curved windows that gave onto the Gulf. As she'd dressed—long crinkling skirt, blue linen shell, turquoise necklace Amelia had sent for her last birthday, aquamarine birthstone studs in her ears—Caroline had thought carefully. How to be kind, but noncommittal? How to accept a gesture gratefully without slipping into debt? As a girl she had gone blithely and thoughtlessly on dates, as you did in those days—but should she even think of this evening that way? All her faculties of romantic discernment felt rusty from disuse.

Now, sipping her gin, she looked at Mr. Keough and said

the line she had practiced in the mirror. "I told you my life story. Now it's your turn."

"Got all night?" In the rain-washed sun through the window, his face above the flowered shirt was a landslide of flesh.

"Well, there's nowhere else I really have to be," she told him.

"Let's just say I've had an interesting life."

Smiling, she said, "That's what people say when they have something to hide."

He smiled back at her, exposing teeth far too white and even to be his own. "Yes, that is what they say. Unless they say their life's too boring to talk about. Those are the people you gotta watch. The boring people."

"Oh, dear."

Again he smiled at her whitely.

A plate of fish was set before her, and she looked at it in confusion. Was this what she had ordered? Her companion was lifting an oyster to his lips, tossing it down like a drink. Outside the sun was slanting over the water and in through the windows. A waiter in black came along lowering blinds.

They had decaffeinated coffee—"No dessert for me. Got the diabetes"—in the dim filtered light. Then, the bill paid, they walked out into an evening still brilliant, though in the upper regions of the sky a dark-blue curtain was descending by unseen degrees. Caroline heard the labored breathing of her companion as he walked beside her. She was afraid that he might try to take her hand, but he only touched her arm and pointed out to sea.

"Looking for dolphins. Keep thinking I'll see some when I'm out fishing. They're hiding from me, I guess."

"My son John used to keep field glasses on the porch," said Caroline. "He used to get up before it was light to watch for them." Smiling to herself, grateful for this vision of John that had returned unasked for—a John who didn't hate *nachr*—she glanced sidewise at her companion to see if he noticed her smile and wondered at it.

But he was still squinting out at the waves, as if at this distance, looking straight into the sun, he might see what his own heart desired. She thought perhaps he had forgotten her, until he said, "Well, it's early, but I'm tired. Been tired lately. I don't know why. Just old, I guess. Mind if we go home now?"

"Not at all," said Caroline.

On the street side their houses loomed close together, nearer neighbors than they appeared on the side that faced the water. Mr. Keough turned into Caroline's driveway.

"Curbside service, lady." In the glowing twilight, he looked at her.

Caroline was gathering up her purse, drawing her light cardigan around her. "Thank you so much. It was a lovely dinner. I can't remember the last time—"

She was going to say, the last time I ate at the club, but he had put out a thick hand and drawn her to him. She felt his lips move against hers, the warm fat flick of his tongue.

Cash, she thought in a panic, wrenching away, how did I come here?

Mr. Keough put both hands on the steering wheel and gripped it hard.

"Thank you," said Caroline. "I had a very nice time. Thank you so much. Good night." She heard the haste in her voice; it was nothing compared to the haste in her heart.

She got out of the car, shut the door firmly, and ran under the house and up the stairs. Stepping into the silent house, locking the door behind her, she heard his car reverse, maneuver, and roll into its own driveway, next to hers.

Across the inlet the Chinese families had turned on all their lights. Spotlights on their dock shone down into the water, steely-dark everywhere except where the light fell on it. There it glowed green and rumpling. In the wavering circles of light floated vague whitenesses: jellyfish. The two Chinese men lay on their stomachs on the dock, watching them rise to the surface, sink back into the opaque depths. A child ran out from beneath the house, writing on the darkening air with a sparkler, a word Caroline couldn't read before it melted away.

On Sunday it rained again. Waking in gray darkness, Caroline heard the water rattling in the downspouts. While her coffee brewed, she stood at the window to see the curtain of rain, the roiled water of the Sound, the cloud closing in, shutting off any long view. She picked up the cell phone Amelia had bought her, to carry at all times: out of charge, and what had she done with the cord? All the newspapers in the house were two years old, at least. There would be no reading the weather forecast, but this one looked like an all-day rain. That was all right, she thought. Like Mr. Keough, she felt tired. She felt tired of Mr. Keough, glad for an excuse not to see him. Happily, with a feeling of rebellion, she took her coffee and a stack of old *Cottage Living* magazines back to her room, where she settled in to spend the day in unrepentant solitude. Even the thought that soon she might be doing nothing but lying in bed did not disturb her. I'm practicing, she told herself. Might as well learn to like it.

In fits, while the rain fell, she read and slept. During one sleep her son John came to her, inside a dolphin. She was swimming in the Gulf deeps, dog-paddling as the waves rocked her up and down, when something bumped her underwater. At first the fin frightened her. Then she saw the glossy taupe skin, the strangely human eye catching hers, the merry snout. She saw, too, her son John, a child, curled inside the dolphin's body like the fetus in a cut-away diagram of the womb. Hugging his knees to his chest, he slept with his long eyelashes on his cheeks. For a time the dolphin swam alongside Caroline. As she swam, she watched John, tucked away in the creature's body, safely dreaming in the roll of the sea. When she put out her hand to touch him, she touched the sleek wet skin of the dolphin. At once it leapt away and vanished beneath the waves. Far out, she saw a finned back curve again out of the water, but she couldn't be sure whether it was the same dolphin or another, a stranger to her. But then she supposed that really, they were all strangers. Or none of them were. Or both at once.

At daybreak the clear light woke her. It was Monday, and she was leaving. Tomorrow she would be at home, waiting for Amelia to come. Now, with trepidation she took her coffee outside, not wanting to see anyone this last morning. Looking across the inlet, however, she saw that the Chinese people had left before her. Their cars were gone. The house was shut up, with an unmistakable look of abandonment. Fishing rods, hats, life jackets, floats: all had vanished. On the patchy grass, a child's red foam-rubber sandal lay where it had been dropped, like any other piece of trash.

Next door, the fishing rod still leaned on the railing. Caroline looked at it for a moment. Then, regretfully, because it was nicer to drink coffee outside, she went back in and shut the sliding door. She stood at the window with her coffee, looking out through the blinds. There, outside, was the water, the sunlight glancing from it, spreading beyond the inlet and away, wide and silver-blue in the morning.

As she looked, a little running wave in the distance seemed to resolve into a brown-gray fin, a shining dark body that surfaced and dove. Then another appeared. And another. Suddenly the Sound was full of them, waves made flesh. Everywhere they leapt and dove, surfaced and vanished. It was like looking at falling stars, she thought. If you looked too hard in one place, you missed them everywhere else. Or maybe, looking so hard, you saw them because you wanted to see them, not because they were there. Maybe it was only the water in the sun. She wondered whether Mr. Keough, in the house next door, was awake and looking out to sea— whether he had seen what she saw, if in fact it was there to see at all.

Moving quickly through the house, she packed the food and wine into the cooler, her clothes into her suitcase. She wiped down the counters, swished out the bathtub. Maids would come from the rental agency before the next people arrived, but she wanted to leave no trace. Bump, bump, bump, wincing at the noise, she brought the cooler down to the car. Turning down the air conditioner, turning off the lights, she stepped outside and locked the door.

Glancing again at the fishing rod on the porch next door, she stopped and thought. It seemed almost an answer to some question that niggled at her. Surely there was one loose end she might tie up right now. Unlocking the door again, she went back inside, found a pen in the kitchen drawer, and, taking up Mr. Keough's card and frowning a little to herself, wrote her phone number and that of her island realtor on the blank side. Amelia would have enough to do without worrying about the beach house. Or would she? Would she want to come back here again? Or was it too much trouble? Would she want to remember, or forget? Would she be angrier with Caroline for giving it away, or for keeping it? It was impossible to know.

Caroline looked at the card in her hand. After a moment's consideration, she slipped it into her purse. Maybe when she got home she'd look at it again. Or maybe she wouldn't.

Once in her car, she drove away without looking back.

As she turned into the main road, she passed a woman and child, bulging in bathing suits, carrying towels and a blue inflatable ring, and marching toward the Gulf. Let them have their day, she thought, as if the day were her boon to grant.

She drove over the spine of the island, past the pale houses, the high grassy dunes. The road rose and became a bridge to the mainland. For a brief while she was part of the sky, with the water spread beneath her like another sky, winking and sparkling. A line of pelicans, waiting to dive, hung in the eye of the sun.

As she crossed the causeway, waves smacked the rocks on the bay side. On the other, the salt marshes lay silver in their sedges beneath the enormous sky. The wooded mainland loomed darkly at their far edge. The next moment, she was there. The trees closing behind her, green and heavy with summer, shut out her view of the sea.

NOT LESS THAN EVERYTHING

Every day in the bright fall weather I visit him. You know
this now, I realize. Maybe it's my fault you didn't know before. Well: it is my fault. I could have told you things, and I
chose not to. Whether those things would have been relevant to you or not I can't say. What I can say, as I'm sitting
here in the lamplight, with my half-finished beer and my
grief journal, is that I feel the need to write it. I feel the need
to drive it home to you. Or just to drive it home.

So now you know the one big thing. Every day, I'm there.
Summer, winter, always. But there's something about the fall.
Just now, the light lying along Hobbs Mountain looks more
concentrated in the short afternoons. Everything's more in-
tense. From my house on the hill above the Institute, I can
hear the plebes drilling on the parade ground. Snatches of
shouting rise on the wind, and if I'm home to hear I think to
myself, "There's Lennox down there. He's doing pushups."

Then I remember. It's not Lennox. It's been long enough
since it was Lennox that people coming into the shop for
their morning coffee don't ask me how I am any more, not
that way. It's been three years since I watched Lennox march
with his brother plebes through the archway into the barracks. If I had known he wouldn't be coming out again, I'd
have gone to the Parents' Weekend tailgate party. I'd have
taken him his birthday present early. I'd have bought it
ahead of time. I don't understand now why I didn't do those
things. I suppose I would have done or not done any number of things it's too late to do or undo now. But of course I
didn't know. I try not to beat myself up.

He was on a run. That much I've told you. It was a routine thing, five miles, the kind of run he could do in his sleep. They'd been through a harder workout the day before, alternately running the perimeter of the rugby field, then doing presses with their rifles, and he had been fine. That was what his cadre said: he'd been fine. They'd noticed nothing wrong with him. If he'd felt bad, he hadn't complained to anyone. He was fine, then he was running, then he was on the ground. The autopsy revealed one of those congenital heart conditions that you discover only because you're dead. Now I know. My own heart, insofar as I still have one, ticks away the long minutes of the rest of my life.

After lunch, when business tapers off, I leave Lydia, the afternoon shift, alone behind the counter to contemplate the empty tables, the dust motes whirling in the slanted sun. Liberated for an hour, I walk the four hilly blocks to the cemetery where Lennox lies among heroes of the Confederacy. Well, strictly speaking, though we have plenty of fallen Confederates, we have only one candidate for heroism, one Stephen Hyke, made a general at twenty-six, late in the war. He died of poison ivy, I think it was, two weeks before Appomattox. He was a graduate of our Institute, which at the behest of the local chapter of the United Daughters of the Confederacy changed its name in eighteen-ninety-six to honor him. Traditionally he is declaimed, when people aren't clamoring to pull his statue down, for his valor, his scholarship, and his gentlemanlike Christian demeanor. Whether nobility, heroism, and unquestioning acquiescence to the evils of an age can coexist in one person, all at once, without canceling each other out, well, God knows. I sure as hell don't.

At any rate, that's our Confederate hero, as you may or may not have remembered. It's not the thing, these days, to have Confederate heroes, but in a Southern town, if you're going to confess to having a history, this is the history you have to confess. It might not be who you are any more, but it's who you've been. Once, in actual Confession, after I'd told the priest some old sin or other that had been weighing on me, he paused before absolving me and said, slowly, enunciating each word as if I were hard of hearing, "You. Are. Not. That. Person. Anymore." And I knew what he meant. If anyone is in Christ, and so forth, and so on. At the same time, what I think is: I may be a new creation, but I remember the person who did that bad thing. She looked an awful lot like me.

You have to pass General Hyke, with his bouquet of little fluttering flags, to get anywhere. To reach Lennox's grave, as you now know, you turn left at the General and keep going, until you find yourself in the new section. After three years of saving, I've only just now put up that rounded granite headstone, whose likeness to the flat modest tablets of the early nineteenth century pleases me. I like to look at it. I like its rose-and-flame motif. I like the sober engraved lettering, telling Lennox's name, his birthday, his death day, and that he was the much loved son of his mother, Elizabeth Reid McNutt. You didn't know that was my name: *Elizabeth.* It was my mother's name, and I've never answered to it. Everyone calls me *Reid.* That's how you knew me. That's how I know myself. Still, *Elizabeth* is part of me, and what's part of me is part of Lennox, laid to rest.

I like the stone's inscription, from Eliot's "Little Gidding," the lines about *A condition of complete simplicity / (Costing not less than everything).* My dad, who loved Lennox, too, wanted me to have something from Plato on the stone. "What the hell, Dad?" I said. Lennox never loved the Greeks. He never loved Eliot, either, but he was my son, and now, when he couldn't argue, I was having something my way.

Lately when I ask Dad, "What do you know?" he's begun to answer, "Only that I know nothing." In this he speaks truth. He doesn't know my name. "Reid?" he says. "I have plenty to read right here, thanks." An inmate of the memory unit, declining fast, he no longer accompanies me to the cemetery. That's all right, actually, because he doesn't know who Lennox was any more, or that he ever existed, and the daily explanations were getting to be a drag. So on days like today, all by myself, I have my Eliot inscription, my son's bones, my complete expensive simplicity, and the sun warming my back. It's enough, I think. And even if it isn't, it's what I've got.

In the years since we last met, you and I, I've made something like a life for myself in this Blue Ridge two-college town. Caldwell College, now a university, sits right there where we left it. As you might have figured, Dad's no longer chair of the Classics Department. In fact, there no longer *is* a Classics Department. Nevertheless, the school's still cranking out liberal-arts majors and coffee-shop baristas, as if those were two separate orders of being. I should know. I hire them. Hyke Institute's parade ground, meanwhile, still abuts the Caldwell lawn. The Institute still feeds cadets into the armed forces, equipped with a useful, if heavily technical, two-year education. The chief difference there is that they have girl cadets now.

As for the town itself, these days we boast three coffee

shops, one of which I own. I inherited it from raucous Vita who ran it, a grungy little diner-type place, all my life, until her varicose veins got bad and her children trucked her off to Florida to sit in the sun. You might remember Vita, or you might not. In our college days it was slum-cool, after all, to drink the bad coffee at Vita's. Now that I think of it, I don't recall you drinking coffee. Other things, yes, but not coffee. I, meanwhile, did not drink coffee at Vita's. I worked for Vita. I started working for her in high school, worked there all through college, worked there after college, through my twenties and into my thirties, and now the place is mine. It's still not as hip as the one around the corner that plays Bob Marley and Van Morrison on a continuous loop, but it's cleaner than it used to be. Also, unlike Vita, I both know and care what an Americano is. Along the steep one-way streets, people with particular tastes in coffee have bought and renovated the old peeling houses with their fanlights of wavery glass above the front doors. No more slum, no more slum-cool. Where Vita would fix you a blackened grilled-cheese sandwich to wash down with your coffee, I offer virtue in the form of organic vegan gluten-free muffins. Presumably these muffins are edible. People buy them, anyway.

In other news, we have more restaurants here than you'd think a little mountain town could possibly support. We have a local craft beer concern, the Flag Pond Brewing Company, which makes a decent Oktoberfest special that lately I like to drink on my hillside front porch in the evenings. Below me, the Institute's barracks glow like a steel mill in the dark, smelting away the dross till nothing's left but the hard ore. I ration my beer strictly, one per evening. A six-pack bought on Saturday night lasts me Sunday to Sunday, as long as Lydia doesn't find it. I skip Friday, which is a day of penance. Every night but Friday, I drink my single beer. I watch the town lights glimmer densely in the mountains' cupped hands, and I try not to think what I'd be doing right now if Lennox were here.

If I'm telling you things you already know, I'm sorry. You know the town, of course, though as I said, it's changed. I've grown up with it, not having left when I meant to, but even from the inside I can see how different it is. Also, I'm not the girl you knew. Then, I was Dr. McNutt's daughter, majoring in English and good times. Now: well, I'm older. I weigh more. I look like any other forty-ish granola-ish woman in a trendy mountain town, with lightweight hikers on my feet, a bandana over my long brown braids, a nose piercing because on his eighteenth birthday Lennox dared me and thought I wouldn't. I don't look like my old self, the one you might remember, any more than I look like the mother of a dead military-school cadet.

Why he wanted to go to the Institute, I couldn't tell you. Dad was a pacifist, and I was a girl. Between the two of us Lennox grew up on soap whittling, tie-dyeing, guitar-playing, cooking, weaving, vegetable gardening, a brief stint at beekeeping. Also, drugs. In ninth grade he grew his hair long and started sleeping through what classes he bothered to attend. In the summer between ninth and tenth grades, he went to rehab and took up with Lydia. The year he was fifteen was a bad year, bad enough that I was willing to welcome Lydia into our house on a permanent basis, if that was what it took to keep the both of them alive and clean. At the time, that was all I cared about: not success, not good grades, not staying out of each other's pants. To say that I looked the other way a lot would be an understatement.

Because I cared that Lennox stayed alive, I had to keep Lydia alive, too, which was more than her own mother cared to do. So when I fed him, I fed her. Breakfast, which no teenager wants to eat, and lunch, and dinner. I made sure the homework got done. Not that it was right, just done and taken back to school. When there were forms to sign, I signed Lydia's, too. Nobody at school ever asked any questions. As everyone knew, Lydia's mother, in a trailer out somewhere on unincorporated county land, was too busy cooking meth to sign her name to anything. This, I figured, was how it was going to be, the rest of our lives.

But all of a sudden, in their junior year, something changed. Specifically, Lennox changed. He cut his hair. He started lifting weights and running stairs. He ran a 5K, then a half-marathon. Lydia stood with me at the finish line, smoking, examining her fingernails, hip cocked sullenly, not looking as Lennox panted past us. Inspired by this—well, it wasn't *success*, exactly, but on the other hand it hadn't killed him yet—he next ran for Student Council at school. He lost that race, too. While other kids had been attending leadership camps, he'd been a freak asleep in the back of the classroom. The only camp he'd gone to had involved daily family-therapy sessions.

And then there was Lydia, who was not remotely First Lady material, even for high school. There were parties he could never have taken her to. There were girls she could never be friendly with, having beaten them up in seventh grade. Of course, even absent a criminal record, an inpatient recovery program, and a girlfriend like Lydia, you don't go from a GPA in the negative numbers to Student Council

President overnight. Well, really, you don't go there ever. But I had to give him credit for taking on the impossible as if it could be done.

"What's this about?" I asked him once, in the fall of his senior year. I'd come across him furtively filling out forms at the dining-room table.

He shrugged. "Just time to think about life, I guess."

I looked over his shoulder and saw what he was doing. He was applying to the Institute. "Really?" I said.

"Well, why not?" He was defensive, but in a way I hadn't heard before. "I've talked to VMI. They won't take me. Hyke will."

"Do you want to go into the military?"

He shrugged again. "I have to do something. I have to go somewhere. I have to *be*—I don't know. Something."

He returned to his forms, and I walked out of the dining room. It was the only conversation we ever had about his future. In hindsight, knowing now how short that future would turn out to be, maybe I'm just as glad we saved our breath. Though for what we were saving it, again I don't know.

The conversations with Lydia were longer and more tearful.

She would pause in the vacuuming I'd set her to do for the good of her character. In the sudden silence she would say, "They'll shave his head."

"Once the plebe period's over he'll be able to grow it again, a little."

"He'll have to *march.*"

"Is there something wrong with marching?"

"I don't know. It's just so—" She would gesture helplessly. "You can't even tell who's who. You aren't yourself any more."

I would say, "It *can* be a good thing to get over yourself."

"I don't want Lennox to get over himself. I want him to *be* himself."

"I don't think the self is something you can lose," I'd say. "But you do have to grow it up somehow."

"Do you have to go *away* to do it?"

"He'll just be right down the hill, Lydia."

"A million miles," she'd say, and storm out, leaving the vacuum sprawled all over the living room. Closing my eyes, counting to five, I'd wait for the door upstairs to slam.

Fun times, fun times. I had no idea what fun times those were.

So today I came up the sidewalk to the cemetery, thinking about nothing in particular and kicking the fallen leaves. I'd come not directly from the shop and Lydia, but by way of the church, where I'd gone to daily Mass. As you would have surmised by now, if I were actually going to send you what I'm writing, I am a convert to Roman Catholicism. Believe me, nobody could have been more surprised by this development than I was myself. Sometimes it still surprises me. The Christian religion is not something I inherited. It's not like a coffee shop, where one day you're fourteen and swiping at sticky tables with a mungy old rag, and the next day you're the boss, interviewing barista hopefuls with tattoos and man-buns, gender-studies-major descendants of what they clearly imagine the ancient druids to have been.

I'd more or less grown up with the coffee shop. I certainly didn't grow up with religion. Dad subscribed to a kind of self-conscious pagan stoicism, probably always a part of his character, but consciously cultivated as a worldview after my mother disappeared. This stoicism was admirable enough in its own way, but, as I have reason to know, hardly an encouraging faith to raise a child in. When I found myself raising a child, I went looking for something better, and this is what I discovered. Dad raised his eyebrows but said nothing. Well, maybe he said, "Good luck."

Good luck, or something, was what I needed. I was not a success at raising my child in this faith. As a toddler he screamed his way through Mass. As a little boy he kicked and whined and complained that he was bored. Sometimes I said that if he was bored, how did he think I felt, listening to him? When he began to outweigh me, so that I physically couldn't drag him out of bed on Sunday mornings—Dad, absorbed in the crosswords, was no help at all—I stopped trying.

Maybe it's my fault that Lennox did not grow up to be an altar boy, let alone a priest. Maybe I should have approached it all more seriously. Maybe I should have gotten married, to some big kick-ass man who could make people do things. But I didn't. Meanwhile, I certainly wasn't martyr material, or even much of an evangelist. I had just enough of whatever it took to get me out of bed, into my clothes, and down the hill to the church on Sundays. If there was a God, I thought, He would have to find Dad and Lennox wherever they were and love them there.

Being short on *the conviction of things not seen,* I was grateful for things to *do.* Go to Mass. Go to Confession. Make a Holy Hour. Pray the rosary. All this I could accomplish. Still can. Even when the Sunday Adult Worship Choir expresses its solidarity with the oppressed peoples of the world by engaging in Spanish songs with maracas, I don't have to despair. I can offer up the experience for the Holy Souls in Purgatory, among whom I imagine my own soul will one day number. In this way I hope to work out my salvation. But first, since it's never too late, I want to work out Lennox's. Then my mother's, in case she stands in need of it. And then, proactively, Dad's. I might spend the rest of my life praying the three of them to heaven. Who'll pray for me? I'll let my guardian angel lose sleep over that.

I'd come from Mass with Father Joe's announcement about the Tuesday spaghetti supper still ringing in my ears. The day was sharp and brilliant, and even the grief I carry always with me seemed a part of that brightness. Like my faith, it was something to do: go to work, go to Mass, go to the grave, make the Stations of my own personal Cross around the town. *Stabat Mater Dolorosa:* not the Latin Dad used to quote.

Go to Mass, go to the grave, go back to work where Lydia, God love her, would have made complete hash browns out of the cash register drawer. My greatest fear, once upon a time, was that Lennox would never break up with Lydia, that I would end up her mother-in-law, biting my tongue while she fed my grandchildren gummi worms for breakfast. Now I can't break up with Lydia, or fire her, or kick her out of my house, and I wish we did have children between us, to give us something to talk about instead of how, again, to make change for a twenty when a twelve-ounce flat white costs two-thirty-nine.

Someday, I imagine, she'll break up with me. It can't go on forever, this basking in stale grief. She's young. Eventually the mileage the past has to offer her will diminish. The cost-benefit balance will tip the other way. Eventually, surely, she'll tire of responding to customers' complaints about their incorrect change, their screwed-up order, with the information that she's a recovering addict and her boyfriend is dead. While this line never fails to shut people up—often they end by apologizing to her, and tipping when they hadn't meant to—I can see that even she doesn't believe it the way she used to. And lately, in the evenings, she's taken to staying out. I don't know where or with whom, and I'm too tired to work up much feeling about it one way or another. Whether Lydia stays or goes, Lennox remains unlikely to rise from the dead any time soon.

Having left her, anyway, to mind the shop for better or worse, I was making my habitual way among the graves. I came past General Hyke, turning left, to the place where Lennox lies. That's when I saw you.

At first I didn't know that it was you I saw. Time has not left you alone either. I was startled, because at that time of day I'm usually alone in the cemetery, except, sometimes, for some elderly United Daughter of the Confederacy, hanging from her walker to snatch at the insulting weeds that do insist on springing up around the General. Today, however, even the General was left to his own examinations of conscience. If I was unprepared to encounter, in my own particular corner of that cemetery, a bulky graying man in a gore-tex jacket, I was even less prepared for him to be you.

"Hello," I said, before I knew. They say that the first thing to do when you encounter a suspicious character is to let him know that you see him. The second thing is not to let on that you're scared. The third is to locate some escape route, preferably toward other people. I glanced around me. In every direction, the dead lay quietly. The hillside sloped away down toward the ragged little river.

You looked up, squinting. *Maybe my voice hasn't changed so much.* Heart pounding, I kept to my course, kicking leaves with great bravado and thinking that probably the smart thing to do, the thing I was manifestly not doing, would be to turn around and walk briskly back into town where everyone knows me.

And then you squinted harder and said, "Reid?"

I will tell you: you look old. And you sound old. Too many cigarettes is right. I remember how much I liked the smell of your clove cigarettes, sweet and heady as infatuation itself. Now you smell like regular old bitter tobacco smoke. I would never have recognized you, not by sight, not by smell, not by the sound of your voice. But then, I hardly knew you to begin with. Maybe this was the real you, always, and I never saw or heard or smelled it for what it was, until now.

"Yes?" I said politely, as if we were speaking across the shop counter.

"Reid, it's me. It's—" When you said your name, I brought myself up short. Because, after all, all these years, I had been avoiding you. I'd stayed away from reunion weekends. I never went to football games. Granted, I hate football, but more than that, I didn't want to come face to face with you in a crowd. I didn't want to have to make small-talk about what I'd been doing since last we spoke.

"Oh," I said. "Well, hello."

"Long time no see."

"Yes. Long time."

In the sunshine, with the leaves sifting down over us, we

stood looking at Lennox's headstone. "Yours?" you said.

"Yes. My son."

"I'm sorry."

"So am I," I said. "But it's been three years. You survive somehow."

"How?" *How did he die*, I assumed you meant. Not *how are you surviving?*

I tapped my chest. "Heart thing. He was running, it skipped a beat, and it just didn't start again."

If I'd expected you to say something like, *Oh, yeah, that runs in my family*, I would have been disappointed, I guess. You looked at the stone, calculating. "He was nineteen?"

"Almost," I said. "His birthday's this month."

Again I watched you calculating. Well might you calculate, I thought.

That was the winter of the big snow, the one that stuck. Most years we get a little snow, scurf that tosses briefly on the wind and dissolves. Real snow that covers the ground, even for a few hours: that's a memorable snow. This one came late, at the end of January, when the daffodils were already pushing up among the campus trees. The days were mildly overcast, with tumbled clouds and warm wet winds that tweaked my hair into ringlets around my face. All through college I lived at home, to save money. I could go tuition-free, but we'd have had to pay for a dorm room. So in the mornings, that humid winter, I walked down the hill from my house to my first class, and I felt that stirring in the blood which the poets seem to feel is the province of young men. It was a feeling of something on the move.

I felt on the brink of something: my life. Every day I

shut the door on the house where I had grown up, just as I imagined my mother shutting the door, that night when I was eleven, and walking out, wearing her nightgown, into a mystery that swallowed her whole. Her body never reappeared, alive or otherwise. Though the soul is sometimes said to return to places it has loved, hers had vacated our place entirely. There was nothing left of her, except things. There were her clothes for the next day laid over the chair by the bed. There was the cereal set out for the morning. There were the pictures of me, abandoned on her dresser and on the mantel, her wedding portrait in the dining room, from which my own face, twenty years younger than I am now, looks out on dust she wouldn't have let lie. Weeks go by when I forget to look at her. When I do, it's as nothing more than part of the decor. The guitar encoffined in its case in the corner means more to me than that girl in her high-necked Seventies fake-Victorian gown, her Juliet cap with its veil of illusion, against a backdrop of flowers fading to mist at the edges.

Why she left, or where she went, we never knew. Whether she left on her own, or under some kind of compulsion, we never found out. She wasn't there to tell us. It was as if she'd been assumed into heaven. At first Dad and I waited and worried. The police searched, questioning Dad, of course, though he never said anything to me about it. The neighbors talked. Later, we moved on, after a fashion. But on those late-winter mornings, when there was a sweetness in the wind, I would come out of our house, shutting the door, and feel that I too could ascend bodily into the sky and never look back.

That day, heavy clouds were piling up over Hobbs Mountain. By the time I was sitting in my ten o'clock Western Civ lecture, the wind had changed. Even in the hot auditorium I could feel it, the sudden chill seeping in through the tall old windows. And then it started to snow. Uncertainly at first, then heavier and harder it came down. By the time I emerged from the history building, the world had changed entirely, to something white, clean, and dark all at once.

And then you came along, skating in your hiking boots over the covered sidewalk. We were friends, remember, in a careless, following-the-same-crowd kind of way. We'd been at all the same parties. Sometimes we had spoken to each other. Without thinking, because I'd worked hard to culti-vate a persona that acted without thinking, I bent down, scooped up some snow, and lobbed it at you. My snowball broke over your face; snow clung to your glasses. Not stop-ping to clean them, you scraped up your own handful of snow and scrubbed it into my neck.

You didn't want to be my boyfriend, not really. One night in your single room with snow falling outside, and again in the morning: that was all you wanted. It was all I want-ed, too. By the time the snow had melted, we were done with each other. By then, we didn't want to be even careless friends. Once you've seen another person naked, in the pink half-light of a snowy midnight, and again in the cold clear morning with no toothbrush, there can be nothing careless between you any more. There's either something, or noth-ing. Either way, it's not casual, but absolute as death.

"Look," you said, leaning back on your pillow, smoking, filling the room with the scent of cloves. "There's this girl back home."

How little did I know you? So little that I didn't know

where *home* was.

"And we're, like, engaged, or—I don't know. There's not like a ring or anything. But, you know."

"That's okay," I said as I climbed back into my underpants, my jeans, my bra, my sweatshirt.

"Was this your first time?"

"No," I lied. "Nah. It was just—"

"Yeah. Just one of those things. Want me to walk you home?"

"No thanks," I said. Though the snow was melting already, classes had been canceled for the day. Inside my clothes I felt wounded, but I shouldered my books and walked home, up the hill, to find Dad drinking coffee in the kitchen.

"Where were you?" he asked.

"With friends. We were playing in the snow, and it got late."

"You could have called."

"Did you wait up?"

"What do you think?"

"Sorry," I said, and poured myself some coffee. "I didn't think."

"No, I guess not." He resumed his labors at the morning crossword.

The next weekend, when the sun had come out, all that was left of the snow were gray lumps and pockets in the shade. I was walking across campus to the library, my feet going schluck-schluck in the mud, when I saw you come out of the biology building hand in hand with a girl I knew couldn't be your hometown honey, because she was in my Wednesday lab. I stopped and looked at you. You looked at me and away. The girl smiled tentatively. Then I went on to the library.

That night I was going to the Epaulet Dance at the Institute, with a boy I'd known in high school. Like you, he was a casual friend. We'd hung out in groups; he and I were the sober non-smokers, which was our chief bond. Our relationship consisted largely of wry glances exchanged while other people were making out or throwing up in the shadows outside the shivering light of a bonfire. After the library, after trudging home up the hill through the long pale-gold afternoon, I spent some time trying to make myself prettier for him. When I curled my hair, one side came out tighter than the other. When I put on my strapless bra, it kept sliding down my torso. Later in the evening I'd go into the ladies' room, take it off inside my dress, and kick it under the sink. I put on the white gown that made my shoulders look like raw chicken wings, bare and pale and stippled with cold. I applied makeup, a bright mask through which my own eyes peered out anxiously at the mirror. In my high-heeled white pumps I wobbled out to meet my date.

I still remember all that; it might have been last night. I remember, too, how we left the dance, went out into the cold darkness, and did what you and I had done the week before, only standing up against the hard concrete wall of the football-field restrooms, because what the hell, I thought. This was who I was now, apparently. I'd already taken the stupid bra off. Why not get all the way naked under my pretty white dress?

So this afternoon, when I saw you calculating, I wanted to say, "Don't assume anything, loser. Because you weren't the only one."

Of course you were the one I went to. Why? Because the other guy was *from here*. If I'd gone to him, pretty soon everyone in town would have known. I was anxious, in those first days, that there be nothing for anyone *to* know. Do I really have to spell that out? You were a stranger. You were graduating. You were out of here. You could help me cover my tracks so completely that even I might eventually forget having made them. And then, soon enough, it would be my turn to fly away free.

I went to you; you offered what you offered, which was what I wanted. You drove me there, and when I came out in tears, you thought everything was over.

I remember that the room was cold. I remember being afraid as I lay on the table with my legs open, my feet in the stirrups, the nurse saying something to me about how I'd feel bad for a few days, and then I'd be back to normal. I remember thinking how strange it was that we were pretending that she and I were the only people present for this ceremony, and that once it was over there could possibly be a *normal* to go back to.

She was smearing K-Y jelly on her gloved hands. "I'm warming this up a little, but it might still feel chilly when I touch you."

"I think I want to think some more," I said.

She went on chafing the K-Y jelly between her hands, with a rubbery clucking sound.

"About this, I mean." I struggled to sit up. I withdrew my feet from the stirrups. "I'm not ready. I might be back, but—"

She turned around now, annoyed, as if I were wasting her valuable time.

"Yeah," I said. "I need to think some more."

So she went out, and I got up and put my clothes on. As I was zipping my jeans over the place where an unseen person lay curled like a stem inside a bean, what I hadn't done struck me like a physical blow. I might have done it. I had come so close to doing it that even though I hadn't, I tasted the full grief of it. You know the feeling: when your child slips in the bathtub and goes under, and you are there to pull him out again, but you might so easily have been looking the other way. You hug your child who's alive, but something in you is weeping over the limp and empty body that you might have discovered instead. Anyway, I was crying when I emerged from the back. You patted me awkwardly, because after all, we weren't even casual friends any more. Then you took me home.

I never said anything to the other guy. We never spoke again. You know how these things go. After the Institute he went into the Marines, then to engineering school. Kansas, I think. Out there he married some girl, and they have a bunch of kids, which I know because his mother comes into the coffee shop, and she's shown me pictures. I'm just as glad, really, that all that has nothing to do with me.

Absorbed as he was in the life of the mind, Dad did notice, finally, that I was gaining weight. Being far less dense than I gave him credit for in those days, he knew why. Over supper, after I'd been confronted and come clean, I saw him trying to square the pregnant woman across the kitchen table with the child whose Barbie Dream House he had had to put together by himself, the first Christmas without my mother. I'd been too old for Barbie already; still, he'd done it. I'd lain awake in the dark of my room, listening to him swear. In the great scheme of things, it hadn't been that long ago.

"Jesus," he said at last.

"All the best people." I tried to laugh.

"It's not a joke, girly."

I mashed my fork around in the tepid scrambled eggs I didn't want to eat. "Have I disgraced you? Are you throwing me out?"

I watched him think for a minute. "No," he said finally. "And no. Why would I do that?"

As I watched, his eyes filled with tears. He set his fork down and left the table. Later I found him in the living room, in mellow early-spring lamplight, reading "On First Looking Into Chapman's Homer," of all things. *Silent, upon a peak in Darien.* I would like to say, for the literary thrill of it, that we looked at each other then *with a wild surmise.* But all Dad said, not taking his eyes from the page, was, "It'll all be all right, Reid. You'll see." As if I were the one in need of comfort.

After that we had Lennox. A slideshow of him plays continually in my mind. Little blanket-wrapped burrito, peering out dark-eyed beneath his striped hospital stocking cap. Running figure in green overalls. Curly hair I didn't want to cut. Bony knees, no front teeth, a soccer uniform, the cheap plastic trophy everyone got for playing on the YMCA team. Rented tux before our stone fireplace, one arm crooked around Lydia's neck, not quite successfully hiding the skull tattoo above her heart. Too-short graduation gown, side-hugging his smiling grandfather. Shaven plebe, severe in dress grays, in a photograph I received only after his death.

My memories of him are still-lifes. In my waking life I can't even remember what his voice sounded like. When it broke and deepened, I mourned because I'd never hear the little-boy treble again. Now I'll never hear any of it, ever, unless I can crawl my sorry way to Heaven, which believe me, I am trying to do, hoping to find him there.

Sometimes he comes to me in my dreams. The other night, for example, we were in the mountains together, walking a stretch of the Appalachian Trail we both loved. The trail took us up through rhododendrons and onto a bald, where the sky opened out and the world fell away around us in blinding sun and wind. Lennox was hiking ahead of me, so that all I could see was his back, sweating a little through the dark green t-shirt he wore, and his head of dusty curls. *Keep up, Mama,* he called over his shoulder. His voice sounded not in my ears, but in my mind, like words on a printed page. Then he was gone. I woke up sobbing in my bed while rain fell on the roof.

More than once I've dreamed that Lydia was pregnant: crazy, I know, but not outside the bounds of a certain dream-logic. In these scenarios I know that Lennox is dead. He's been dead far longer than the requisite nine months. I know this. Still Lydia comes to me with a smile, an ultrasound picture, a miracle. Sometimes the dream lasts long enough for her to have the baby, but inevitably it turns out to be a monkey, or a puppy, or a whoopee cushion. That last one was a particular disappointment, let me tell you. In real life, I have no grandchild, no part of Lennox left to me at all, except Lydia, to whom I don't wish to cling. If she could get on with her life, then perhaps I could quit dreaming about whoopee cushion babies.

Of course, it's only some hours later that I've thought of telling you all this. When I saw you, as I came across the grass in a state of grace, having gone to Confession before Mass and then received Our Lord as bread and wine, the way He offers Himself to us, because His real Self appearing before us would strike us dead, all I thought was, *what the hell?* Recognizing you, who look nothing like Lennox, let me hasten to say, was in its own way as weird as all those baby dreams. It had its own surreality, our whole relationship, a paradoxical quality of intimacy and estrangement that I suppose makes sense when you think about it. Get naked with a stranger, and this is what grows between you. Seeing you, I felt all that sensation well up again. *Here is someone I do and do not know.*

Outwardly, though, I was all serenity. "What brings you back here?" I asked, the polite and expected thing to say.

"Oh, well." You shifted uncomfortably.

I took you in: untidy graying hair, faded green anorak, cargo pants, hiking shoes as scuffed as mine. I noted your smoky smell. For a moment, stepping outside myself to look at us side-by-side, I considered who had worn better with the years, and decided that I won. I don't smoke. I drink the one beer at night. I sleep. I eat. I talk to people over the counter, because if you serve coffee, you can't not talk to people. And I go to church. All those things, I think, have given me clear skin and the ability to meet someone's gaze without looking away.

You, on the other hand, were looking at the ground. "Well, officially, my daughter is visiting colleges. My ex-wife's taken her to Duke, Chapel Hill, UVA, you know. The biggies. I figure she'll go someplace impressive, but I wanted to bring her to see the old alma mater, just—you know. Be-cause. She's still just a sophomore, got some time to think about it—"

"You said *officially*," I prompted after a moment. "Was there some other reason?"

"Oh, well." You went on not looking at me. "Since I was coming this way, I Googled you. I mean, not that—I didn't even know if you'd still be here. I mean, I was looking up a bunch of people we went to school with, you know how you do. Anyway, what came up was your son's obituary."

"Yes," I said. I hadn't thought about that before, that if anybody searched for me online, they'd get Lennox's death.

"You know, I thought—"

Uncanny that I could read your meaning. "I know," I said. "I changed my mind." Watching your face, I added, "I'm sorry. I never said anything. I really wasn't thinking."

We stood there a while, you and I, looking at the grave of my son. Maybe he was our son, and maybe I owe you more than a lame apology for my silence. Maybe he wasn't, and I don't. Maybe you were thinking you owed me something. Or maybe you weren't, and you don't.

Maybe Lennox has a bunch of brothers and sisters running around at this moment on the clean wide prairies of Kansas. If I told you nothing, remember that I told their father even less. But then I asked less of him, too. And as far as I know, he's never looked me up on the internet.

On the other hand, maybe Lennox has one sister, whom I've now met, a nice enough blonde girl with your smile that means nothing—to me, anyway. She came loping up, bored with General Hyke. You introduced me as an old college friend. You had been sorry to learn that this college friend's child had died. You had thought, since you and she were there, that you would pay your respects. That is, you didn't say all that exactly, but it was more or less what you conveyed to her. She took my hand damply; she looked me briefly in the eye, or close enough; she smiled your smile. I'm sorry that I couldn't care about it. I'm sure she's a lovely girl. I'm sure she deserves all the love that comes her way, and more. As a Christian, I'm supposed to love everyone, even my enemies. But it wasn't Lennox's smile.

"Well," you said at last. "We were going to have some coffee before we take off. Gotta get her home to her mama, you know how it is. But I want to spend just a little more time—would you join us?"

I laughed. How easy it was to laugh at you, how blessed and clean to be able to say, "I live and breathe coffee. I honestly don't want any now. But I can tell you where to go."

I named the shop and said to tell Lydia the drinks were on me. I scrabbled in my bag for a business card and pen, and scrawled a note to that effect. You handed it off to your daughter. Megan, I think you said her name was? Or Morgan? Or Jordan? You told her, "Go on ahead, babe. I'll catch up with you."

Together we watched her drift away among the graves, the afternoon brilliance touching her hair to a steel-cold flame. I think maybe you said something about tennis scholarships, hoping she'd save her old man some money. Yeah, I remember thinking bitterly. That's the thing about kids. They cost you.

One last time you turned to me. You leaned in close, so I could smell what you'd drunk for lunch. Not coffee, that's for sure. I was glad to be sending you to Lydia before you took to the roads with your child.

You said, "So you didn't go through with things."

"No," I said. "I didn't. He was a person with a life, and I couldn't."

"And now he's here." You nodded at the stone.

Looking away over the graves to the river beyond, I wondered again whether I owed you an explanation, or an apology, or any response at all. Were you thinking that if I could go back again, knowing the end of the story, and do things over, then hell yes I'd flush eighteen years away without another thought?

So a little joy would have swirled down the drain with the heartbreak, but joy is cheap, you might have thought. You might have thought, *She can always find more joy.*

Well. Thank you for your possible thought. And forgive me for my lack of charity, if I've misread you. I was granted a child. I accepted him as a gift. And these were the terms.

"He was worth it," I said, and there I let it rest.

Tonight, though, it's on my mind, not resting. Lydia's out, doing something without me, thank God. In solitude I've eaten my frugal supper. Although it's Friday I've broken my fast with the week's last beer, the one I'd ordinarily have saved for Saturday. Before I opened it, I made an Act of Charity, telling God, with my mind's fingers crossed, that I loved Him above all things and my neighbor as myself, for His sake. I wished Lennox an early happy birthday. Then, for both of us, I took the first sip, the Oktoberfest brew, savoring its amber fizzle on my tongue.

As I drank, I thought of what I wished to say to you. In this grief journal I was encouraged three years ago to keep, I began to write it down, and here it is. But maybe I shouldn't have written it. At the very least, maybe I shouldn't have mixed journaling with beer. Reading back over what I've written, I find that the words I wish I'd said to you are every bit as faulty in their way as the words I did say. If I knew your address, if I were going to track you down on the internet, would I tear these pages out and send them to you? I don't know. I don't know what earthly difference it would make if I did.

Maybe there is nothing to say, nothing in human language. Maybe our guardian angels converse and make themselves understood. That's about the only way it wouldn't be too little, too late. By now you're gone again, back into your mystery. Lennox, on the other hand, lies where I can always find him, under the high, dry autumn stars and the soft-stepping wind. At least, his body is there. All my life now, my going to bed and my rising, my work, my leisure, my prayer, is bent on finding his soul, and Dad's, and my mother's, and mine, together in some good place.

Now, having finished with you, what I'll do with the rest of my evening is visit Dad before they put him to bed. It's one last good work I have it in my power to perform today: to see Dad, for whom, now, Lennox never existed, for whom the wrongs and rights of the past are like blank snow, un-printed by any human foot.

I'll take his hand and see the surprise in his eyes. How nice of this strange woman to come and see him. He thinks maybe he was married once to a woman who looked a little like her. Her sister, perhaps. Or maybe it's that woman herself, stepping out of the night, home from a brief trip abroad.

I'll say, "It's me, Dad. Reid."

"Reid?" he'll say. "Reid? I've got plenty to read right here. But thank you."

I'll sit in the chair beside him, there in the bare little

room that's all the world he recognizes. I'll pat the hand lying resignedly in mine.

"Well, Dad, what do you know?" I'll say.

He'll look at me, as if—stranger that I am—I ought not to have to ask that silly question.

"Only that I know nothing," he'll tell me.

A FIRE IN THE HILLS

Really, I have no complaints. I love my husband. Our life is good. Our little house, high up in the Avenues, suits us perfectly: nice kitchen, spare room for Declan's study, built-in bookshelves in every room. We live there comfortably, Declan and I. Every week or so, his three grown sons join us for dinner. The easiest offspring, I have found, are the ones you inherit as adults. They come to your house, they drink your wine—sometimes they bring *you* wine—they engage in polite conversation. When they've gone, you sit on the couch with your sweetheart before the open window, through which the city lights below you, a great grid narrowing to a point at the south end of the Salt Lake Valley, shiver in the restless summer night. You tuck your bare feet beneath you. You drink a good-night glass together, and you are happy. I, that is, am happy.

*

Every summer some dry part of the mountains is burning. Potentially, I suppose, it could all burn right up. Potentially the flames could come down and swallow us, too, but so far it hasn't happened. Most of the time the fires are nowhere near us. But at night, when darkness descends, it all strikes closer. You'd think it was your neighbor's house, or maybe even your own, starting to smolder.

Your husband gets up dutifully and goes around feeling walls and floors, smelling everywhere, to calm you down.

"The smoke alarms are working, Vinnie," he says to reassure you—if you're me, that is, and Lavinia is your name. "If there were really anything wrong, they'd go off. Everything's fine. It's just a wildfire somewhere. Far away. Go back to sleep."

You—I—lie back down. The nightmare you've been having is over. Chances are that it won't ambush you a second time. The house is flooded with moonlight and quiet. Declan gets back into bed and turns so that I can lie spoon-wise with him, my cheek on his cool shoulder blade. The peace is blessed and unbroken. There's no storm, no lightning, no flood, no telephone call, nothing to shatter the night. When your love's made sure, you can go to sleep.

*

If sometimes I see Bernard, it's by accident. I know people who maintain friendships with exes, but I'm not one of them. Until I met Declan, I was a bridge burner. In high school, I would like a boy for precisely as long as it took him to call me his girlfriend, and in my twenties I wasn't much better. When Bernard and I parted, we did not part as friends.

But I can't help seeing him sometimes. Declan and I hold season tickets to the Nguyen Chamber Ensemble. The music, by contemporary and experimental composers, is excellent. It's not a personal thing. We go in spite of Bernard, not because of him. Anyway, that kind of seeing only partly counts. It's only me seeing him from a distance in the dark, when he doesn't know I'm there. Most of the time I see his back, arms upraised to the expectant musicians. The stage lights shine on his long black hair. I used to run my hands through that hair, but this seems impossible to me now.

When I first moved here as a student, knowing no one, I constantly mistook strangers for people I knew: people from back home, maybe, or from college, people whose names hung on the tip of my tongue, just out of reach. More than once, before my vision cleared, I almost cried out in surprise and delight. Sometimes people glanced at me oddly, reading the inexplicable recognition in my face.

Seeing Bernard these days, I have the opposite sensation. Once upon a time, I knew him. I knew him in the biblical sense, for which *intimacy* is only another euphemism. Watching him onstage, however, I behold a stranger. That I once made a *life* with this person: did I hallucinate the whole thing? Am I hallucinating now? Occasionally Declan and I will attend some arts function, a fundraising dinner, a silent auction. I'll glimpse Bernard in the crowd, and he'll glimpse me. Our eyes will meet for an instant, until one of us decides to pretend not to recognize the other.

Of course, just as I've got Declan, Bernard has a wife. I still remember the first time I saw her, at a children's cancer benefit some years ago. In all that pressing intermission crowd, she stood with Bernard, her hand in his. She was small, silver-blonde, wearing red lipstick, a severe black dress, funky Mary-Jane-style heels. I observed all these details with fascination. I took in, also, that she was pregnant. The black dress fit the swell of her body like a boast.

*

There is a technique I use with clients in my counseling practice, as a way of rewiring how the brain reads its contents. An abused woman, for example, may remember the first terrifying moment when her husband's face changed, when a stranger stepped into that familiar body and raised his hand to strike her. She may despise herself—almost certainly she despises herself—for having submitted to that blow.

What I have her do, in the safety and comfort of my office, is call up that moment in her mind, place herself in it again. I take her back to herself as she was right then, not as she thinks she should have been. Doubtless she has been tormenting herself: what she ought to have said and done, either to defy him or to escape him or to keep him from wanting to hit her in the first place. She is certain that whatever has happened, it's her fault, and she deserves whatever suffering has come to her in consequence. No one, she thinks, can ever love her or forgive her. It's my job to prove her wrong. I take her back to that moment, that woman who sobs or cowers, and I invite her to forgive that woman, and love her. Only thus can she set herself free.

Of course it's a process. I don't claim to be some kind of psychological miracle healer, only a wielder of tools. Because I wield them for myself, too, I know how limited they are, how long things take. But I'm good at it nonetheless.

As an exercise, to keep myself limber, I return to a particular moment.

I seat Bernard beside me on our cracked leather couch.

"Earth to Lavinia," he says. "Come in, Lavinia."

"Hello," I make myself say.

He peers at me, solicitous. "How was your day?"

Shrug.

"That good?"

Shrug again.

Outside, the day of my memory fades to a dry golden twilight. I remember that as well as anything else: the quality of the summer light, arid and pitiless, and the way the mountains, only a few streaks of snow still caught in their folds, stand harshly on the sky.

"I was thinking," he says. "Do you feel like going out?"

"No."

He puts his arms around me. I sit stiffly in the circle they make, the child in the mush pot, waiting to be released.

*

Bernard, as everyone who reads the local arts section knows, is a Vietnamese adoptee, one of a sprawling Provo family of children from various continents. He has three sisters from the Ukraine, another from China, two brothers from Haiti, two more from Guatemala. When I met him, his parents were awaiting final approval to adopt a Tongan-American five-sibling group from foster care.

Bernard's full legal name is Bernard Hyram Nguyen Christiansen. Professionally, and perhaps tellingly, these days he's Bernard Nguyen. *Musical Instrument,* his Vietnamese name means, coincidentally enough, from a Chinese word for *plucked string.* It's also said, less authoritatively, to mean *original.*

"Yeah," he told me over beers, on what would become our first night together, "we all have these stuck-in ethnic names that mean stuff, supposedly. I have a Ukrainian sister whose name, I am not lying, is Abilene Bogdana. Bad Texas Town The Lord Has Rendered Christiansen. My parents look this shit up and slap it on whatever kid is coming through the door."

Giddy in his presence, I believed him. Why not? I never met the parents or the siblings. In all the time Bernard and I were together, I knew his family only through the bitter filter of estrangement. Knowing nothing, I could laugh with him about them. After a time I felt I did know this Abilene Bogdana, and all the rest, who didn't need to be on drugs, Bernard told me, because life itself was a psychedelic.

"Your parents seem like nice people," I sometimes said. "They mean well. They're doing the best they can—"

Bernard would laugh. "Yeah. People who go to the pound and take home *all* the dogs mean well. I'm sure people who do things like that are perfectly nice people. Divorced from reality, maybe. Abusive, maybe. But nice people."

*

What did I know about it? Nothing. That was what he meant. Shut up, Vinnie, he meant, but was too politic or something to say. In those days I didn't have, yet, anything like a professional opinion. These days I do have a professional opinion, and according to it, a vast gulf yawns between *I think my parents were abusive* and *my parents were actually abusive*. I meet the fallout of *actually abusive* every day. It is, by and large, not doing well.

Of course, my professional opinion is also that all parenting leaves some kind of mark. Declan's three sons are a case in point. They love Crazy Imelda, their mother. They don't doubt that she loves them. They are flourishing young men: investment banker, sociologist, inventor of some new kind of rock-climbing harness. But when they mention their mother, it's with words like *tiptoe* and *eggshells*. Her emotions are legendary and volcanic. There are wrong things to say, and she is always waiting for someone to say them, so that she can treasure them up in her heart and bring them out over dinner, when there's a lull in the conversation. "It's never boring at her house," Brendan, the oldest, the banker, confided to me once. "Come to think of it, I *like* boredom."

*

Most of the time, naturally, I don't think about Bernard at all. My life is full, and my work consumes me. I have my private practice, seeing these patients, mostly women, with various forms of PTSD. This being Utah, I treat a lot of women coming out of the polygamist subculture, which seems unambiguously defined by trauma. Or maybe it's just that I never meet the happy ones.

The unhappy ones get referred to me by a foundation that sponsors safe houses, clothes closets, job fairs, all the necessary resources to help these women integrate into the world of the fully human. It's my job not to restore them to happiness, but to help them restore themselves to happiness. If your brain, in its default mode, tells you that you're incompetent to manage your own money, that you can't choose your clothes, that beatings are what you asked for, that sex is a series of payments you make toward the privilege of existing, then I am here to help you change those messages. Change the message, change your life. This is my credo.

*

Our house is a duplex, with a large central unit where we live, and around the side, a smaller mother-in-law apartment, which contains my office. I have the best commute in Salt Lake. Every morning, rain or shine, snow or thermal inversion, I finish my first cup of coffee at my kitchen table, then I pour a second. I step into my work shoes, which I keep lined up beside the kitchen door. This year I bought six pairs of pumps in the same brand, in black, gray, nude, fuschia, cobalt, and blood-red. Every day, on my way to work, I choose my color. With my coffee I walk out the kitchen door, around the side of the house, and into my office, where in the little kitchenette I start a new pot to power me through the day. I plump the cushions on the green sofa, run the Bissell over the rug, glance at my notes, and I'm ready to go to work.

Through the magic of technology, my secretary, Marianne, is able to work remotely from home, taking appointments and typing up my notes while she cares for her new baby and her toddler. This suits her, and I am happy to have my office to myself. There's no front desk cluttered up with someone else's family photographs. I like to receive my patients at the door, as if they really were entering my home, to offer them coffee or herbal tea, and to settle them on the couch for a good long talk.

This is a safe space. I've given my whole life to making it happen. And when someone has spent an hour here, telling me things she's never breathed aloud, ever in her life, then having a good hard ugly cathartic cry, and she steps out again with new resolve into the hard dry light of day, I feel the throb of pride and joy I imagine a woman must feel after giving birth, when the child is placed in her arms and she sees clearly for the first time that the thing she thought was part of her own body has become, or was always, a whole person whose life opens like a new door in a wall.

*

That summer, I shared an apartment with Bernard in an old building downtown: beautiful dark millwork, original art-deco bathroom tile in yellow, mint green, and black. Our decorating, sadly, didn't do the place justice. In our life vision, this apartment occupied the level of the purely functional. That is to say, we had a *relationship,* or, as the kids say today, a *situation.* We lived together, but where we lived together wasn't a *home.*

Bernard's piano filled what would have been the dining room. Without the piano, we might have lived upstairs and had a view. By the window, looking into an overgrown foundation planting of junipers, I'd set a green plastic patio table, salvaged from the curb, to hold my books and papers in their disarray. In one bedroom stood our bed, a confusion of stale sheets on a Hollywood frame. The second bedroom was empty; we had talked about making it an office for me. In the narrow kitchen, the textured gold linoleum caught grime and kept it forever. Outside, the sun shone in its hard-edged way, though it never quite penetrated the junipers. The August heat wavered whitely on the sidewalks.

The building itself was a world of sorts, with familiar rhythms that marked the progress of its day. Because I was home most of the time, writing up my research, I was able to mark this progress. My own consciousness began to be shaped by the bang of the foyer door, for example, right outside our own front door, and the rattling that meant the mailman. It was a daily noise, the background to my dissertation notes. But it was also, always, an instance of interest and diversion.

The mailboxes, a bank of brass-fronted pigeonholes in the wall beneath the stairs, provided the one locus of community in our building, though it was a community more of evidence than of interaction. Just above us lived a group of

LDS girl missionaries; how many there were, and whether they were always the same girls, or different ones who moved in and out, I was never sure. They wore black skirts, white blouses, nametags. They all worked as tour guides at Temple Square. In the mornings I heard them on the stairs, clattering and laughing, calling each other *Sister* like a bunch of religious postulants. By the letters they clipped to the front of their mailbox to be collected, I knew that one of them was dating an Elder Chad Sorenson, on a mission in Ecuador. All of them, in fact, seemed to be dating missionaries scattered across the world. Clearly they awaited the bright morning when those missionaries would return, and they themselves could hang up their nametags and put on wedding dresses. They wrote every day, I thought, to make sure the men on the other end remembered all that.

Bernard was scathing on the subject of the missionary girls. "That's exactly what I got the hell out of, Vinnie. Two years in Bora Bora with a bicycle and some other twerp in a tie, asking strangers if they want to talk about family. Yeah, no thanks. And there's nothing cute about those girls. They're just pathetic. I can't imagine why you'd even be curious about them."

"I'm not curious about *them*," I said. "I just think it's interesting what you can infer about people's *lives*—"

"Some people's lives aren't worth inferring anything about."

I don't meant to paint Bernard as an ass. He wasn't. That is to say, even when we're not casting off the shackles of our parents' religion, we're all like that in our twenties. Our own lives rivet us completely. Declan says that if I'd met him at any time before the age of thirty-five, I'd have hated him. And

I know myself well enough. I wasn't interested in those girls as people. I was interested in them as foils. I couldn't help thinking that there but for the grace of whatever went I.

*

I've plumped the throw pillows on the couch and tweaked the vase of flowers—midsummer blooms, black-eyed Susans and coneflower with a little lavender—into a composition that pleases me. My first client of the day is a young woman, barely eighteen, who's left an abusive polygamist marriage, and is now being steadily gaslighted by not only her husband, but her entire extended family, including the four other wives and her own mother. Just before she left, her husband took her up in the mountains to some secluded spot, to rape her and then beat the living shit out of her, as a punishment for some perceived infraction. Now they're all united in trying to persuade her that it was for her own good.

She has two children already and is not allowed to see them. Meanwhile, despite the beating, she hasn't yet miscarried the third. Her belly is just starting to swell inside her flowered prairie dress, one—I am certain—of a matched set of five. I've seen those wives, all of them dressed identically, like little girls in school uniform, superintending actual little girls in the same uniform. This girl still wears hers. She still has the straggling long hair, the large unfashionable eyeglasses, the hunted expression, that identify her former state in life. She's late this morning, and I have to admit that this worries me. Has she gone back? Have they talked her into thinking that I'm an agent of evil, that the way for her to ensure her eternal exclusion from the celestial realm is to be convinced of her own personhood? Sure, honey, you can have your human dignity, but nobody you love will ever speak to you again, for time and all eternity.

Through the wall I can hear Declan singing as he washes the breakfast dishes.

*

If I rummage around in the past, there's much to bring up that seems, on the face of it, inconsequential. What do I do with these shards of detail? What do I make of Miss Genevieve Macbeth, for example, who lived at the top of the building? She and I were the only people home all day, and we both listened for the mailman. Though she was in her eighties, Miss Macbeth could hear a dropped circular rustle to the floor, five stories down, and could be there to pick it up almost before it settled. We ran into each other often outside my door.

Miss Macbeth had occupied her apartment, she had told me, since 1949, when she had come up from Manti to work in the ZCMI department store. Her perfectly good stove was the same one she had had when she moved in. In the beginning she had made, and forever after had kept, a resolution to use it only on Sundays, to preserve it in excellent working order. Like new, she said. In those days the apartments had come fully furnished, with silverware and linens, even. She still possessed two blankets from those lost days of luxury.

Whether she still had the furniture and silverware, too, or what had happened to it if she didn't, I never found out.

Here are details: Miss Macbeth turns from the mailboxes. As always, her hair has been shellacked into a kind of double fold on top of her head, with a precise little snail-shell curl at each temple. Beneath her black cat-eye spectacles, her long nose and tiny, drawn-in mouth make her look like some exacting species of bird.

She sees me wavering in my doorway, still dressed in the t-shirt and pajama trousers I've been wearing for days. "Are you all right?" she asks abruptly.

"I'm okay, thanks. I've been kind of sick, but I'm better now."

"Well." A quick, birdlike movement of the head. "I hope that husband of yours has been taking care of you." She pronounces the word *husband* as if it meant something like *drain clog* or *dog vomit*.

Miss Macbeth is an innocent. As usual, I let *husband* pass without comment. Generally when Miss Macbeth mentions my *husband,* it's to complain about his piano. Even at times when he isn't physically present, she hears it. If I must have such an appendage as a *husband*—which of course I do not—then hopefully, she seems to imply, I get something out of the arrangement besides earworms.

"Oh, he's always good to me," I murmur.

"Well." She looks at me again, long and piercingly. Then she's gone, up the stairs.

It's a kind of friendliness we have. It pleases me far more than my few exchanges with the missionary girls, though you'd think we had much in common. "Hi!" they call, bouncing past me and out the door, turning to each other as if for protection against this unwashed woman, living in sin, who has stepped out braless in her boyfriend's t-shirt to fetch the newspaper.

"Sister, did you check the mail? Well, later, then. We have to hurry . . ."

Always the missionary girls were cheerful, in an impervious way that you wouldn't mistake for a desire to get to know you. Maybe Bernard was right, and they weren't cute. I still see girls like that downtown, clustered at the stoplight, waiting to cross over to Temple Square. I know exactly how they sound, those hard, bright voices that chip away at the air.

Miss Macbeth, I reflect, was the elderly version of those girls, the one whose missionary never came back. Or did come back, but married someone else. Or simply wasn't. If he ever existed, I didn't hear about him. If Miss Macbeth had hoped for anything besides perpetual blankets and kitchen drawers pre-filled with cutlery, she never told me. The friendliness we shared didn't penetrate that deep. Still, the part of me that thought about her at all wanted her not to have had the missionary, or the hopes. How much less dreary it was to have *meant* to live alone.

*

Right at the fifteen-minute mark, my client calls.

"I'm sorry." She's crying. "I'm in the emergency room."

"Are you all right?" Even as I ask, I know it's a stupid question. People don't go to the emergency room because they're fine.

"I'm bleeding." She cries harder.

"Is anyone there with you?"

A long pause.

"You're not there alone?" I say.

"No." I can hear her breathing. "My mom's here. She just went out to the bathroom, so I thought I'd call and tell you."

"Is that—are you okay with that? With your mom being there?"

I can hear her quick breathing. "Well, I had to call some-body. And, I don't know. She's my *mom.*"

Yeah. Your mom who's one of seven wives, herself. Your mom who thought it would be just dandy to pull you out of school at fourteen and hand you off to her cousin, to be *his* fifth wife. Your mom who thinks you need beating for the good of your soul. Your mom who's colluding to keep you away from your kids. Yeah: your mom.

"Anyway," she says. "That's why I'm not there. I'm sorry."

"Don't be," I tell her. "Don't apologize. It's not your fault." None of it is your fault. That's what I keep trying to tell her, though it's clear she doesn't believe me. "Look, take care of yourself. That's your priority. And just call me when you can. I'll work you in, any time."

"Yeah," she says. "Maybe. I have to go now."

Silence. Around the corner of the house, the door shuts. Declan's key turns in the lock. A moment later, he passes be-neath the window where I stand with the phone in my hand. The sun bears down on his crisp faded hair, his flushed face. In the hard light his pale summer jacket is so bright I can hardly look at him. Seeing me, he kisses his hand and waves. I kiss my hand and wave back as, cheerfully, on his way to daily Mass, he gets into his car and drives away.

*

In the space of half an hour I can send Bernard out for Chinese food and bring him back. He spreads our dinner picnic-style on the floor.

"Ar lighty, now," I'll have him say. "You gotcher Genelar Tso's Chicken. You gotcher veggie flied lice. You got, ret me see now—you got Vinnie's Favolite Mu Shu Polk with the ritter pancakes and prum sauce. Aaaaaand two egg lor."

It could almost be, but is not, our first night together. "Asians mocking Asians. Nothing racist about that, babe, yo." Then, I laughed with delight and recklessness. I thought him the funniest, most interesting, most subversive, most attractive person alive. Now, maybe, he's still funny. But for some reason, I can't laugh.

He sits cross-legged on the carpet and pats the place beside him. "Come sit. Have a picnic."

His hands are small, neat, and plumpish. The way he spreads them out to play arpeggios reminds me, oddly, of a snake unhinging its jaw to swallow a tapir. Lately his hair has been growing out of its neat short cut. The straight black layers stand out raggedly from the sides of his head and straggle over his shirt collar. He's not yet the sleek ponytailed artist you see in pictures, barefoot in a black suit so sharp you could cut your own hair with it, leaning on an instrument that you know without looking is a Bosendorpher. Here, he's just a guy who plays studio sessions with the Osmond Brothers because money is money, and he and his girlfriend, who's not yet a psychologist, have rent to pay somehow.

I don't want to run my hands through that hair. I don't like the way it looks, in its awkward growing-out stage. In this moment, I don't find Bernard gorgeous. I don't want to touch him. I'm tired of him. Or else I'm experiencing some other, more ambiguous emotion concerning him.

People say that you don't stay *in love* forever, that you lose the feeling, that in the end love is a *will,* not an emotion. Well, then. I *will* myself to slide off the couch and onto the floor. I *will* myself to accept the egg roll he hands me. I *will* myself to bite into it, chew, and swallow without gagging. But I experience no hunger of any kind.

*

I've told everything to Declan. "You're not that person any more," he'll say, when the same old dreams return. "You're not there. It's not happening." Nevertheless, in his arms I shake and pant, consumed with terror.

Of course it doesn't happen that often. Things fade in your mind. I can, for example, these days, operate a vacuum cleaner without the support of alcohol or Zoloft. Still, it comes back to me sometimes, and I need Declan to say that the past is not who I am. I don't believe a word of it, of course. I don't believe there's anything healthy about severing yourself from your history, even if such a thing were possible. But when I wake up in a sweat, this is what I want to hear.

*

I've been keyed up to work, but now my first hour falls flat. That poor girl. Right now, for all I know, her baby's bleeding away to nothing. Perhaps that's a kindness. But for all I know, even as I think about her, her mother's remarking that this is what happens to bad girls: not a kindness, to put it mildly.

My next client drinks coffee, and she likes it black. Though she won't be here for another half hour, I've got a good strong pot going for her. Of course this woman has her traumas, too, but there's a lot about her that's easy. She's close to my age. She's funny, in a dry, devastating way. If she couldn't laugh things off, she tells me, she'd be dead. She mocks her own obsessive habit of checking and rechecking the locks on her car doors, whenever she gets in or out. I've seen her do this. In front of my house, she'll clamber from the car and press the lock button on her key until the horn has bleated several times. Then she'll walk around the car, testing the doors. Sometimes she does this three or four times before she can walk away.

It's an obsessive-compulsive behavior, and she knows it, though what drives it is cold hard reason. One day her ex-husband will get out of prison and come to find her. I have my nightmares, and she has hers. In her nightmare she's driving, when he sits up in the seat behind her. His dead blue eyes meet hers in the mirror. "It's time," he tells her. He puts a gun to her temple and pulls the trigger. That's what wakes her up, sweating.

I've come to love her a little, the way you do sometimes

in my job. She's one of the people whose names I'm glad to see on the appointment book, for now. When she's done with me, someone else will take her place. I'll forget about her, but she'll still be there, somewhere in my mind. Everything always is. People are like plastic, which never totally biodegrades. Once you've used each other up, there's nothing for it but the landfill, but it's all still there, the people, the past. You're not pretending it isn't. Still, you cover it over, you build a park on top of it, and you move on.

*

"Look, Vin," Bernard says. "Do me a favor. No, scratch that. Do *you* a favor."

"What?" I'm too tired to be irritated.

"Number one: eat that food. You'll feel better if you eat. No, really. You will." He pushes the little carton of Mu-Shu Pork at me, and the foil-wrapped pancakes. "Number two: go take a shower."

"Do I smell?" I'm too tired to care.

He sniffs me. "Nope. But you'll feel better."

"Who says I don't feel fine?" I pick at my food, which I'm too tired to eat.

"I'm not finished. Next I want you to put on something clean and fresh, and get into bed. Don't worry about this mess. I'll clean it up. And—"

"What?" I'm too tired, really, to want to know.

"Tomorrow we'll do something."

"*Do* something? Do *what*?" I'm too tired. I don't care about tomorrow.

"I don't know. Go up in the mountains. Hike a little. Have fun."

"I'm still kind of bleeding." And I'm tired. Good Lord, I'm tired.

"I'll go buy you more pads."

"That's okay."

In truth, the bleeding has almost stopped. The heavy, clotty flow's reduced now to a faint brown smear. Any day now the whole thing will be behind me. Over and done. And Bernard is not being an ass. He is being—though I'm too tired to realize it—heroic. It's by no means every man who'll offer to make a public purchase of feminine-hygiene items. But I don't love him for it. I can't even *will* to love him. I'm too tired.

*

The light is brilliant and dry on the stand of rosemary by our front walk. Yes, yes, I've seen *Hamlet*, and I know what rosemary is for. Maybe sometime today I'll walk out and pick some, to add to my vase of summer flowers. Then my whole office will be full of its sharp, antiseptic smell; I'll breathe it the rest of the day.

Even as I think about it, my second client's out there already, parallel-parking her beat-up Subaru. She's early for her appointment, but that's all right. She'll sit for a while in the car, gathering her thoughts. Then, getting out, she'll perform her ritual, walking twice, three times, four times, around the car, to be sure all her doors are locked. Surreptitiously, from behind my blinds, I watch her grip the steering wheel, steel herself to look in the rearview mirror one last time. Nobody there.

*

At the summer's end, Bernard went away to play some concert gigs in Montana, Idaho, and Wyoming. *The Cowboy Tour,* he called it. Three weeks. While he was away, I found a garage studio, tucked behind a Victorian house, several blocks up the hill on C Street. When Bernard came back, I was gone. The nights, though they still smelled of smoke, had turned chilly. Often I sat up through the dark hours, working. Though I was glad to be alone, I didn't trust myself alone with sleep.

One day in the early fall, the apartment manager called; some package had arrived for me at that address, and could I come pick it up? It was easy enough to walk down in the afternoon, after I'd finished my day's dissertation work. Walking in the brilliant air, sunny and cold all at once, with the aspen flaming gold on the mountainsides, I felt as if the summer hadn't happened, or had been a bad dream. Whoever that woman had been, that woman who couldn't get dressed or leave her apartment, except to bring in the mail, she hadn't exactly evaporated somewhere between my former and current addresses. But she had been transformed. Or perhaps it's better to say that she was restored to herself. This was the real me, the true, strong, smart me, striding along the cracked sidewalk with my parka unzipped. I was afraid of nothing, and though I didn't sleep, I felt no longer tired. As if on a dare, then, before stopping in for the package, I gambled on Bernard's being out. Stepping among the junipers outside our old living-room windows, I looked in to see what I could see.

The piano had disappeared: I noticed that first. I could see the dents its feet had made in the carpet. The rest of the apartment, what I could see of it, was empty. Well, then, I told myself. He's moved on, too. Except for the dents in the carpet, I might have imagined the whole thing.

As I stepped back onto the sidewalk, brushing off the juniper needles, a new idea seized me. I'd go down and collect my package in due time, but first I would walk up and visit Miss Macbeth. Why I wanted to see her I couldn't have said. But I did want to see her.

Details: Five flights of red-carpeted stairs. The radiators on every landing, the familiar dry heat-smell mingling with the smell of walked-on carpet. Reaching the top floor short of breath. My heart crashing.

Knocking at the door. The building is silent except for a muffled radio talk show, twittering voices that emanate wordlessly from behind the door opposite. Who lives there? No idea. I never knew that anyone else was home during the day.

Knocking again, louder.

From the apartment opposite, with the radio, a man looks out: sixtyish, maybe, with little darting eyes and black hair combed greasily back from his forehead. His forearms blue with tattoos.

"You looking for Miss Genevieve?"

"Yes," I say. "I used to live downstairs. I was just over this way and thought I'd say hello."

"Yeah, well." The man runs a meditative hand over his hair, as if to flatten it down more. His eyes rove over me, down the stairs, back over me again. "Yeah. You're a little late."

"Has something happened to her?"

"Same thing that happens to us all, honey." He watches me, not quite catching my eye, to see if I understand. "Service was kind of small. I went. I'm not of that faith, if you know what I mean, but it seemed like the neighborly thing to do."

He looks me full in the eye for an instant. Glances away again.

"I had no idea," I say at last.

"Yeah. Well. Nice lady. Wound a little tight. Used to complain about my radio. But a nice lady."

"Yes," I say, "she was. I'm sorry to hear this. Thank you for telling me."

"Yeah. You want to visit people. Visit people *before* you think about it."

The door closing. Left alone to contemplate this paradox. Stifling heat of all the radiators in the building, risen and gathered there at the fifth-floor ceiling.

*

No, I don't want to leave myself there, on that landing in the rising heat. Better, though not much, the steamy shower where Bernard has steered me. In the shower, I can't lift my hands to wash my hair. I'm too tired to do anything but stand there.

Into bed, with its soft, cool percale. I spread my toes, finding pockets of greater coolness. The t-shirt I'm wearing smells like Bernard: one part fabric softener to two parts Dove body wash.

Through the bedroom door, the piano. Let me locate myself: I am *there*, in bed. I am this woman who has not yet left her boyfriend. She has not evaporated; I know this now; she will not evaporate. Outside the door, the boyfriend is playing the piano, in the desultory way that this woman used to love. He's thinking aloud in music, drifting chords, soft and clashing all at once.

Detail: Miss Macbeth, five floors up, in her own bed, hands folded on her breast, her twin curls speared with bobby pins. I don't see her, of course, but I know she's there. *Sleep,* I command her. *Sleep. You hear nothing.* This woman who has not yet left her boyfriend is angry with him for waking the neighbors.

After a moment he comes in and opens the window above the bed. Fading blue of the summer evening, cool air bearing in smoke.

"What's on fire?"

He turns. "It's someplace up in the Uintas. I heard it on the news driving home. Miles away. You relax and go to sleep."

He stands over me, stroking my hair until my eyes close. This woman still lets her boyfriend stroke her hair, though she cringes inwardly at his touch. Then he's gone, shutting the door softly behind him. Getting out the vacuum cleaner.

It's easy enough to fall asleep. There seems so little point in being awake that I welcome the drowning of each long day. Falling through the black depths into some lost undersea trench where things move about with little lights suspended at the ends of tentacles which waggle enticingly. Beyond that point of light, the toothed jaws opening.

Screaming. The voice belongs to this woman, who hears this noise that is not the vacuum cleaner. An overhead light, yellow in her eyes. In the stirrups, her bare cold feet. Her toes curl. She doesn't know why she's screaming. There's nothing to scream about. Still, she's screaming. She didn't scream then, in fact, but she's screaming now. This too is a detail.

The noise outside the door stops. Bernard appears in the doorway, haggard. "Sorry. I'm sorry, babe." Murmuring apologies and endearments. His hands, his arms, his voice are full of love. This woman accepts that love limply. "It was the vacuum. I thought you were asleep. Foltune cookie say: Crean up lice on calpet—"

Not so limp after all, she sits up. Details: her snarling face, her voice. "Stop talking like that. It's not funny. It's never been funny. Just stop. You're not funny at all."

I'm this woman. She hasn't gone anywhere. Though she keeps quiet these days, she's still right here with me.

*

"You're not that person," Declan says. I know better, but I let him say it anyway.

It's important to him to think what he thinks. He's not the same person, so he believes, as the man who was married to Crazy Imelda. That segment of his history has been proclaimed, officially, not to have happened, or at least to have no binding claim on him. The annulment declares that there was no marriage. There are, of course, these three boys who happen to turn up now and again. There are memories attached to them. Still, somehow, Declan has slipped free of it all. He is that happy person, a new creation.

Sometimes I go to Mass with him, if it's not too early on Sunday morning. As, disinterestedly, I watch the priest lift the little white disk, a halo with no head to wear it, I think: Bread. God, if you exist, that's what you are? That's it?

Well. If it satisfies Declan, then I'm happy for him. I admire him for being faithful to this idea. But it's not my idea. I can go to the cathedral, sit in the pew, surrounded by frescoes and the thin, accurate voices of the choir-school children. And when it's over, I can walk out into the light of day, unchanged.

※

As I've told Declan, I have to go about things in my own way. I can't separate the woman I am now—standing at the window, coffee in hand, watching my client confront her rearview mirror—from the woman who wakes up screaming, accepts the beer Bernard brings her, and falls heavily asleep again.

It is myself I find there, again, familiar and abiding, deep in the night.

Detail: wind through the open window, meandering, dry, cool, sharp with smoke from the distant wildfires, riffling the pages of a book left open on the moonlit floor. With a soft sound the pages lift and settle, are never quite turned.

I put out my hand to touch Bernard. His place beside me is empty, cool and dry as the wind. Tensing, I listen for him. He's back at the piano, thinking in vague soft fragments of music, as he always does when he can't sleep. This woman, who is me, past, present, and always, lies listening to the murmuring open-ended phrases.

After a moment the fragments resolve into scales, up and down, down and up. But there's something wrong about them. It's a broken scale he's playing, incomplete—*do re mi fa sol la ti*—the song of the brain-fever bird. *Ti la sol fa mi re.* Smaller and smaller. Then the brain-fever bird's whole song again.

Five flights up, as I imagine, the bedsprings creak chastely. Miss Macbeth is disturbed, in her all-too-temporary sleep. As if he imagines her, too, Bernard plays louder. *Fa sol la ti do,* the brain-fever bird sings to her. *Do re mi fa sol la ti.*

Climb and fall short. Climb and fall short. Somewhere, far away, the wildfires burn on. *Do re mi fa sol la ti.* High above us, the barren moon burns in the sky. *La sol fa mi.*

Everywhere the darkness smells of smoke.

*

At last my client climbs from her car, pointing her key like a gun. Blat, goes the horn once, then twice, then again. Next she walks around the car, yanking at the handles. I can see her channeling the ferocious strength of her ex-husband's rage. He would rip the doors off the car if he could. She's trying to convince herself all over again that he can't, and this entails trying to rip them off herself. What if she succeeds? Well, I guess we'll laugh about that, too. We'll agree that it's good that she knows her own strength. Now she's striding up the front walk. Her husband will get sprung someday, but not today. Her life is a gift she is always, every moment, until that moment, receiving.

I'm prepared to help her receive it a little more. Breathe in, breathe out. Lay the examined past away. It never changes, and will keep. Right now, in the present, I'm ready to go to work. I am happy and strong and whole. The fires may burn in the high elevations, the brain-fever bird may sing its midnight song of sorrow, but down here in the sunlit city we are fine.

THE HAPPY PLACE

Amelia's mother died, but the beach house remained. Through illness and decline and grief, Amelia had forgotten the house, except as a relic of childhood memory. Nobody had spoken of it. Nobody had gone to see about it. There had been assisted living, then the memory unit, the private caregiver. There had been the sale of Amelia's childhood home, the dispersal of her mother's furniture and goods. In the end there had been the funeral: the tracking down of some kind of minister, the inevitable eulogy with its vague assertions that the deceased had been a good woman who loved God. Last, there had been the cremation, a whole existence going up in smoke, the ashes gathered and decorously shelved in a columbarium. Well, that's over, Amelia had thought.

But it wasn't over. Death was not the end at all. Here suddenly were taxes coming due. Here was paperwork from the management company documenting the rental income, the company's percentage subtracted. There the house stood, right where they had left it. It had not gone up in smoke at all.

"You got yourself a waterfront property, all right," said the lawyer, son of her father's old law partner, who had handled her mother's affairs. Technically Amelia was the one who handled these affairs, but until now, *handling* had meant signing the papers the lawyer faxed her, not always looking that closely at what she was signing. Yada yada. Same old, same old. Scrawl scrawl scrawl, fax it all back.

Then on with her real life, which was complicated and

demanded her full attention. There was her counseling practice. There was her divorce, which had turned out to be, in its own way, as demanding as the marriage had been: a whole other full-time job. There was the whole business of co-parenting, of keeping straight which weeks were hers and therefore which class parties demanded that she burn a pan of brownies the night before, then lock herself in the bathroom with the fan on to cry. And then her mother had entered her long decline. Amelia, the only living child, had had to go back and forth to visit her, to take her out driving, to consult with the staff and with her private attendant, to worry about what her mother ate or didn't eat, felt or didn't feel, knew or didn't know. It had been, as Amelia's daughter Mallory liked to say, *a lot.* It had been yet another job, layered over the other two. She hadn't had time to read every word of every document that came her way. If the school office hadn't sent it, her *modus operandi* was to skim and sign. And who could blame her?

But how could she have managed to overlook a whole house? If the lawyer had entertained an opinion about this lapse of attention, he'd kept it quiet. Well, she told herself in her own defense, on top of all her accumulated strata of responsibility, nobody had been down there in years. Her father and brother were dead. Her mother had lived in North Carolina, while Amelia lived in Texas. Though they might have called it a midway point, a good place to meet up, the Alabama coast made an inconvenient drive from either direction. And then her mother was ill, first with cancer, then with dementia. As her mother forgot things, Amelia tried to hold them in her mind. In one limited human mind there was only so much room. As a psychologist, Amelia thought much about the marvel of the human mind with its plastici-ty, its regenerative powers. Still, you couldn't stretch it past its breaking point.

Amelia's grandfather had built the beach house when he came home from World War II. When Amelia was a child, the family had gone there, always. Nowhere else—where else was there to go? Her mother, Caroline, had been going there all her life. To the child Amelia, it had seemed as if there were only two places in the world: her own small Pied-mont town and a sandy half-moon island looking out on the Gulf of Mexico. It had felt to her as if all summers were concentrated in this one spot, caught between the Gulf, the Bay, and the gray rustling water of the Mississippi Sound.

When Amelia was a child, her father would come home early on a warm, daylit Friday evening, and the four of them, Cash, Caroline, Amelia, and John, would bundle into the packed station wagon to make the long drive to Palmyra, Tennessee, where her grandmother lived. Arriving at mid-night, they would camp out in her grandmother's uncon-genial living room with the plastic-covered sofa, to be ready to drive down all together, more jammed-in than before, in the morning, before it was light. These had been arduous trips, but it had never occurred to them to go to the Atlantic coast, so much closer to their own home. In those days, they hadn't thought in terms of *convenience.* Amelia's grandfather had built this beach house, so they went to it. It was the way things were. They never thought of doing anything else.

And then, so subtly that Amelia couldn't remember no-ticing the change, things weren't that way anymore. Her grandmother died. Richard and Paula Emerson, her par-ents' oldest friends, divorced and seemed to evaporate, with their son Rick, into nothingness. They had owned the beach house next to the Mallorys', but suddenly they didn't. From then on, that was the way things were. Amelia had gone on growing up. She had found better things to do: high school, college, graduate school, marriage, motherhood, divorce, remarriage. She had not evaporated, though maybe her mother would have said that she had. In any event, she had lived her own life, in which trips to the Alabama coast had not figured at all. Even before her mother's dementia set in, erasing first the immediate past, then working its inexorable, obliterating way back through the whole timeline of their lives, the beach house had faded from everyone's mind.

"I don't have the heart, I guess," Amelia's mother had said vaguely after John's death. Still, there had been that one weekend. Toward the end of Amelia's first marriage, when her daughter Mallory was two, Amelia's mother had conceived the idea that Mallory should see the Gulf of Mexico. Amelia's mother had insisted on it, had gone so far as to buy Amelia a plane ticket. At the time, Amelia's father had just died, and this, of all the things in the world, was what her mother had fixated on.

Amelia, preoccupied with other worries just then, had scoffed at the idea. "She won't remember anything, Mother. You're making a whole lot of fuss for nothing."

But her father was dead, and the ticket was bought for her, so she had gone. She had taken Mallory. She had figured that giving Mallory to her mother for a few days at the beach was better than the nothing she had been offering as consolation. At the same time, she herself was going to say goodbye: to the Gulf, to the Sound, to the house, to her life as a child and all that had filled it. Goodbye, she had said to the island as she rode away in the back of her mother's car, returning to the Pensacola airport, while Mallory shrieked, red-faced, in her car seat. At the time, Amelia had meant it: Goodbye.

"Well," said Kurt, when she had hung up the phone and told him the news, "it's paid for, isn't it?"

"Of course it is. My grandfather built it. He didn't believe in debt."

"So it's actually an asset. The rental income is actual income."

"I suppose so. But we have to pay taxes and insurance. Hurricane insurance, for crying out loud. And would we use it ourselves? Ever?"

"We haven't yet," said Kurt. "But we might."

No, Amelia said, that was ridiculous. They had one house. The last thing she wanted was to be tied to another. If they had a beach house, they would feel obligated to use a beach house. She had grown up going nowhere but the beach house, not even knowing how the rest of the world might beckon to her. Too, she was a redhead, with a redhead's vulnerable skin. In the aftermath of her sunburned childhood, she examined herself nightly for misshapen freckles and strange moles. Every now and again, she went to the dermatologist and had some odd spot shaved off. What would a person with that kind of skin do with a beach house, except use it to commit slow-motion suicide? She called the management company that very afternoon and told them to put the house on the market.

Then, almost as an afterthought, she relented. She and Kurt, with Mallory, who was twelve, decided after all to drive across Texas and through the dark-green woods of Louisiana to the Alabama Gulf Coast and the island, to look over the house themselves before the *For Sale* sign went up.

As Kurt drove, Amelia stole little glances at his profile. After two years, it still struck her as incredible that she had managed to marry this kind man. He was older than she was, widowed. He had four grown sons who approached Amelia with wary courtesy, when they approached her at all. She didn't hold out much hope that these relationships would ever deepen into actual warmth, but then she saw them only once or twice a year. There were no marriages or grandchildren yet to complicate things, which was a relief. Amelia squinted at complications.

Kurt, however, was blessedly uncomplicated in his history: a long, happy marriage concluded by the one thing that was supposed to part people. During the day he wrote code for his latest software start-up. At night he liked to cook for Amelia, or to go out for dinner. He was short and round, built like a man who loved food. He wore his graying beard close to his face and shaved his head daily. On his first wife's death, he had had his left ear pierced, her tiny engagement diamond set in an earring that he would wear until his own death and be buried with. As he drove over the island causeway, the westering sun caught the earring; Amelia saw it flash like a distant lighthouse, a warning. Well: it was a memory. Together they lived with it.

Less tranquilly, they lived also with Amelia's ex-husband, Michael, who was Mallory's father. Not that he lived with them literally, in their actual house, but he was a constant presence. Mallory spent alternate weeks, whole weeks, with him, so there was much picking up, dropping off, back and forth, negotiation. Amelia and Michael would never not have each other's cell numbers. Under the terms of their divorce, Amelia, who made more money, paid child support. Somehow what she paid was never enough to support the child in question. Left to herself, Amelia would have said no to some of Mallory's more expensive activities. Did one twelve-year-old really need drama camp, and guitar lessons, and horseback riding, and soccer, and swim team, and cheerleading?

"Cheerleading?" Amelia had said.

"She's a girl. It's what girls do."

"I never did cheerleading." What a laugh, she had thought, the idea of her string-bean short-haired bespectacled self as a cheerleader.

"Would have done you good," said Michael. "Besides, she might as well be busy. Otherwise she's just got to sit in after-care. They have cheer scholarships for college, too."

Last time we talked, you were all about soccer scholarships, Amelia thought but did not say. Just like you're all about having your kid be a tax deduction. The things I shut up about, she remarked to herself, not for the first time, while Michael continued to talk. Meanwhile, she still had to fill out paperwork and receive Michael's permission in writing if she wanted to transport Mallory across the Texas state line.

"School's not out," Michael had responded. "You better check if this little jaunt conflicts with STARR testing."

So what if it did, Amelia had thought. Would missing the state achievement test wreck a twelve-year-old's future in some irreparable way? She thought not. But she did check just the same.

In the back seat, Mallory, her long amber hair tied up in a purple bandana, was watching the brown waves of Mobile Bay roll up to the stony causeway-side and smash. "Have I ever been here before?"

"Once when you were little," said Amelia. "We came here with Mimi. You wouldn't remember."

"Did I dig in the sand under the house?"

"I'm sure you did," said Amelia absently. What little children had not dug in the sand under that stilt-legged beach house? She could remember Rick Emerson burying her up to her neck, then lugging a bucket of water from the inlet to pour over her head. She remembered her brother John, who was dead, bulldozing the fine sand with his hand. She remembered the smell of lighter fluid and hot dogs, of fish in the deep fryer, of Coppertone suntan lotion, Jack Daniels, beer in a can. If she shut her eyes and thought about those smells, she could hear her grandmother's voice: *Y'all come eat.* And her mother's, gentler, more querying and marveling, with a note like a mourning dove's, asking rather than telling. *Did you see those stars last night? Do you think if we looked we might see a dolphin? Now, where did I set down my sunglasses?* It was her mother who would take a child's hand, to look at something, to go somewhere together. It was her mother, too, who would smack a child, without warning and for no reason. Her gentle mother: someone to approach with caution, after all.

"There's the pier," Amelia said, to shift her thoughts. Before them the bridge rose. They rose with it, and all around them, opening out on either side, lay the water, silvering to the west where the setting sun was about to touch it. Turning around to look at Mallory she said, "When I was a little girl there wasn't a bridge. We had to take the ferry. And look, those condos weren't there. But we used to eat at Captain Bodine's sometimes. There it still is. They had a big aquarium with angelfish."

"Sounds like dinner tonight," said Kurt. "Want to stop now, or come back in an hour?"

"Stop now." Mallory was craning to right and left, taking in the restaurant, the marina where the charter boats tied up, the dock for the deep-sea fishing rodeo.

But Amelia said, "No, let's go on. Let's put our things in the house. Then we can come back."

She had thought she could navigate by memory, but the island had changed. So many more houses had gone up, new ones since the last big hurricane. In the old days, their house on its narrow inlet had been visible from the main road. Now two streets of houses hid it. At last, however, after several turnarounds, because she refused to let Kurt GPS it, they pulled up in the driveway. Almost before the car had stopped, Mallory was out of the back seat, running under the house and out to the dock. Amelia followed more slowly, her arms full of groceries.

She looked about her. Miraculously, through so many years of storms, the house had stood. Others had been swept away, or else had been torn down to make way for new ones. But here it was, the same old house, a weathered cypress box raised on pilings, a new metal roof overhanging the familiar wrap-around porch. The old picnic tables were long gone, of course. They had had one under the house, one on the porch. Now there were only a row of recycled-plastic adirondack chairs, all red. Inside, too, the house had been transformed. The wall between the living room and the little galley kitchen had been knocked out, the whole interior drywalled. It might have been any other anonymous house, rented out week to week, that people claimed briefly as if it were their own, then left behind without another thought. In bemusement Amelia watched Mallory, childish again as she could still sometimes be, run first into one bedroom, then into the other.

"Which one was your room?" Mallory called.

"Depended," Amelia called back from the kitchen counter, where she was taking boxes of organic macaroni and cheese out of her shopping bag.

Mallory put her head around the door from the little side hallway. "Depended on what?"

"Lots of things. Who was here, mostly. When I was a really little girl, I slept with your Mimi and my daddy in that bedroom." She pointed in Mallory's direction. "Or I slept with Muh in the one through that door by the fridge."

"*Muh?*" Mallory ventured into the kitchen.

"My grandmother. That's what I named her." Amelia smiled at the memory. "She hated being called that, but once I started, she was stuck with it. Poor Muh." She hefted a gallon of milk into the refrigerator. "And then when Muh got too old to come, I shared her room with my brother John. And then sometimes we slept in hammocks under the house."

"So you didn't have your own *room?*" said Mallory, with an only child's incredulity.

"At home I did. But this house was always kind of small. Back when it was built, it was a luxury just to have a house at the beach. You didn't mind sharing and roughing it some. It was like going to camp, but with your family."

"Can I sleep in a hammock under the house?" Mallory, rummaging now through the drawers, to turn up some treasure that was not a fish knife or a corkscrew, glanced up from her search, her eyes bright with the idea.

"No," said Amelia.

"Why not? You did."

"Those were different times," Amelia said.

Kurt had been prowling around the living room and kitchen, opening cabinets, looking inside storage ottomans. "One bathroom still?"

"Afraid so," said Amelia.

"That's going to make it harder to sell."

"Tressa told me that." Tressa was the island realtor. Over the phone, in the space of days, she had become practically a member of the family. So Amelia had said, jokingly, to the woman with whom she shared her counseling practice. Amelia could remember her grandmother's using this phrase when she spoke of the maid. What it meant was that the maid knew everything about Amelia's grandmother, who didn't consider it her job to know anything about the maid.

Now, as Kurt turned from his examination of a basket beneath the coffee table, she drummed her fingers on the kitchen island. "Tressa says what will happen is that somebody will buy the lot and knock the house down. They did that with the Emersons' place next door."

On that lot, a strange sea-blue cottage levitated on stilts. It had a round tower at one end, an open gazebo at the other, all floating above sand and golden beach grasses. A widow's walk sat like a crown on an improbable flatness behind the raised eyebrow of its front gable. Amelia remembered the old house, unpainted cypress like her own, with its steep

A-frame roof, its little deck like a tongue sticking out at the Sound. She remembered her parents' friends, Richard and Paula. Richard had been the kind of father who clamped a cigarette in his teeth while he swung you around by your arms and let you go flying into the water. He would say to the closest available child, "Bring me another Schlitz out the ice chest." Bunch of little bartenders, Amelia thought, Rick and John and I. They would gather up the empty cans and drink down the last drops inside, lick the little residual ring of beer around the top. That flat taste, that thin metallic smell: now, as she offloaded a six-pack assortment of craft-brewed beers into the fridge, she could conjure the small, sharp memory. Summer had tastes as well as smells, and cheap beer was one of them.

How strange, she thought, too, that of them all, only she was left. There was nobody for her to turn to, to say, *Remember?* Her parents were dead. The Emersons had divorced and vanished from their lives. At some point or other her mother had heard from somebody back in Palmyra that Rick had *not done well*, as she would have put it. In her mother's language, a phrase like that almost certainly meant alcoholism, drug addiction, unemployment. You were left to fill in the blank, but those were the choices.

John too was gone. *Gone,* they had always said. Not *dead*, though what else could he be? From the first, though it made her mother slam the kitchen cabinets, Amelia had refused not to use the word *dead*. John too had not done well, despite having been to law school and given every sign of following their father into the firm. Amelia remembered the palpable sense of relaxation that had gradually pervaded everything in those first-year law-school days. After a worrying start—John hadn't talked until he was five—his strangeness had begun to level out, his brightness to take over. At last, at last, her parents had seemed to say without saying it, everything was all right. And it hadn't been. Amelia might have told them that, if only she'd been there. For nearly as many years now as he had been present, *absent* was John's permanent state of being. If her parents had expected him to reappear, they had gone to their graves expecting. Did they expect to see him again on the other side? If they had, if they had believed in any *other side*, they had never said so to Amelia.

Well, she thought, expectations were dangerous things. You had to know how to have expectations: which expectations were good to have, which were not. What was realistic, what was delusion. What was *doing well*, and so on. She had been expected to *do well*, and she had. She had gone to college, then to graduate school. She had received her PhD. Somehow, though, that wasn't quite what her mother had meant. Her mother's idea of *doing well*, for a girl, had been to marry, bring up children, and be happy. Did a girl need anything else? Not really, her mother had thought.

For the last twelve years, Mallory's whole life, Amelia had been practicing, with great deliberateness, her own carefully considered expectations. She did not tell Mallory what to wear. She did not make a fuss over grades. She did not say that there were things boys did, and things girls did. She said, *Everybody has a path in life, and the thing to do is find it.* She hoped that her own expectations at least canceled out Michael's, which were that girls should be cheerleaders and win soccer scholarships and live with their fathers who needed to claim them for tax deductions.

"Bastard," she said under her breath.

Kurt glanced up from the photo album he had discovered. "Beg your pardon?"

"Nothing. Just thinking. Should we go have dinner now?"

Afterward, in the dark, the three of them walked on the beach. Amelia brought the flashlight she had found in the pantry closet—left there by whom?—to show Kurt and Mallory how you could surprise the ghost crabs. As they walked, their feet kicking up the mild surf, crab after crab, large or small, shining like the photo negative of a black spider, skittled sideways into the dark water ahead of them. Every time she saw one, Mallory screamed and did a little dance on the wet sand.

"They won't hurt you," Amelia said.

"I know, I know. They're more scared of me, blah blah blah." Having, for the moment, exhausted the childish part of her, Mallory had shrugged on again her pre-teen guise, the persona that had heard everything already a thousand times. A thousand times twice, she sometimes implied, since she had to hear it all from Amelia and Michael separately.

Or thrice, now that she had Kurt. To his credit, Kurt did not hand out cigars of paternal wisdom that often. "I have *had* children," he said. "I'm off the clock." Still, when Amelia declared some house rule, some directive or prohibition, she was careful to say, "Kurt and I think . . ." It was his house, after all.

But actually, that too—their house in Texas—was Amelia's house. She had bought it after the divorce, a modest little flat-roofed rancher in a down-at-heels nineteen-fifties subdivision full of live oaks and multigenerational non-English-speaking households. It had been her settlement house, her single-mother house, the house of her new life. Now Kurt lived there with her and, on alternate weeks, so did Mallory. Amelia's new life was theirs now, together. Kurt had assented affably enough to her suggestion that he integrate into this existing arrangement. He had required only that the backyard shed be floored, insulated, plumbed, and wired for electricity, so that he could make it his office. When his sons visited, as they had done at Christmas, they slept on air mattresses on the floor of this backyard office. Nevertheless, it seemed right to Amelia that she should suggest some authoritative role for Kurt. It seemed right, too, that now she should drop behind him a little, hand him the flashlight, and step into his footprints as she carried her thoughts down the beach.

The moon was rising in a pale fug of cloud. Directly overhead, the Big Dipper pointed out the North Star, exactly as it had always done. Amelia could remember standing on the dock with her father and John and Rick Emerson, the water of the inlet sloshing at their feet, the stars so bright above them that they seemed to crackle on the sky.

"See the North Star?" her father would say. "See how those two stars point at it?"

Amelia would squint at the sky. "Which two stars?" There were thousands. Which two were the special two? Of course she had been little then, only eight or nine. The shapes in the night sky were an idea she understood, but when she looked, she saw only chaos.

In bed, stretched between sheets that hadn't had time to get sandy, Amelia lay thinking. In the morning Tressa would come to walk through the house with them. They would talk about how to stage the house: what to get rid of, what to leave, what to repair, what to paint over and hope for the best. In the likeliest scenario, of course, the house wouldn't matter, only the waterfront land beneath it, with its long grasses and blanket flowers, its one enormous white oleander which even now was tossing outside the window of the room where they lay.

By the time they had gone to bed, clouds darker than darkness had risen over the Gulf and moved in, wiping away the stars. Now she heard thunder. A second later came a flicker of lightning. *A storm could wash this house away any time*, she thought, *for all it really matters. One good hurricane could save us all a lot of work. Of course, it would be nice if we didn't get washed away in the process . . .*

She yawned. After the long drive, she felt inside-out with tiredness. But her mind kept clicking along, an electric train that refused to switch off. Around and around it went, clickety clickety, on its tiresome little track. At one bend she was thinking of the torn screen to the sliding door, the pipe dripping under the house, the bamboo starting to take the little side yard. At another, she was seeing her mother turn breaded fish in a cast-iron skillet full of spitting-hot fat, leaping back as it popped so as not to get burned. At yet another, her brother John stood at the edge of the dock, fishing, thin and deliberate as the blue heron that waited down the dock to see what would get tossed its way. And in the homestretch she was thinking about paint: a refresher throughout the house? Plain white? Off-white? Could Mallory paint without dripping on the floors? Should they refinish the floors? Another crackle of thunder and lightning; Amelia started inside her skin. As if in answer, Kurt turned over and laid his arm across her, so heavy she almost couldn't breathe. Click-ety-clack went the train of her thoughts.

Silently and suddenly, Mallory appeared beside her. "Mama."

"What?" Amelia feigned waking from sleep.

"Do you have any *supplies?*"

"Did you start?" asked Amelia, fake-sleepily, slipping from beneath Kurt's arm. He sighed and rolled onto his back. Now he would snore.

Mallory's whisper was agonized. "Yes. It came early. Please don't wake Kurt up."

"I won't. Go look in my bag in the bathroom. I did pack some things." As Mallory padded away, Amelia lay back against her pillows. Above the house, the sky broke open with a bang and a flash, and rain hammered down.

At six in the morning it was still raining. Having slept fitfully, slipping beneath the surface sometimes but never really submerging, Amelia gave up altogether and slid from bed to make coffee. Glancing from the living-room win-dows, she saw the green-brown sound puckering hard be-neath the sky. The bridge lay hidden in fog. She had wanted to drink her coffee on the porch, watching the sun rise above the eastern curve of the island, but the sun, already up, was only a whiter whiteness on the sky. Realizing that she had forgotten the chocolate coffee creamer—one of the few real decadences she permitted herself—she said, "Damn," out loud, and slammed the fridge shut. No one else woke up.

At seven, while Amelia sat making a list, Kurt came yawning in. "This would be a good fishing day."

She looked up from her writing. "I didn't know you liked to fish."

"I don't, really. But it's the kind of thing you do in a place like this. I used to take my boys, you know. I thought men ought to know how to fish."

"Why should *men* know how to fish?" Amelia frowned. This was the kind of thing she expected from Michael, not Kurt. "Why not women, too?"

"If I had had a girl, I might have taken her, too. Maybe I thought everybody ought to know how to fish. Everybody in my house happened to be a boy."

"Except Julie," said Amelia.

"No, Julie most definitely was not a boy. And she didn't want to fish. She would cook fish if we brought them home cleaned, but that was as far as it went."

"Like my mother." Amelia smiled. "You could take Mallory out to fish. We used to fish off the dock." Well, she thought, Daddy and John fished, and Rick and Mr. Richard Emerson. Sometimes they went out on a boat. What did I do? No memory presented itself.

"Are there poles and things?" Kurt was pouring coffee. He came and refilled Amelia's cup, until a meniscus of milky liquid shivered above the rim of her blue mug.

She leaned over and sipped the coffee down. "There used to be poles and things. Down in the closet under the house. But Tressa's coming this morning, remember? I could use your input."

"Off the hook," said Kurt, and laughed at himself. "I didn't want to fish anyway."

"I don't feel good," said Mallory when Amelia woke her at nine.

"How don't you feel good?"

"Cramps." Mallory stared up in pathos from her crumpled pillow. "And we forgot the ibuprofen. And I don't have my own pads or tampons or anything."

"I can send Kurt to the Ship and Shore," said Amelia.

Mallory clutched at her arm. "No. I'm fine. I'll just take a shower. And then you have some more stuff, right?"

Kurt buys me pads, Amelia thought tiredly. *He knows that women menstruate, for crying out loud.* But it wasn't worth fighting about. She tried and failed to imagine her own father buying feminine supplies. Her mother had never said the words *menstruate* or *period* aloud, even to her. It was always *that time.* Kurt's wife Julie had called it *Aunt Flo*, so that was what Kurt said. *Going to buy some napkins, Aunt Flo's coming to dinner.* This, apparently, had been a standing joke between them. When Amelia tried to think of jokes she had had with Michael, she came up empty. From the beginning, theirs had not been that kind of marriage. Sometimes she wondered how long it would take for jokes to grow up between her and Kurt. So far they mostly recycled the ones he had had with Julie. Watching Mallory thump down the little hall to the bathroom and shut the door, Amelia felt faintly let down, though she couldn't have said by what.

At ten, Tressa the realtor knocked at the sliding glass door. Amelia, dressed now in a short black jersey shift but still drinking coffee, sprang up to let her in out of the rain.

Was there a realtor factory somewhere that turned them out? Amelia studied Tressa with fascination: the standard streakily blonde hair, the loose twisted updo, the soft bangs falling over a face that had surely belonged to a cheerleader, a member of the Homecoming Court. Though it glowed, dewy-fresh with moisturizer, the skin was starting to slide, ever so gently, from the delicate bones. Amelia noted, too, that beneath her beautiful melting face, Tressa had a ropy neck like a guinea hen's. Pink and green sleeveless dress, brown muscular arms, flip-flops. Painted toenails, a double row of pink shells. Amelia glanced down at her own naked feet. Her hair was so short that, of a morning, she could wet her hands and run them through it to make it behave. Her face and body were bony and taut. *We come from a long line of hat racks*, her father had liked to say.

"*Look* at this cute *house.*" Tressa's liquid voice rose and fell on waves of urgency. Having offered her damp, lotion-y hand first to Amelia, then to Kurt, then to the glowering Mallory, Tressa advanced into the living room, gesturing with her clipboard. "And it's just about the oldest one *left* on this end of the island. Is that *not* so special?"

"My parents were pretty invested in it," said Amelia. "The only vacations we ever took were to this house."

"Honey, there's so *many* worse things you could do." Tressa was exploring the kitchen, opening and shutting drawers. "Now, these appliances? How old do you think they are?"

"My mother put them in at some point. I really can't remember. Fifteen years maybe? Twenty?"

"*Normally* I would say that some new appliances would be worth the investment, you know what I mean? Not *expensive* ones, but shiny-new, maybe stainless steel, because it's *on trend*, you know? But in this case I'm *thinking . . .*"

"You really don't think the house itself is worth anything?" Kurt said.

"Well?" Tressa paused. "I think it depends what you *mean* by *worth anything.* It can be worth a fortune to you, because all your memories are here. And you know, what was your name again? Karl? You *might* get lucky and somebody else come along and this house would just *speak* to them in their *heart*, if you wanted to wait for that person. Now, for that person, you could put on some fresh paint and maybe, you know, *freshen* those appliances and maybe your bathroom, and just wait. Like you're waiting for the big fish to come along. And that person might come along and pay what you're asking, because the house *speaks to them*."

"Or?" said Amelia.

"*Or*, honey." Tressa turned on her heel. "You could just decide you're tired of fishing and want to cut bait. Price it for the lot, not the house, sell it to the first person who makes you an offer, and be done with it."

"That sounds kind of good to me," said Amelia.

"Well, I want y'all to talk it *over*. You don't have to make any big decision right now. The house is rented all summer, so it's gone make you a little income and give you some time to *think*. How long are you here for right now?"

"End of the week," Kurt told her. "More or less. We thought if we wanted to paint, or if we see something that needs fixing—"

"That's good. Y'all are doing the *exact right thing*. Take time, and get some things *done*. Maybe a renter this summer will really *feel* this house, you know what I'm talking about? And if things are nice and fresh, that'll help them feel it. Now, why don't we keep walking through and make some notes?"

After Tressa had gone, Mallory retreated to her room. Kurt, list in hand, drove off to the Ship and Shore. Left alone, Amelia stepped onto the porch and stood looking out at the Sound. The rain had stopped; the air touched her face softly and damply, in a way that recalled Tressa's handshake. The clouds were breaking up, and the water had changed from brown-green to slate, with hard wrinkles instead of whitecaps. At the mouth of the inlet, a fish jumped: a flash of motion, a splash. A pair of black-headed gulls arced past, sawing the wind and laughing as they went.

Across the inlet, as she watched, a boy carrying a fishing pole came out of a house and stepped onto the sea wall, where it curved at the mouth of the inlet to meet the wide Sound. Against the silvering water he stood up straight and black, flicking his pole so that the weighted line flew over the inlet's mouth, where she had seen the fish jump. Perhaps he would catch that very fish, she thought. Did she want him to? Which side was she rooting for? Up and down went the water. Coming in, or going out? In this wind she couldn't tell. That moment, there was a commotion at the end of the boy's line, a white flapping and splashing, and he was reeling in something wide and winged: a skate. She saw him turn and call toward the house, though what he said got lost in the wind. A man came out and consulted; a moment later, the skate was flying back into the water. The man went back into the house. The boy shrugged and cast again.

How many times in her life had she stood at this railing, looking at this view? Only it wasn't the same view, the familiar one. In her childhood, the bridge hadn't been there. Neither had all these houses, each with its dock and boat lift, its sharp white cruiser riding the air above the tossing water. The house behind her, too, had been different. There had been a wall dividing a tiny kitchen from a tiny living room, where her grandmother had so often ended up sleeping on the couch with the television on, playing static all night. The house had felt overflowing with family: her parents in one room, John on a cot, Amelia in the other bedroom, stepping around her grandmother's suitcase to get to the door. All those voices, all those separate breaths rising to the ceiling as they slept. When she was allowed, she had loved sleeping in a hammock slung beneath posts beneath the house. There, in a sleeping bag, she had breathed the clean salt air all night, heard the rush of the water, in and out. And then everything had ended. All that breath had dissipated. Of them all, only she still breathed in this world. As she watched the boy, a stranger, unknown and unknowable to her, casting again and again across the inlet, she hugged herself against a sudden chill.

She'd last seen her mother after Christmas—she didn't count those final unresponsive hospital days. At Christmas, her mother had still been conscious, more or less. Still, Amelia hadn't visited for the holiday itself. She and Kurt were hosting his sons as well as Mallory, having what she had agreed would be a family Christmas. Even Michael had been invited, to forestall any tug-of-war over Mallory's time that day. All of this had been enough to consume Amelia.

Over the phone, LaKisha, her mother's attendant, had reassured her. "She won't know it's Christmas. She'll just think there's some pretty decorations when we go in to supper. They have a kids' choir that's going to come and sing, and she'll like that. But otherwise, I'm going to be honest with you, the less disruption the better."

"What can I send her that she would like?" Amelia had asked. It was almost like asking permission—to send a gift to her own mother! But then, she reasoned, her mother didn't remember that she was anyone's mother. For a time after she had forgotten Amelia, she had still remembered that she was John's mother, but even that was gone now, or at least locked inside her, with all the other things she might still know, but couldn't find words to say. In her world there was only LaKisha. She liked to hold LaKisha's hand.

So when LaKisha had said, "Oh, just send a card," Amelia had done precisely that. She had found a card that played music when you opened it: "Winter Wonderland." Though it made no difference, she had signed it, had had Mallory and Kurt sign it, too. *Love, All the Strangers in Your Life.*

In January, when she visited, driving from Texas to North Carolina, staying, like any stranger, at the Comfort Suites, signing herself in at the memory unit's reception desk, because understandably they liked to keep track of people, she had found the card on her mother's nightstand.

"Look." LaKisha had picked up the card and handed it to Amelia's mother as she sat in her wheelchair, staring at nothing. "Here, Caroline." LaKisha's voice changed, became the voice of a mother coaxing her baby. "Here. Look at your pretty. Show Amelia how you like your pretty."

Without looking at the card, Amelia's mother had opened it, and the music had begun. *Sleigh bells ring, are you listenin',* went the tinny little audio chip inside it. Amelia's mother sat holding it as if this were her duty, the one task that gave purpose to her day, though she didn't enjoy it much. After a moment, she closed the card again. LaKisha, solid, square, no-nonsense in purple scrubs, took it gently from her hands.

God, I'm crying, Amelia thought now, clutching the porch rail. *Well, there's nothing wrong with crying. It's healthy.*

It's cathartic. It's part of an emotion, and emotions are neither good nor bad. They just are, like the weather. Still, she didn't want Kurt to drive up and find her in tears. Because no one watched her—the fishing boy across the way had gone inside—she twisted her face momentarily into a mask of anguish. Her whole body tensed, a soundless scream. Then as the car did pull beneath the house, she relaxed, ran her hands over her wet cheeks to dry and smooth them, and went downstairs to see what Kurt had brought.

All morning it was cloudy, with spatters of rain. While Mallory stayed holed up in her room, Amelia and Kurt sat at the kitchen island and figured.

"I mean, we *could* paint," said Kurt. "There's a Walmart in Tillman's Corner. I could get some white paint, and we could roll it on everywhere. Cheap and quick."

"What if the new white paint is off from the trim and the kitchen cabinets?" Amelia looked about her. She hated dissonance, even the tiniest deviation from harmony. White on the wrong white would drive her bats, even temporarily. The memory of it would bother her.

"Or beige. Or cream." Kurt was persistent. "Then the trim would be just a highlight. We wouldn't have to worry about matching it."

Amelia sighed. "I think we'd be wasting our time. We can give it a good clean, declutter anything that looks junky. Stage it a little more. Those magazines in that rack are twenty years old. I think we can pitch them."

"The fishing rods are totally done," said Kurt. "I looked."

"We'll have to find out whether we can just put them in the can for the garbage men, or what. They're picky."

Kurt was doodling something in the margin of the notepad on which he had been making their to-do list. Now, looking up, he set down his pencil, and Amelia saw that he wore his business face. "I think it would help us to identify a goal here. We're spinning our wheels over these tasks, but what do we actually want?"

"To get this house sold," said Amelia.

Kurt looked at her steadily over his reading glasses. "Are we sure about that? Are we all agreed?"

"Aren't we?"

"What does Mallory think?"

"Mallory is twelve." Amelia tapped her own pen on the white-tiled surface, then rubbed with her thumb at the accidental mark she made.

"This was her grandmother's house."

"She doesn't even remember being here," Amelia said.

"But now she is here."

"Well, I mean—"

"I'm not telling you what to do," said Kurt.

"Good," said Amelia. "Don't."

This was as close as they came to fighting.

Remain solution-focused, Amelia told herself as she turned the pen in her fingers. *You are an adult. There is a solution. As long as you stay in your calm adult-mind, you can find that solution.*

This was advice she handed out professionally all the time. It was advice which, had the shoe been on the other foot, she would not have listened to, or considered relevant, while she was married to Michael. Staying in her calm adult-mind would not have affected Michael's ability to hang on to a job, for example. He was always smarter than his superiors. His ideas always eclipsed theirs. Over and over, it was because they couldn't handle truth spoken to power that they let him go. Now he managed a rundown little store that sold used and factory-seconds outdoor gear: backpacks, tents, sleeping bags. The owner was a friend of his from high school, a laid-back guy. The store was a place where a person who spoke truth to power could slouch around speaking truth to whoever wandered in. The gear was cheap, and the few return customers knew what he was like already. Perhaps they themselves were solution-focused people, who figured that the deal they were getting on the Kelty internal-frame backpack model of several years ago was worth fifteen minutes of curmudgeonry from the man behind the counter.

Though she would not have listened to her own wise counsel, in the end Amelia had had to become solution-focused. Her solution had been to take Mallory and leave. Michael, naturally, had not thought much of this solution. "Do you know," he would still sometimes say, as if she had never heard it before, "that seventy percent of divorces are initiated by women? Do you know the percentage of cases where the man loses his children, his house, everything he has—and pays the woman for the privilege? Do you really think I don't know that women are predators?"

Amelia had initiated her divorce, as it happened, but what had Michael lost? She paid him child support. He lived in their former home. Half the time, their child lived with him. He could claim Mallory as a dependent for tax purposes. Mostly he seemed satisfied with these arrangements, but at some point, as he occasionally intimated, he might want more. One false step on Amelia's part, and full custody, for example, could be his. He didn't mind reminding her of this fact.

"I don't understand why you give him so much power," Kurt often said.

"He's Mallory's father. It's in her best interest for us to be as amicable as possible," she would reply, but this was only a partial truth. The real truth was that she was afraid. Apart from the question of custody, she very much did not want him to be right about women. That is, she did not want what Michael said about women to be the truth about *her*. Had she divorced Michael because he was a feckless asshole? Or had she divorced him, really, because of something fundamentally wrong in herself, some bottomless well of selfishness, some obdurate refusal to be satisfied? Was Michael the problem? Or was she herself the problem she carried with her and never confronted or solved? All day every day she asked other people these questions about their broken relationships. But when the life was her own, it was hard to say.

Impatiently she got up and went to the sliding glass door. The rain had cleared away. Beneath the high blue sky, where the storm clouds had dissipated into streaks and strands of leftover moisture, the restless water rustled and whispered. Around the curve of the island came two teenaged girls on jet skis, bright in their bathing suits, crisscrossing over the open water, leaping each other's sharp white-edged wakes.

Amelia turned to Kurt. "Forget all that now. Let's go to the beach."

"Hm." Hunched on his stool, he was still listing and figuring. "Why don't we wait a couple of hours, let the sun get down the sky? I hate to see you burn."

"Yeah." Amelia looked at her thin freckled arms and sighed. Kurt was right. It annoyed her, sometimes, that he could be as right as he was, as often as he was. With his skin, he could go out shirtless for three hours and come in looking well-rusted, nothing more. By nightfall his rust would turn to bronze. She could kiss his chest in the dark and taste how brown it was. He worried about her, and that made her twitchy. Still, he was right. Despite all her hopes, her freckles had not grown together, over time, to give her a permanent tan. They just multiplied, leaving, somehow, between them, skin enough to burn.

For an hour she sorted old magazines into two stacks: *pitch* and *keep*. The *keep* category were the least out-of-date, the most decorative, and the significantly smaller pile. Onto the *pitch* pile went all the *Cooking Light* magazines. Why had her mother subscribed to this magazine, thin as they'd all always been? Amelia picked up a magazine and read the cover. "A Week of Heart-Healthy Pastas." "Ten Filling Salads for the Non-Rabbits in Your Life." Oh, please, she thought. Nobody believes this any more. We all eat zucchini noodles because pasta's going to give us diabetes. And who the hell wants to live on ten kinds of salad?

"Mallory," she called. "Come help me haul these old magazines down to the trash."

Mallory appeared in the hall. "What?"

"Come help me."

"What is that?"

"Old magazines. I'm weeding them out."

Mallory advanced into the room. Amelia looked at her. "Have you been doing something to your hair?"

"I just put peroxide on the ends. To make them, like, ombre."

"Did you ask before you did this?"

"It's my hair," said Mallory. "Do you like it?"

"What do you think your dad's going to say?"

"If nobody tells him, he won't notice." Mallory's smile was gloating.

"Well, then." Defeated before she could even pick the fight, Amelia struggled up from the floor, gathered a pile of magazines, and dumped them into Mallory's arms. "Take those down and put them in the garbage can. I'll bring another load. If we work together, we can have this done in five minutes."

"The family that works together," said Mallory, and stopped to think. "Twerks together."

"Does *what,* did you say?"

"I said, *are a bunch of jerks together.*" With her toe Mallory nudged open the sliding door.

Late in the afternoon they went to the beach.

"I don't want to go." Mallory's whisper was agonized. "You know why."

"All right." Amelia, already in her bathing suit, was rubbing SPF 100—solid zinc plating, Kurt said—into her shoulders. "You're old enough to stay alone while we go."

"You'd leave me?" Mallory's voice rose in lament.

"Only for a little while."

"Well, wait, then." The bathroom door slammed. If they had been alone, Amelia would have asked Mallory if she was sure she could handle a tampon, but wisely she forbore. Since Kurt's entry into their midst, any number of subjects, including but not limited to feminine hygiene, had become taboo. To speak of shaving and razors, for example, or of brassieres or deodorant or creative writing, was not permitted. Despite having married Amelia, to Mallory Kurt remained in essence an alien: a male alien. Personal girl topics were none of his beeswax. Anyway, Amelia reassured herself, Mallory was competent, far more than she herself had been at twelve. She was the kind of person who not only researched how to bleach the ends of her hair, but worked out how to play the adults in her orbit so that none of them could possibly object. Now here she came, tying the ends of her tankini top, needing no help from Amelia, shrugging off the offer of sunblock.

On the beach, though, they might have been any family. The sun lay low now on the western end of the island and flamed out over the water that lifted itself up and laid itself down, over and over, in a rumble of welcome collapse. Walking barefoot, hand in hand with Kurt, Amelia watched Mallory run to the water's edge, then skitter away as a new wave rolled in higher than she expected, with a little shriek and dance as she'd done for the crabs the night before. Was this how Mallory would approach all of life, putting her toes in, running away, edging back, approach and avoidance?

Could you do that, Amelia wondered, and be healthy? At the back of her mind niggled the old anxiety that she had broken Mallory somehow. She had broken her by divorcing her father. Or, worse, she had broken her in the very act of conceiving her with that father, who would have to be divorced eventually, and had been. Now she had broken her further by bringing in this new father, saying, Here, let this guy buy your tampons, little girl.

"All right?" Kurt squeezed her hand.

"Yeah. Why?"

"You seem kind of meditative, that's all."

"I'm fine."

"Look at that sunset."

"I see it. It's beautiful."

Kurt stopped and turned her so that he could peer into her face. His engagement-diamond earring flashed in the sun. "Sure you're all right?"

"Just tired. It all feels like a lot."

"You don't have to hurry," he said. "You don't have to decide anything right now."

She took some steps ahead of him. "I want to get it done."

"Why?" He broke into a trudging little jog to catch her up.

"I don't want it hanging over my head."

"What?"

Amelia choked down her irritation. "The house, of course. All the details about the house. Why the freaking hell didn't she sell it ten years ago? She never came down. It was just here. She could have taken care of it while she still had her mind, and then I wouldn't have had to deal with it."

"It's okay." Kurt spoke soothingly, as to a child. "I'm glad she didn't sell it. I like it here. I like being here with you. And you know, I keep thinking—"

Oh no, thought Amelia, hugging herself as she walked. Don't think.

But Kurt did think. "I keep thinking what it would be like to have everybody here, have the guys come." By *the guys* he meant his sons. "We could fish. Get a boat, even. It could be cool to come here for Thanksgiving. Or Christmas. Ever been to the beach in the winter?"

"Never," said Amelia.

"It would be different," Kurt said.

"Different from what?"

"I don't know. The traditional thing, I guess."

"What traditional thing?"

"Well," he said, "like, having everybody at our house. I mean, it's nice to do that. The tree. Dinner. All that. But sometimes I think—"

"What?" she said, when he didn't continue.

"Sometimes I think it's good to get everybody out of their normal environment. That's all."

"You couldn't fit everybody in this house for Christmas," said Amelia.

"Cots. Sleeping bags. Surely one of those couches folds out. We could do it."

"Sounds like chaos." She inhaled, held her breath, exhaled. "Look, Kurt, that's a really lovely vision, but what I'm feeling is—"

"Just think about it." His voice was pleading.

Mallory, who had been puttering along the water's edge, now ran splashing to overtake them. "Aren't we going to swim?"

"Do you want to?" said Amelia.

"Well, yeah." Mallory took a few exploratory steps into the water. "It's kind of cold," she called back over her shoulder.

"Still early in the season," Amelia began to say, but Kurt had dropped her hand and gone charging into the surf, with elephantine strides that sent the water flying.

"This is how you do it," he said, and dove into a cresting wave. Mallory danced up and down for a second, then as Kurt surfaced, blowing, she plunged headlong into the next wave. Amelia, watching, felt a pang of terror. The water rose, curled, fell back flat. Her eyes searched its retreating skirl for Mallory. What if she never came up? What if some shark smelled her blood and came hunting her, there in the shallows? It could happen; you didn't have to be way out deep. Or a riptide . . . As Amelia took a few halting steps forward, Mallory exploded from the water five feet in front of her, shaking back dark strings of wet hair and laughing at her mother's face. The sun burned on the distant rim of the sea.

They returned cheerfully over the dunes of waving sea oats, past the pale houses arrayed on the darkening sky, over the main road on which nothing was driving just then but the rising wind. In turns they showered the sand and salt from their bodies. Kurt, who had stopped at the seafood market on his way home from the Ship and Shore, stood red-faced over the stove, turning shrimp in oil laced with fresh ginger, chilis, and lime juice, while Amelia opened beers for them, and Mallory drank a usually-forbidden Sprite.

"Is the beach where people come to poison themselves?" she asked.

Amelia laughed. "It's where the rules get relaxed a little, let's just say."

"Can I taste your beer, then?"

"Sorry. You're not legal anywhere on this planet."

"Somalia," said Kurt over his shoulder.

"Somalia has no government to speak of." Amelia set his beer on the counter behind him, where he would have to reach for it. In the corner of her eye, she caught Mallory sticking out her tongue. At Kurt? At her? At all the nations of the world that would conspire to deny a twelve-year-old a sip of prickly-pear-flavored IPA?

They ate on the porch, looking east over the Sound. Behind them, the sun had set, but the sky was still filled with an amber light that faded by degrees from white to blue. The water rumpled darkly beneath it. Down the way, beyond the house that stood where the Emersons' had been, a dock light switched on and shone whitely on a patch of shifting green.

Kurt eyed the dock and the light with approval. "Now, that's the place to fish. Look at that guy's setup. It's got to be a private place, that dock's way too nice. And check out his boat. Two boats. I wonder if anybody's there now."

"Mm," said Amelia, disinclined to encourage this line of thinking.

Kurt drained the last drops of his second beer. "Look at that, the fish are jumping already."

"There's the guy." Mallory pointed to a hulking figure that had appeared on the dock and stood watching the illuminated water.

Kurt leaned back in his chair with a little moan of satisfaction. "Want to go talk to him, Mal?"

"Me?"

"Yeah, why not? I want to find out what's running, what tackle he uses. You can come with me. And then we can go shopping tomorrow. You can be the fishin' magician. Show the guys, next time we see them."

"Girls don't fish," said Mallory fastidiously.

This roused Amelia to protest. "Who says girls don't fish? Who says there's anything girls don't do?"

"Dad says—"

"Well," said Kurt, "your dad's a good guy, but he's not here right now. And in the great scheme of things, I don't think fishing is going to make you any less a woman. Do you?"

Mallory granted him a rare smile. "Not really."

"So, if your mom doesn't mind getting stuck with the dishes—"

"Oh, thanks," said Amelia. But they had pushed back from the table and left her. A moment later she saw them going single-file, with cat-steps, along the narrow stretch of sea wall where the Emersons' old dock had long since washed away.

She sat back in her own chair, content to nurse her beer a while longer, alone. Around the side of the house, in the white oleander, a mockingbird tried some experimental notes, then burst into full song. Funny, of all the island birds she remembered—pelicans, gulls, the little fleet sandpipers on the beach—she hadn't thought of mockingbirds. That song took her someplace else: the cavernous old house she had grown up in, the little North Carolina town she had been happy to put behind her. *Nothing ever happens here,* she could hear her teenaged self declare. What did you want to happen, she asked that girl now. And she answered herself: anything that wasn't what *was* happening.

Her mother had liked to sit on the front porch in the long spring evenings, reading until it got too dark, and re-marking on the birds. "Look at that thrush, now," she might call to the passing Amelia. "She has a nest in those laurels. Look, now. She's carrying something to her babies."

"That's nice," Amelia would murmur, scanning the street for some sign of a friend on a bicycle or, later, in a car; someone to come by unexpectedly and fetch her away. To do what? Anything. The summer she was fourteen, they used to go down into the ravine behind the old high-school gym. A boy named Jeff, whom she liked then, poured off whiskey out of his parents' bottles into a metal Boy Scout canteen, refilling the whiskey bottles to their old level with water. In the dark, the first fireflies blinking around and above them, he would pass the canteen to the person beside him. There had been, always, four or five of them, people Amelia knew from school. She hadn't kept up with a single one of them. But she could remember the taste of that whiskey, faintly impregnated with aluminum, and a mockingbird singing above them in the dark.

"Listen," her mother would have said. But did anyone ever listen when her mother told them to? Her father would nod absently, thinking of work he had to do. Her brother John might look up from his book, or he might not. He had always been someplace else, far away in his mind. When he opened a book, he found himself already there. And she, Amelia, was always going someplace, desperate to go, always on the brink of something more exciting than to listen to an old bird trot out his mating call, the way birds always did and had always done, forever, as long as there had been birds.

Now, though, she sat back and heard the clear song with its queries, feints, and improvisations, unscrolling in the restless evening air. In it she smelled not only the salt wind, but also the damp musty air-conditioned breath of that other house, the almost fetid honey-sweetness of the laurel blooms in the gathering darkness, the lingering scent of whatever her mother had cooked for dinner borne in on her when she went inside.

Behind her in the house, her cell phone, set down and forgotten on some surface, began its own warbling. Amelia hesitated. Did she want to answer? It was an intrusion. But the phone's noise was imperious. With a sigh she got up from her chair.

"Hey," said Michael.

Instantly she was wary. "Hello, Michael."

"How's the beach?"

"It's fine."

"Nice weather?"

"Yes, very nice."

"Mallory okay?"

"Yes," said Amelia. "She's fine. Having a good time."

"Let me talk to her."

"She and Kurt went over to a neighbor's dock," said Amelia. "Kurt wanted to ask him about fishing."

"Well, I want to talk to her."

Amelia inhaled, exhaled on a count of five. "All right. Hang on." Phone in hand, she went out and down the stairs. Against her palm, as she went, she could feel the vibration of Michael's voice protesting, complaining, pronouncing. With a thrill of anxiety she thought that he might very well be formulating some case against her. Letting Mallory go alone somewhere with Kurt, who was only a stepfather: she had been told and told the statistics for abuse at the hands of step-parents. She had been reminded and reminded that it was out of consideration for Mallory that Michael had not remarried. Never mind that Kurt wasn't that kind of stepfather, any more than Amelia was the kind of stepmother who would leave children in the woods to be eaten by witches. In Michael's mind, letting Mallory go alone with Kurt to the home of some strange man constituted an instance of criminal neglect, even though Amelia, as she picked her way unsteadily over the narrow sea wall, could see them clearly, silhouetted against the deepening blue of the sky. All they were doing was talking. The other man was cleaning fish.

All around them, gulls hovered, flailed, cried for scraps. Pelicans, wings folded, pendulous chins tucked, rode expectantly on the swells just off the dock. Amelia hadn't taken her eyes off Mallory, except to answer the phone. She was safe. Everything was safe.

The Emersons had had a dock like their own, but some storm long ago had washed it away. The house that stood where the Emersons' house had been loomed with all its turrets and gables against the sky. The water slopped at the sea wall. Amelia set her feet carefully. The wall was narrow, its concrete top broken and crumbling in places, as if the storm that had taken the dock had slammed it down repeatedly on that wall before carrying the wood away in splinters.

Mallory, sighting her, called, "Mama!"

Mallory was waving. Behind her, the sky swam. Mallory swam on the sky. Amelia stepped forward, then wavered, one foot in front of the other, a narrow base, as if she were an Egyptian woman in a frieze of hieroglyphics. An eye, a bird. A line of pelicans sailed past her, out of the neck of the inlet.

She was watching Mallory. She was watching the pelicans. She held the phone. She held Michael's tinny voice in her hand. The sky swam. Mallory swam in it. Beneath that sky, Amelia wavered. She reached out instinctively to grab—what? Then the sky was water, cold and full of motion, closing over her.

Her fingers scrabbled on the slimy sea wall. Reaching up, she found the rough top edge of it and hoisted herself a little out of the water. As her head broke the surface, something cold bobbed against her shoulder: a grouper's severed head, missed somehow by the birds, floating in on the rising tide, trailing torn white flesh. Its flat eyes gazed at her; its gray mouth frowned. Its touch was unspeakably dead.

"Get away," she panted. "Get away, get away, get away from me."

Above her, Kurt's face loomed. "Amelia!"

At the panic in his voice, Amelia's own panic crystallized into anger. She wasn't dying. It was no big deal. She spat out water.

"I'm fine. It's not even deep here. I'll swim around to our dock and get out by the ladder."

Steeling herself to touch the grouper's head, she shoved it away. Then she kicked off from the wall, leaned into her stroke. She was a strong, good swimmer, and the tide was coming in. How silly of her to have been afraid, just because she'd lost her balance. With practiced efficiency she swam around the dock and climbed out, to stand shedding salt water. Only salt water, she told herself. Like in the ocean. But the inlet was dark. Eels lived in it, and marine catfish with their toxic spines. And people cleaned fish and threw the heads and guts—the grouper's blind, dead head bobbed before her again, and she shuddered.

Kurt was putting his arms around her, but she pushed him away. "No need for us both to get soaked."

"I saw you go in. I saw you go under." To her surprise, when his arms closed around her anyway, he was shaking.

"I grew up swimming in that inlet," she said. "I was fine."

"The water was so dark. I couldn't see you."

"Well, you see me now. I'm fine." Suddenly, remembering, she looked at her hands: both empty. "My phone. Dammit, my phone—"

"It's just a phone," said Kurt. "We'll get another one. No problem."

"Michael was on the phone. He wanted to talk to Mallory. He'll think—"

"Was he on the phone when you fell in?" When Amelia nodded against his chest, she could feel him laugh, deep inside himself. "Then I imagine he'll know you fell in. Don't you think?"

Somewhere beyond, another man's drawling voice said waggishly, "Nice night for a swim."

Later, showered and dressed in a clean t-shirt and shorts, she sat on the couch with Kurt. They had opened the sliding doors on all sides to let the cool damp air pour through. Except for the little light above the stove, the house stood dark. Outside, the enormous, brilliant night held them, the house and the people in it, on its palm, as if they were a tiny black stone it wanted to treasure a while. Mallory had retreated to her room with her iPod and was texting friends back home.

Kurt held Amelia's hand and told her about the man with the big dock. The man had a name now: Rex, a dermatologist, practicing two days a week in Mobile, living full-time on the island so he could fish. Rex said the speckled trout were starting to run. White trout were in already. You could catch specks with live shrimp, which Kurt was going to buy tomorrow. Rex would lend them rods, Kurt and Mallory both. The whites would strike at lures, sometimes, and Kurt had seen some in a tacklebox under the house, so he thought—

"That's nice," said Amelia automatically.

"Mallory was really interested. We might go back out later tonight, when they start some serious biting. Rex says he'll be fishing until one or two in the morning, and we're welcome—"

"That's great," said Amelia.

Kurt let go her hand and laid his heavy arm over her shoulder. "If it's okay with you, that is."

"Sure. Why not?" What could Michael say, she thought? Her phone was at the bottom of the inlet. Perhaps already the tide was raking it out to the middle of the Sound, and from the middle of the Sound out to sea. Michael could text Mallory, of course, on her iPod. The house had Wi-Fi, and Mallory had found the password already. As cleverly as she'd figured out her internet access, Mallory could also shake Michael off. She could tell him, in gnomic text-speak, an abbreviated version of things that left her cracks to slip through. That, thought Amelia, was freedom. Not to lie, exactly, but to telegraph only true fragments. A pity she was too old for all that: not for texting, but for fragments. She texted whole words, complete sentences, with punctuation. Or she would again, anyway, once she had a new phone.

Kurt was still marveling. "I was never so happy in all my life as when I saw your head come out of that water."

"It wasn't that deep, you know. And I can swim."

It was important, she knew, that she not die. And, this time, without even trying hard, she hadn't.

At ten Kurt and Mallory went over the sea wall again to fish with Rex. From the porch Amelia watched them go, picking their way with the black water slopping at their feet. She remembered the grouper's head and shuddered. Rex's light shone whiter than ever on the water, greening it; even from that distance she could see the fish rising and darting, slivers of quickness, not things, not nouns, but movement itself, drawn to the light and animated by it. She watched as Rex detached himself from the shadow of his big boat on its lift to shake hands with Kurt. Mallory was handed a rod. Amelia saw her jerk it back, then forward. Mallory looked quizzically at the men, whose laughter came floating on the gusty night air, then Kurt was helping her cast. Far away over the bridge, sheet lightning blinked behind the clouds. Shrugging at them all, Amelia turned and went into the house.

How late into the night they fished she didn't know. For a long time she lay in bed, awake as always, hearing the mockingbird—did it never sleep?—try its phrases, over and over, in the oleander. The ceiling fan above her sifted down coolness, and she set herself to concentrate on the sensation of the soft air on her skin. Breathe in, she ordered herself. Breathe out. Tweedle tweedle, went the mockingbird outside. Breathe in. Breathe out. Screw that bird. Breathe.

At the end of things with Michael, she hadn't taken Mallory and stepped into her new life, just like that. She had come here. Let that baby see the Gulf, her mother had said, and grateful, maybe, after all, for what was extended to her, Amelia had come. Her father was dead and buried. *With John,* nobody had piously said, thank God. Amelia, a good daughter, had gone to the funeral. She had gone with Michael: a married woman, desperate that nobody should know how badly married she was. But coming to the beach, she had come alone with her child. She had lain awake in the room across the hall, as she had done in childhood, sharing with her grandmother. She had been an adult; she had a baby, sleeping in the Pack-N-Play at the foot of the bed Everything had been different, changing even as she lay there. Across the hall, her mother had slept alone. But outside, as always, the water had been hurrying beneath the troubled sky. Amelia had lain on her back, watching the fan's blades row the air like shadowy wings, as if some dark bird hovered above her with its eye on her vital signs. *Am I leaving?* The thought had thrummed in her mind. *What am I breaking that can't be fixed?* To her mind, the question was not at all rhetorical. It seemed to her that no matter which way she turned, she would break something, some fragile treasure. The baby murmured in her sleep, and Amelia's heart clenched. *What will I do? Screw that bird. Breathe. Breathe.*

She didn't hear Kurt and Mallory come in, laughing and talking. She didn't hear the shower, or feel Kurt, warm, flushed, fragrant with coconut-milk body wash, slide into bed beside her. She didn't hear when the mockingbird stopped singing, or when a fresh storm broke, with thunder, lightning, clattering rain.

In the morning, while the others slept, she drank coffee and cleaned the kitchen. Away with the years-old containers of Tony's Cajun spice mix, the Zatarain's fish breading, damp in its box. She tossed out half-grinders of salt and pepper, bottles of basil and thyme, sage and oregano, all reduced to dust. From the refrigerator door she took down menus from now-defunct restaurants, and put the magnets that had held them into the drawer with the corkscrew and bottle opener. She sprayed the refrigerator, inside and out, with bleach cleanser and wiped it down. The stovetop, the sink, the cabinets all received the same treatment. On her knees she scrubbed the toe-kick. The kitchen stank of bleach.

"Whew," said Kurt, appearing from the bedroom. "That's some clean."

"A pretty minimal investment, though." With a special eraser, Amelia was rubbing out a scuff mark on the wall.

"Look, we really could just paint. It wouldn't take us half

a day, and you wouldn't have to track down every single ding on every single wall. There aren't even any pictures to take down." Kurt poured coffee for himself and topped off Amelia's cup. "And then the house would smell like fresh paint instead of a covered-up crime scene."

"I don't want to paint."

"Then I will. Mallory and I will. I'll show her how. Life Skills 101. You won't have to do a thing." Kurt smiled at her over his coffee.

So they painted. While Amelia rampaged with bleach spray through the bathroom and bedrooms, Kurt drove with Mallory to Tillman's Corner for cheap cream paint, pans, drop cloths, and rollers. While Amelia hauled the hopeless corpses of plastic floats and aluminum beach chairs out of the storage closet under the house and stuffed them into the trash, Kurt and Mallory plugged Mallory's iPod into the stereo system—when had that been added? Before or after the Wi-Fi?—and turned up her music. Sweating, sticky with cobwebs, muttering to herself, Amelia could hear them laughing overhead, breaking into the chorus of some dumb song about dancing all night. Is it them against me, she wondered. What exactly are we fighting about?

When she came upstairs for a drink of water, she found all the living-room furniture dragged together in the middle, clustered and ghostly beneath drop cloths. In the bedrooms, beds and dressers were pulled out from the walls, suitcases piled on beds. All the doors and windows stood open. A bright salty wind blew straight through the house. As Kurt had prophesied, it did smell less like a covered-up crime, more like something new.

Mallory waved her roller at Amelia, spattering her with

paint. "Dad says why'd you hang up on him last night?"

Amelia stopped. "Did you tell him I fell in the water? I lost my phone. I didn't hang up on him on purpose."

"I didn't tell him anything," said Mallory. "I just said I was fishing and didn't know anything about it."

"Great," said Amelia, half to herself.

Kurt had bought, or found, an aluminum ladder, on which he teetered close to the ceiling. "Use my phone to call him back."

"Thanks. Don't fall." Forgetting her drink, Amelia picked up his phone from the counter and went downstairs again. On the swing under the house, she tapped in Michael's number.

The space beneath the house, the storage closet that still stood open, breathed on her some vague scent, timeless and larger than the present in which she sat with Kurt's phone to her ear, waiting for Michael to answer. Mustiness clung to everything down there, a dampness that never entirely dried out. It was seawater, she thought, evaporated and re-condensed, that she might have swum in when she was seven.

Clearing out the storage closet, she had been reminded of one summer when her brother John had been lost. He had vanished, a tiny boy, and nobody had known where to find him. The whole summer, in her memory, was reduced to that one afternoon. Her father had gone around yanking open every closet, not only in this house, but all up and down that stretch of the island. Each closet had given up to him only this same smell of emptiness. In the end they had found John in the Emersons' house, locked in somehow. Nobody ever knew how. John had never said. It had happened before he started to talk. Looking back, Amelia had often wondered whether, having no words then, he had also had no memory of that day. She had had words, and she had memories, too. In the midst of their terrible searching, when they all thought he had fallen into the water and was gone forever, Amelia's mother had slapped her for some forgotten infraction. In her flip-flops Amelia had turned and run back to their own house, not crying but grinding her teeth and saying to herself—in words she remembered even now—that if she had been lost, her mother would not have slapped John. I wouldn't *get* lost anyway, she had said to herself, loud in her own mind, to drown another voice that said, You *can't* get lost, ever. Nobody would put up with *you* getting lost.

"Unavailable to take your call. Leave me a message," said Michael's voice on the other end. Caught off-guard, Amelia began to speak in hurried fragments. She was sorry. They had been cut off last night. She had fallen off the sea wall. She was sorry. She had dropped her phone in the water. Everyone was fine. Mallory was fine. She was sorry. He could text Mallory or call back later. Everything was fine. Sorry. Goodbye. With a gasp she ended the call.

Taking up the push broom, she began to scrub the concrete floor. Outside, the water stirred, brilliant in the sunlight. From where she stood, Amelia could see the bridge set like a comb to hold back the water from the sky. No other person was visible in the clear afternoon. The fishing boats were either far out to sea or had come in, to go out again at dusk. Everyone else, no doubt, had gone to the beach. It was just herself, there beneath the house, working, and the birds, who did no work at all, but swam industriously across

the air all the same, with vigorous oar strokes that suggest-
ed purpose. Her own arms, pushing the broom, might have
been wings, taking her somewhere. They did take her somewhere: across the cool floor, by degrees, to its edge, where
she swept sand off into waving grasses that grew in sand.
There, she thought, though she knew that what she had
accomplished was precisely nothing. Even as she set the
broom aside, the wind was blowing sand back under the
house. Shrugging, she went out to the dock and sat down
cross-legged in the sun.

On three sides, the water, green now up close in the
sunlight, surged and ebbed against the dock with a noise
like Mallory chewing with her mouth open. When Amelia
looked down, concentrating on what she saw, little splinter-
ing fish materialized out of the murk, which as she watched
it became less like murk and more like a shifting clarity, with
layers in which different things lived and moved and had
their being. *Their little lives are fun to them in the sea*—who
had written that line? Somebody who had never observed
actual fish, thought Amelia.

For a time Mallory had had an aquarium, a birthday gift
ostensibly from both her and Michael. They had gone even
so far as to accompany each other to the store and argue
over the selection of fish. The idea, of course, had been Michael's. He had thought an aquarium would be educational
but because he hadn't wanted to fool with it himself, this
miniature ecosystem had ended up in Amelia's kitchen, not
his.

The aquarium had lasted precisely as long as it had tak-
en all the fish to eat each other. Some fish had disappeared
overnight, in silence and utter mystery; others had disap-

peared gradually in visible bites. A couple of platys had succumbed to the suck of the filter before whatever was eating them had time to finish them off. The interest of the aquarium had become, for both Amelia and Mallory, something on the order of a whodunnit.

"We'll know," Mallory had said wisely, "when there's one fish left. We'll know that fish is the one."

But in the end, they hadn't known. There had been three fish left: one last nervous neon tetra; a male guppy whose beautiful fanning orange tail had been disappearing by the mouthful; and an ugly, glaring algae eater, which skulked along the bottom casting sidewise yellow glances at everything about it. And then one day, as the rhyme goes, there were none.

"What the heck?" Mallory had said.

Amelia had not known how to answer. What, indeed, the heck? Together they had dumped out the water, half-dreading what they might find at the bottom, buried in the gravel. Finding nothing, they had put the empty tank away in the garage, where it still sat, years later, furred with dust.

That time John was lost at the beach, what everyone had feared was the water. He had been little then, three or four, and the water was what would scare you, if it were your child you couldn't find. That time when she had come to the beach house with Mallory, in the wake of her collapsed marriage, Amelia had lain awake at night, imagining Mallory toddling through the house, managing somehow, with the sort of genius you'd be a fool to think a baby didn't possess, to unlock the sliding door—and then what?

In general, for Amelia to have Mallory with her, but not

to see her, meant to panic. To freak right on out, Mallory said. How many times had they gone to the mall together and experienced what Mallory called the freakout? More times than Amelia cared to dwell upon. Even now, they could be in a clothing store, and Mallory—almost thirteen, surely old enough to look at jeans on a rack ten feet away from where her mother stood fingering little cotton-jersey dresses of a type Mallory had last worn when she was seven—would step away. Amelia, looking around, would feel her heart stop. She had learned, by now, not to alert the mall's security department until after she had counted to ten. But, well. There was no avoiding the mall.

If Amelia closed her eyes, she could hear her grandmother, Muh, snap at her mother: *Did you forget that baby's life jacket?* Who was the baby, John or herself? Did it matter? She could hear, again, her grandmother issuing orders not to go near that dock, or she would jerk a knot in somebody's head. Amelia's mother had never talked like that. Except for those moments when she broke open and you saw something else inside her, she had most often spoken in wondering tones to a child. *Goodness, look at this! Heavens, did you ever?* Even as a child herself, Amelia had thought that there was something in her mother that was not quite grown up. She would come back flushed from shopping and show Amelia some extravagant little item she had bought—a potted succulent for a windowsill, an empty bottle in a pretty color that would catch the light—and say, "Don't tell your daddy I spent money on a thing like this!"

She was always a little guilty about something, and that made it easy to boss her. *Mama, I need shorts for gym class— well, really, I needed them last week.* That was how to get her into the car and off to the store where, once inside, she might buy anything else you said you needed.

Or: *Mother, Daddy doesn't look so good. How long has he had that cough? So what if Dr. Murrah said it was nothing? Dr. Murrah is seventy years old. Haven't you thought about seeing a specialist?*

Or: *Mother, I put you on my cell-phone plan. Here's your phone. I want you to carry it with you so I can reach you. Or if you have an emergency. Look, here's how you work it. Now, put it in your purse. And when it rings, answer it.*

Or: *Christ, Mother, this is the bicycle path, not the street. Pull over. I'm driving.*

Or: *Mother, it's Amelia. A. Mee. Lee. A. Say my name. No, not John. Amelia. Mother, look at me. In my eyes. Look at me.*

John was still lost. No amount of bossing would bring him back, only that short in her mother's mind that had found him, caught and held him in the living world. *Is John back yet? I sent him to get me some cigarettes*—when Amelia had never seen her smoke. *Did John take the car?* It seemed that John was always taking the car. Or was about to call on the telephone. Or was there, in the room with them, holding Caroline's hand. As Amelia watched, her mother draped her hand over the arm of her wheelchair and, with her thumb, stroked the air where John's hand hovered, invisibly pressing hers.

Amelia shook herself. There was nothing she could do, now, about any of it. All those people were gone, and she would never find them again, either to set them straight, or to tell them she was sorry. But *what am I sorry for?* She stretched out her legs and kicked them, off the edge of the dock, to see their reflection scissoring on the water. In the shadow of her legs, the fish showed frantically white. Behind her, the mockingbird sang on.

Footsteps sounded on the deck above her, and Mallory's voice called down. "Kurt made scrambled eggs for lunch, Mama. Want some?"

By evening the living room and kitchen shone with fresh paint. In the setting sun, with all the doors open, the house glowed inside, almost yellow. "It's like buttermilk," said Kurt, pleased with himself.

"My grandmother used to drink buttermilk," Amelia remarked. "I tried it once. I thought it was disgusting, but she loved it."

Mallory lay on the couch, leafing through a magazine that had somehow escaped the trash. "Butter is good. Why wouldn't buttermilk be good?"

"I guess," said Amelia, "because you're expecting milk, and it tastes like really watery yogurt instead."

Kurt was cooking the fish he and Mallory had caught the night before: little ones, Amelia thought, though perhaps they had looked bigger before they were cleaned. As she watched from her stool at the island, with her misted-cold glass of Sauvignon Blanc, he melted butter in a deep stainless-steel skillet she didn't recognize, and dredged the fish filets in cornmeal he had gone out again to buy. A second later, they were hissing in the pan.

"I wonder whatever happened to the deep fryer," she wondered aloud, but nobody answered. Nobody knew.

In their bedroom, later, Kurt found her rubbing aloe into her arms. He put his arms around her and kissed her neck.

"Aren't you and Mal going out fishing?" she asked.

He kissed her neck again. "In a while." His breath flamed on her skin.

Conscious of Mallory in her room nearby, they made quiet love beneath the turning fan. Desire, she thought as she lay on Kurt's chest beneath the turning fan. What was it? Even now, she wasn't sure that she felt it. Giving in to Kurt was like giving in to weariness, knowing that sleep would come. It was like seeking comfort and finding it. And what did he feel? Julie had been sick a long time. The last three years of their marriage, he had told Amelia, had been years without sex. But, he had said, what he had learned was that holding someone while she vomited was a form of lovemaking. Brushing the last of her hair from her shining scalp: lovemaking. Changing her catheter bag: lovemaking. Holding her hand as she ebbed away at the end: lovemaking. Now, married to healthy Amelia, he had sex again. Still, feeling his hand resting warmly on her breast as he slipped into a brief light sleep, Amelia thought that on balance, if she were looking for the most primal form of self-giving, she might well choose the catheter bag.

Some time later, Mallory knocked at their door. "Are you done with your little nap?" she called. "I can see Rex out on his dock."

Kurt groaned. "Yep. Getting up right now." He rolled away from Amelia, and she heard the thump of his broad feet on the floor. "Be right there." He leaned over Amelia and stroked her short hair as if she were a cat. To oblige him, she purred, vibrating her tongue against her teeth, and stretched out again beneath the sheet.

At daylight she woke to the noise of gulls, a mingled smell of paint and frying fish, and Kurt and Mallory's voices. For a time she lay in bed listening to them.

"Careful," she heard Kurt say, over an aluminum clanking that signaled the moving of the ladder.

Mallory said, "I put a dropcloth down. I'm not dripping on the floor. I can get this hall done before breakfast is ready."

"Go for it." Fish sizzled as Kurt turned them.

"I didn't think fish were a breakfast food," said Mallory after a moment.

"You can eat fish any time. In England they eat smoked herring for breakfast. Kippers."

"Huh," said Mallory without interest, but Kurt continued down a thought-trail of his own.

"I could get a smoker," he mused. "No reason why you couldn't kipper a white trout, or a redfish, or whatever you caught down here. We could have kippers for Christmas breakfast. Just like in E. Nesbit, or Narnia, or something."

"Are we coming here for Christmas?" Mallory was incredulous. Slap slap went the sound of her paintbrush outside the bedroom door.

"Don't you think that's a good idea? The guys could come—"

"What about my dad?" said Mallory. "Would we invite him, too?"

Amelia heard Kurt sigh. "We could."

"We'd have to. Otherwise I couldn't come. I have to spend Christmas with him."

"Well, then." More sizzling.

Slap slap went the paintbrush. "I thought we were selling this house."

Amelia heard Kurt hesitate. "That's up to your mother. I don't think she's decided yet."

Oh, yes I have, thought Amelia with her eyes closed.

Mallory, right outside the door, said, "Could you swim at Christmas?"

"It'd be too cold to swim," Kurt said. "But you could surf-fish."

"I don't know if I like to fish that much," said Mallory, painting away. Then, in a voice identical to Amelia's, she added, "I didn't think *you* liked to fish that much."

Kurt laughed. "I'm discovering new things about myself all the time."

When Amelia emerged, the hall outside the bedroom was glistening with wet paint. Kurt and Mallory sat at the kitchen island, eating fish together in a manner that struck her as far too conspiratorial. She decided to be irritated with them.

"That's what's for breakfast?" she said.

Kurt smiled at her. "Cereal's in the cabinet, my darling."

"Delish."

"Try this fish, Mama," said Mallory, chewing loudly. "We caught it last night."

"I'm sure it's totally scrummy." Amelia found the cereal and with ostentatious fastidiousness poured herself a bowl. "I love fish for supper. I *had* fish for supper. Now I'm going to eat this Kashi stuff."

"More scrummy fish for us," said Kurt serenely.

After breakfast, Amelia picked up a paintbrush and began on the third living-room wall. By afternoon, working together with the fast-drying latex, they had finished a credible first coat: both little hallways, both bedrooms, the bathroom. If you looked closely, Amelia thought, you could tell that they hadn't gone over it a second time yet. Maybe they would get to a second coat, and maybe they wouldn't. The different whites, walls and trim, weren't so jarring after all, she decided. From a distance, it looked just fine.

"This is a lot of white," said Mallory from the middle of the living room.

"Technically it's off-white," said Kurt. "A warm off-white. The trim is white-white."

"Whatever. There's a lot of it."

Amelia smiled. "It's clean. That's what matters. And when people come to look at the house, they'll see a blank slate, which is exactly what you want them to see. You want them to see themselves in the house, not you."

"Yeah," said Mallory. "Whatever. Can we go to the beach now?"

Kurt and Amelia looked at each other.

"Sure," said Amelia. "Why not? We'll put on lots of sunscreen, and I'll wear a shirt and a hat. It's our last day—"

Now Kurt and Mallory looked at each other. Some spark passed between them. Amelia was sure she saw it leap, from Mallory to Kurt, from Kurt to Mallory.

"Tomorrow's Friday," she said. As they turned to her, aghast, she added, "Isn't it? Or have I lost count?"

"I guess it is," said Kurt.

"And Mal, you've got to be at Dad's first thing Saturday morning. We have to leave early tomorrow. I'm sorry, but that's the way it is. It's been great, but we knew we weren't staying forever."

"I know," said Mallory glumly. "I know, I know, I know." She thudded away to her room.

Kurt, too, was glum, pulling on swim trunks damp from the porch rail. "Yeah, I know we have to get back, but damn."

"Stop making me the buzzkill." Amelia turned so that he could tie the back of her bathing-suit top.

Kurt came to her and scrabbled with his thick fingers at the strings. "I'm not making you the buzzkill."

"Yes, you are. I heard you and Mallory talking. It's two against one, isn't it?"

Kurt kissed the back of her neck, where her hair grew silkily in a deep coppery vee. "I'm on your side, babe."

Her neck prickled. She twitched her shoulders impatiently. "So you say."

"I am on your side, Amelia. I'm always on your side."

"But you want to keep the house. You and Mallory."

"Maybe. But it's your house. Your decision."

"And I'll be the buzzkill forever if selling it is what I decide."

Kurt turned her to face him. He was smiling. "Not forever." He moved to kiss her, but she ducked her head, and the kiss landed on the part in her hair.

"Yes, forever. It's not funny, Kurt. I can tell what the two of you want, and I wish you'd just come out and say it."

"I thought we had." Now he wasn't smiling. "Were you listening?"

"Of course I was listening. But we have to be sensible. Not get carried away. It is beautiful here. I love being here. Selling this house is like selling my whole childhood." Furiously she blinked away tears. How stupid to cry, when sensible was all she wanted to be.

"So why sell it?" said Kurt.

"Because it's over." Amelia snatched up her sun hat, the

kind of sun hat she would have ridiculed her mother for wearing, and jammed it onto her head.

Again, though, on the beach, they were like any happy family, all their real-life troubles left behind. Mallory and Kurt dove into the waves, while Amelia sat on her towel watching them. The wind had risen. The water was rougher. The waves, rising brownly, turned over and came crashing down with a noise like a child's block tower kicked over. Amelia saw Mallory get caught and tumbled, all flailing white legs like Icarus in the painting by Brueghel. Starting up, she was ready to dive in herself and pull Mallory to safety, but by the time she had skinned her shirt off, Mallory was standing up, coughing and laughing, shaking the water out of her ombre-bleached hair.

"I thought I was dead," she said, and Amelia wanted so badly to smack her that she turned and ran down the beach a little, her feet slapping the wet sand, until the feeling dissipated. So that was what it felt like, she thought. You built your levees, but if the waters rose and pounded hard enough, the levees could break.

But her levees were high and strong. She hadn't come all this way, through the maze of her life, to break down. Even at her mother's funeral she hadn't broken. It was a primal wound, the loss of a mother. Everyone knew this. She had clients whose lives had been broken in childhood by the deaths of their mothers. They were so broken, some of them, that they didn't even know they were broken. Broken was normal; they had never known anything else. Amelia, poised in her armchair, listening to them, could tell that this was so. But she had not been broken.

After the funeral, she had stood with LaKisha in the fu-
neral-home vestibule. Kurt was inside, still, talking to people he had never met before. Mallory, for the moment, had
vanished altogether. It was raining, a dull drumming rain
that made the very asphalt outside look impregnated with
water. Through the glass door she had seen the long, low
wing of the memory unit. Though the funeral home did not
actually occupy the same property as the transitional-living
community where her mother, through several transitions,
had lived out her last years, it was close enough to stand as a
reminder to anyone with enough mind left to think about it.

LaKisha was wiping the tears from her cheeks. "You'd
think after all this time I wouldn't cry, but I get attached to
them. Every single time. I always tell myself I won't, but I
do."

Amelia had patted her shoulder. Even through the unreality that always seemed to accompany a death, she felt
that this was backward. Shouldn't she be the one grieving?
Shouldn't LaKisha, the professional caregiver, be caring for
her a little? But then, Amelia was strong. Death couldn't
break her. Even if all this was backwards, it was the way it
was. She went on patting LaKisha.

"She was a good lady," LaKisha said. "It was a privilege."

"You saved our lives," said Amelia, the expected thing to
say. The next thing, she supposed, was to say that LaKisha
had become one of the family, but they would both know it
wasn't true. The family, what was left of it, had kept its distance. LaKisha wasn't part of them at all. They had paid her
not to be part of them, to do what they wouldn't do. LaKisha
wouldn't have done it for free.

But there she was crying for Amelia's mother, all the

same. And there was Amelia, dry-eyed, patting her through the navy-blue polka-dot dress that looked like a costume, so accustomed was Amelia to the sight of LaKisha in purple scrubs. Now LaKisha stood, dignified, even elegant, in her dress and heels, her lipstick. She's a pretty woman, Amelia thought with a little jolt of surprise. She went on patting LaKisha, to comfort her in her loss. Finally LaKisha turned and hugged her. Amelia was aware, briefly, of the scent of Jergens Lotion, the same lotion her grandmother had used, and through that, the warm smell of LaKisha's own skin. Then she was alone in the vestibule with the pummeling noise of the rain.

They had made a transaction, Amelia thought. She had sold LaKisha some human grief, and what had LaKisha paid her for it? Sole rights, again, to her own mother? LaKisha would go on to care for someone else and, eventually, to weep at that person's funeral. She would forget Caroline. Eventually someone else would sit holding a Christmas card that played a tune. The face would be different, but the expression would be the same. That person, too, would like colored lights and carols. That person, too, would never notice whether his or her children were there. LaKisha would hold that person's hand as she had held Caroline's. But at death, the memory of that person who had had no memory would be folded up, handed back to the family to keep.

Here was Amelia now, walking down the beach, seeing the little sandpipers that skittered before her to the water's edge and back again. Their tiny v-shaped prints faded almost instantly into wetness. She was thinking how she had wanted, only a moment ago, to slap Mallory for having been tumbled in the surf. The greater your love was, the more it could make you want to break the person you loved, to keep them from some worse harm. But if you hadn't loved them enough—what then?

Oh, well. She shook herself. It was a long time ago. She had grown up. She understood things, had arrived at terms. She had left Michael, and the world hadn't ended. Mallory, whom she had agonized about, was fine. She had Kurt, her whole new life that shimmered before her now like the Gulf. It was the Gulf, though, she thought, that washed up these bits of memory like beach glass, driftwood. It would take them back again, too. It would tumble and polish them until their sharp edges wore away, their clarity dimmed and softened. You could pick them up then and run your fingers over their satin surfaces that wouldn't cut you. You could make jewelry of them, wear them out to dinner with your lover.

"Amelia!" Kurt was calling her. She turned. He and Mallory stood waving, beckoning her back.

They walked over the dunes, their feet skidding and slipping in the dry sand. The wind sprayed the backs of their legs with more sand, which stung.

"It's kicking up some," Kurt said. He nudged Amelia's shoulder with his and nodded at Mallory, trudging before them, her arms full of towels. "Also, somebody needed an Aunt Flo break."

Amelia stopped and stared at him. "She told you that?"

"I mean, in code, but yes." He smiled at her.

"Well."

"What can I say? Turns out I'm good at this stepfather thing."

"Yes," said Amelia. "You are. You amaze me." She took his hand.

Hand in hand they came into their own road.

"We've got company," said Kurt. Following his gaze, Amelia saw two cars parked behind their own car in the driveway: a white sedan with an Island Realty badge on the door, and—

"Dammit," said Amelia.

Ahead of them, Mallory broke into a toiling run. "Dad!"

Michael stood in the driveway, leaning on his rusted Subaru wagon, talking to Tressa the realtor. Talking *up* Tressa the realtor, Amelia thought. He stood with his arms folded over his bulging chest. Michael believed in physical discipline for himself. Amelia had to give him credit for that. His calves beneath his baggy shorts were hard, the muscle like a clenched fist beneath the white skin. The wind was blowing his ragged graying hair. Now, hearing Mallory's voice, he started.

"Well, hey, puddin'."

Mallory flew into his arms. "What are you doing at the beach?"

"Wha'd you do to your hair, girl?"

So Mallory was wrong. Michael did notice things.

"Mama told me I could."

Over the top of her head Michael's glance fell on Amelia, still holding Kurt's hand. "Where the hell have you been?"

Kurt put out his free right hand to shake Michael's. "At the beach. Ever heard of it?"

"Nice to see you, Michael," said Amelia through her teeth. "Obviously you've met Tressa."

Now it was Tressa's turn to shake hands. She went

around to everyone, not shaking their hands, exactly, but squeezing them in a damp little vise grip. "Hey," she said. "Hey, *hey*. How are *you*? I just came by to see how y'all were getting *along*."

"We painted," Mallory told her. "You should come see. Me and Kurt painted the whole house."

"That's a real educational thing to miss a week of school for," Michael said. As the rest of them moved toward the stairs, he caught Amelia by the elbow. "Why did you hang up on me the other night?"

Amelia held her breath. Then she let it out. "I did not hang up on you. Did you not hear the message I left? I was walking over the sea wall to give the phone to Mallory, and I lost my balance and fell in."

"Uh huh."

"I did."

"Uh huh."

"Look, Michael, if you want to hunt for my phone, be my guest. You won't find it. It's at the bottom of the inlet. Didn't Mallory tell you what happened?"

"She did. But sometimes I like to see the lay of the land for myself."

The others were going up. Their footsteps rang hollowly on the wooden stairs, then the deck. Still Michael gripped Amelia's elbow.

She willed herself not to struggle. "Why don't you come on up? Have a beer. I'm not sure what's for dinner, but of course you're welcome to stay."

"Nah. I'm not staying. Just tell Mallory to pack her bag and come on down. I'm taking her home."

Amelia jerked her elbow. Michael's hand opened, releasing her, and she staggered a little.

"Your week doesn't start till Saturday," she said. "You're violating the terms of the parenting plan. Is that really what you drove all this way to do?"

"Let's just say I'm concerned about my daughter's safety and well-being."

"Michael, that's ridiculous. And we agreed—"

"I thought better of our agreement. I decided I didn't think it was wise."

"Wise?" Amelia screeched.

Again Michael reached for her arm. "Aren't you the one who's all about presenting a united front? Aren't you the one who's all about not upsetting the kid? You made her a child of divorce, babe, not me."

"Look, Michael—"

At that moment Kurt put his head over the railing. "Are you people coming up or not? I put out chips and nuts and stuff, and there's beer. Michael? Mallory's wondering when you're going to come see this paint job."

Michael glared up at him. "Yeah, yeah. I was just having a little talk here with my *ex-wife*." Then his expression softened. "Tell Mal I'll be right up."

Everywhere the paint had dried. Tressa, in heels today instead of flip-flops, was clonking from room to room, cooing over it. "Honey, what a big *girl* you are," Amelia heard her say, somewhere at the back of the house. "To *help* your daddy like that."

"He's not my daddy," Mallory's voice replied. "He's my stepdad."

"Well, you're a *good helper* anyway, honey, and that's what matters."

Kurt turned from the fridge. "Michael? What's your pleasure?"

"Just water for me. I'm driving."

"Driving?" Kurt filled a glass at the fridge door and handed it to him. "You just got here."

"Well, I'm not staying."

Amelia heard her own voice, still too high-pitched, hysterical. "It's such a long way, Michael. Why don't you stay over, at least until tomorrow? That's when we were going to leave, anyway. Have a little beach vacation with us. Mallory would be so glad."

"Plenty of room," said Kurt stoutly, backing her up.

"Dad," called Mallory from a bedroom. "Come and see. I'm showing Miss Tressa all the places I painted."

When Michael had gone, Kurt looked at Amelia. "You want him to stay?"

"Hush," she said. "I can't do anything about it now. He's here."

"I really think—" said Kurt, but whatever he really thought, he seemed to think better of it. Mallory, followed by Tressa and Michael, sloped back into the living room and grabbed a handful of chips from a bowl.

"Well, it all looks *good*." Tressa brushed back her falling blonde bangs with a languid hand. "And I see you polished up that fridge and stove, too."

Amelia said, "I cleaned out all the closets down below, and weeded out magazines and other clutter. Do you think it'll do?"

"I think it looks *real* nice." Tressa glanced at the cell phone she held. "I've got another appointment in ten minutes *all the way* at the west end of the island, but I *totally* wanted y'all to know I hadn't forgotten you. Why don't you stop in the office, whenever you're on your way out, and let me know if you're ready to put the sign up?"

When she had clonked down the stairs and driven away, Mallory said to Michael, "What do you think? Doesn't it look good?"

"It's okay." Michael sipped his water virtuously. Both Kurt and Amelia had cracked open beers, a decision Amelia thought she might live to regret. "I mean, it's not professional or anything."

"For a first outing," said Kurt, "I thought Mal and I did a pretty good job."

Michael shrugged. "Yeah. So, you're selling this old house at last?"

A long pause.

"Amelia's mother used to talk about this place like it was the Holy Grail," Michael said.

"She loved it," said Amelia. Since when did Michael know what her mother had talked about? Amelia had hardly ever brought him to visit her parents. At Christmas she had called home, pled both their work schedules, letting her parents think that they both had work schedules, that Michael was supporting her, that everything was fine. Only when her father died had they come to visit, all three of them. As soon as she could after the funeral, she had sent Michael outside to push Mallory on the swing, so that her mother wouldn't have to talk to him.

"This was her happy place," she added now, the conventional thing to say. Had it, in fact, been happy? Happier than anywhere else? Chiefly it seemed to her that life had gone on here as everywhere, sometimes happy and sometimes very much not.

Mallory spoke through a mouthful of chips. "I think we should keep it."

"Cost a lot to keep," said Michael. "House like this."

Amelia watched him. *If I sell this house and make a pile of money, I'll have to give some of it to Michael.* She hadn't thought of that before. Of course, it might be worth it: to unload the worry of the house, and to settle things further with Michael. If she threw more money at him, maybe he would go away a little more. In her heart, though, she knew this wasn't, couldn't be, true. It irked her to think that whatever she did to free herself from complication, she would still be tangled up with Michael.

"Let me get cleaned up," she said, for something to say. "And I'll make a run to the Ship and Shore. What do we all want for supper?"

"Let's go out," said Mallory. "Daddy hasn't been to Captain Bodine's."

"Sure, why not?" Kurt was expansive. Amelia sighed. Sitting around a restaurant table with her current and former husbands, angelfish drifting in predatory uprightness through the tank in the background: not her idea of a good time. Then again, nothing they might do that evening was going to be a good time, if Michael had consented to stay. Looking at him, she saw that he had. He had ceased to emit waves of impatience. He wasn't looking at his phone. He was still drinking his water, but now he eyed the fridge where the beer was.

Let's all get good and buzzed, Amelia thought. That way, if there's a disaster, there's also a chance that none of us will remember it.

As it turned out, there wasn't a disaster, not really. They

had gone decorously to the restaurant and had sat around the black formica table drinking sweet tea. From where she sat, Amelia could see the angelfish hanging like medallions in the brilliant water of the fish tank that occupied the wall opposite her. They didn't seem predatory. Perhaps, as she had always heard that angelfish did, they had already eaten everything smaller than themselves. That was why Mallory's tank hadn't had angelfish. Michael had wanted to buy them, but Amelia, in whose house the fish tank would reside, had balked.

"They'll eat the other fish," she remembered protesting in the aisle at Walmart, several days before Christmas. Michael had glared at her. What did Amelia know about anything? Here we are, she had thought wearily, just a couple of ex-spouses partaking in the holiday spirit. But in the end, for once, he had listened to her, not that it had done any good. The fish had eaten themselves all up anyway. It was years ago, but she still wondered how they had managed it. Watching the Captain Bodine's angelfish, large as her palm, striated in black, floating along with every appearance of innocence, she mistrusted their nonchalant expressions.

Here we are, she thought again. *Just another American family: three parents, one child. All of us being good together. Having a lovely, relaxing time here at the beach.* The waitress set before her a steaming platter of fried fish, fried jumbo shrimp, fried oysters. A moment earlier she had thought she was starving, but now, suddenly, she had to excuse herself to the ladies room.

She shut herself in a stall and sat down. Once away from the table, she didn't feel sick anymore, only reclusive. Coward, she reproved herself. Leaving Kurt out there to make small talk with Michael.

She heard the restroom door open and shut.

"Mama?" said Mallory. "Are you okay?"

"I felt a little woozy. You okay?"

"Yeah." The stall door beside Amelia's banged, and the metal bolt slid. There was a rummaging, as in a purse, and a ripping of paper. "I hate this," said Mallory.

"I'm sorry. I shouldn't have left you alone out there. Are Daddy and Kurt—"

"No, I mean my stupid period," said Mallory. "It just goes on and on. Can I get my whole uterus yanked out, please?"

"Of course not. What if you wanted to have a baby some-day?"

"I would never want to have a baby." The toilet flushed. "What did you say about Dad and Kurt?"

"Nothing," said Amelia. "Just wondered if everybody was all right."

The stall door banged again. "Kind of quiet. But all right, I guess." Mallory washed her hands and went out.

For a while longer Amelia sat contemplating. It was quiet in the ladies' room, all right, quiet and vaguely vanilla-scented. I could sit here forever, she thought. Just tell them to lock up the restaurant and leave me here in the dark. The angelfish are out there, on patrol. Nothing could get in to hurt me.

But at last she had to go out. As she sat down at the table, Kurt reached over—glancing first at Michael, as if to ask his permission—and took her hand. "Okay?"

"Fine. I just felt a little off for a few minutes." She picked up her fork and started to eat. Beside her, Michael studied the remains of his flounder lagniappe. How odd, she thought, to be sitting next to him at dinner. Next to Michael, across from Kurt. She wondered how Michael felt. It wasn't like him not to announce to everyone how he felt about something, whether everyone wanted to know how he felt or not. Generally, the less everyone wanted to know, the more Michael would proclaim whatever was passing through his mind. Amelia could remember a time when she had found his openness compelling. He was a straight talker, she had thought. No games. A little blunt, maybe, but you knew where you stood with him. Now, when it was too late, she knew that this was precisely what you didn't want to know.

That night, prevailed upon, Michael went with Kurt and Mallory across the sea wall to Rex's. From her chair on the porch with her after-dinner beer—God, how she needed it—Amelia saw him accept a rod and cast into the rumpling white-lit water. Please, God, let them stay there a long, long time, she thought. After she drank the one beer, she had another. Then she went to bed.

At daybreak, when she came into the kitchen to make coffee, she found Michael stretched on one of the couches in his clothes, an empty bottle on the floor by his dangling hand. He breathed with his mouth open, sucking in the salty air like a vacuum cleaner and expelling it with a pop. His morning beard bristled thickly on his cheeks, giving him the look of a man struck down in the process of turning into a werewolf. If he had been anyone else, she would have bent to his ear and shouted, "Good morning!" But because he was Michael, she tiptoed.

Mallory appeared, rubbing her ears exactly as she'd done as a baby, waking up. "Do we have to go home today?"

"That's the plan," said Amelia in a whisper, glancing at Michael, who slept on.

"Yeah, but we only made that plan because I had to be at Dad's. Now Dad's here."

"Well." Amelia looked about her. The creamy walls glowed in the early light. "I think we've done everything we came to do, haven't we?"

"I don't know." Mallory was pouring cereal.

"All that's left is to stop by the office and tell Tressa to put up the sign."

"Really? *Really?*" Mallory spoke through a mouthful, spraying Rice Krispies onto the island countertop.

Amelia shushed her. "Don't wake Dad up. Of course, really. What else did you think was going to happen?"

"I don't know. It's just—I had no idea we had all this. No. Idea. All my life, we could have been coming here. And we didn't. It's like we let something go to waste." Mallory turned her tearful gaze on Amelia. "And now that we are here, and it's like the best thing ever, we're just going say, Too bad, so sad, bye-bye? *Really?*"

"Look." Forgetting Michael, Amelia steeled herself to use the mother voice Mallory most hated. "Yes, it's great here. Yes, I am sorry we didn't come here more often when we could. Life has been complicated."

On the couch, Michael opened his eyes. "Pipe down, you bunch of hens." His eyes fluttered shut again.

Swallowing, Mallory lowered her voice. "Dad had fun last night. He caught about ten thousand croakers and had to throw them back, but today him and Kurt want to go get some live shrimp. See, *we* have plans, Mama. We can't go home."

Plans. Amelia sighed. "*He* and Kurt."

In this way, the day's outline was sketched and colored in. There was nothing Amelia could do about it. Presently Kurt got up and was given a cup of the coffee she had made. She had already given Michael some and received his grunted thanks. Mallory was out on the dock throwing torn-up bread—perfectly good torn-up bread, that people could have eaten—to a battering crowd of seagulls. Once, Amelia remembered, she had stood with her mother on some earlier version of that dock and thrown leftover pancakes to the gulls. Throwing perfectly good food away on birds was one of those timeless beach experiences. That kind of waste, she supposed, never got old. While you were doing it, it didn't seem like waste. You were trying, it seemed, to fill up hungry nature, all of it. And you didn't know yet that the kind of hunger nature brought to you, open-mouthed, screeching, squabbling for its turn, was a hunger you could never fill, even if you stood there forever, even if you gave it every scrap of food you had and went hungry yourself. It would always want more.

It was the same impulse, she supposed, that sent Michael with Kurt and Amelia to the bait store for live shrimp. Last night they had had the wrong kind of bait, and in consequence, had caught all the wrong kind of fish. Tonight they would have the right bait. What would they catch? There were only so many shrimp in the little aerated bucket they brought home. That meant only so many fish. Still, when they climbed from Michael's car, all of them laughing and splashing water out of the bucket as they lugged it under the house out of the sun, it was clear that they were operating, for the moment, anyway, on a new and seemingly limitless budget of hope.

Well, let them. Amelia washed the dishes, then looked over the linens in the closet. The sheets would do, all cheerful blues and yellows. Tomorrow, when they left, because tomorrow they really were leaving, she would strip the beds, wash and dry the sheets they had used, fold those sheets and put them away, make up the beds with new ones. Leave No Trace, as the saying went. Today they could all imagine whatever they wanted to imagine. Sky's the limit, thought Amelia. But tomorrow they would go home.

In the afternoon they went again to the beach, Michael plastered in zinc oxide, with a spare panama hat of Kurt's pulled low over his ears. He wore Kurt's other fray-cuffed year-before-last's white dress shirt buttoned up to his neck. Amelia waded and picked up shells while the men horse-played with Mallory in the water. First Michael hefted Mallory on his shoulders, from which height she wrestled with Kurt until he unseated her, screaming, and ducked her in the waves. Then, as if she were little, Michael and Kurt took turns lifting her and throwing her back and forth. The waves today were bigger and rougher than they had been, and after they tired of the throwing game, the three of them body-surfed, swimming in on the yellow-foamed breakers, then going out again, breasting the waves until another big one came up to be ridden back to the beach. Under her sun hat, Amelia sat in the sand and watched them.

When the sun melted, all blood, into the silver water, they came home and ate gumbo and white rice. Michael had bought more beer, an entire case of something called Emergency Drinking Beer, in yellow cans. It tasted like something you'd be glad to drink after a hurricane, with no overtones of ginger, prickly pear, or grapefruit. Afterward, the men went onto the porch to talk over the fishing some more. On their outing they had also bought new rods, as an act of conscience. "Can't keep borrowing Rex's," Michael had said piously. He had bought Mallory a fishing rod, too, and took her down to the dock to make her practice using the spinner reel, learn where and when to put her finger down to stop the line spooling out. Apparently, after all, in his mental economy, there were times when a girl could take a break from cheerleading and learn to fish with the men.

While Amelia was washing the dinner dishes, however, Mallory came in and flung herself on the couch. "I'm bored."

"I thought you liked fishing," said Amelia.

"I mean, I do. But you know."

"How are the cramps?" Amelia asked her.

"Better. Kurt told me Julie used to take two ibuprofen, then five sips of beer, and that stopped them. I tried it, and it worked."

"Who gave you beer?" You talked to Kurt about menstrual cramps, Amelia did not say.

"Well, Kurt did. Just five sips. Dad was right there. He didn't mind. It was for medicinal purposes."

Julie, thought Amelia, I get tired of you sometimes. Aloud she said, "Are you going out with them tonight?"

Mallory shrugged. "I don't know. Dad said I have to put the shrimp on the hook myself. And they're gross. They have swimmy legs." She waggled her fingers to show Amelia. "And a hook or a barb or something. They poke you, and it hurts."

"Maybe Kurt can help you. You ought to give that pole at least a trial run."

"Yeah."

After a moment Mallory swam back up from the depths of the couch and wandered away to her room. Amelia took the broom and began to sweep the kitchen, then the living-room floor. Through the windows, she could see the Sound, silver turning to blue in the last light. Then it was dark. She was just going to open the sliding glass door, to let in the night breeze, when it opened, as if on its own, from the outside instead. Michael came in.

"Having fun?" Amelia clutched her broom.

"Yeah. Just came in for more beer." He moved toward the fridge, but she was in his way. He stopped and studied her. "You look all right, you know."

Foolishly she flushed. "Thanks."

"Like old times." He put out a hand, touched her hip. "You always did have a bony ass, girl."

She moved away from him. "Michael—"

"Yeah, yeah. You married marshmallow boy out there. I know."

"Yes, I did."

"Well. I kind of like him. He's not nearly as much of a pussy as I thought."

Michael studied her for another moment. Then he reached for her, pulled her to him, and kissed her hard, pressing his tongue between her teeth. He tasted of salt and beer. Then either he let her go or else, still holding the broom, she used the handle to lever herself away from him. One way or another, they separated. For a moment they looked at each other. Then Michael stepped around her, opened the fridge, collected an armload of beer, and went out, leaving the sliding door open.

Amelia sprayed down the kitchen island with bleach

and wiped it until it dazzled. Then she sat on the couch and read *Cottage Living*. From beneath the house came shouts of laughter and, every now and then, the tinny clatter and skid of an empty beer can. Ignoring these noises, Amelia went on reading an article about a woman who lived in a renovated dovecote. Then she read recipes for Five Irresistible Backyard-Barbecue Cocktails, and an article about propagating hydrangeas. At some point, surely, Amelia's mother had held this same magazine and flipped through its pages. Had she envied the woman in the dovecote? Had she made even one of the Irresistible Cocktails? She had had enough hydrangeas already. But the rest was mystery. Amelia would never know what her mother had thought about any of it.

Twilight glowed blue at the windows. For a while Amelia dozed, upright on the couch with the magazine in her hands. The laughter beneath the house migrated over the sea wall to Rex's dock. Between the dock and the house, Kurt had told her, there was a graveled yard with adirondack chairs around a firepit. Rousing, stepping onto her own porch for a last breath of air, Amelia saw down the way, the glow of the fire, the sparks gushing up to meet the stars. Then she went to bed.

Late in the night, she was awakened by their voices. The men's laughter, in the house now, was loud and ragged, punctuated by stumbling footsteps. The bathroom door slammed. A minute later, through the wall, she heard someone peeing copiously, with much plashing and plunking. Thinking how carefully she had scrubbed that bathroom, she sighed.

She had almost relapsed into sleep when Kurt came in. Dimly she heard him unbuckle his belt, unzip his shorts. His clothes fell to the floor, with clicks and a noise of soft collapse. When he climbed into bed, his kisses, like Michael's, tasted of salt and beer. He reached for her with urgency. Half-conscious, she felt her body open to him.

"Julie," he said. "Julie."

Then he rolled away and was asleep. For a long time after, beneath the ceiling fan, Amelia lay wide-eyed.

Sometime before dawn, Mallory tugged at her. "Mom."

"What?"

"I want to go home."

Amelia opened her eyes. In the half-light Mallory loomed over her, dressed in an oversized black Panic At the Disco t-shirt and clutching her iPod.

"Well, we are going home sometime today," Amelia whispered. "But why the sudden change of heart?"

"McKenna just now texted me, and she's having this sleepover—"

"What time is it? McKenna's texting you *now*?" Amelia's whisper became a hiss. "Does her mother know?"

For answer, Mallory tossed her back her hair. Something gleamed in her earlobe.

Amelia narrowed her eyes. "What's that?"

"What's what?"

"In your ear."

Mallory put up her hand to finger the little shine. "Oh, um. An earring."

"Pierced?"

"Um, yes."

"Who said you could get your ears pierced?"

Mallory shuffled her feet on the sandy floor. "Nobody. I

just did it. I saw these earrings in the Ship and Shore, and I had my own money, so—"

"When did you do it?"

"Last night. While Dad and Kurt were fishing. You were asleep."

"What did you pierce them with?"

"I found a sewing kit. Somebody must have left it. Don't worry, I sterilized the needle with a match. I'm not going to get blood poisoning."

"You didn't ask Dad?"

"Nope."

"Well, great." Amelia sat up and swung her legs over the side of the bed. Kurt, sprawled on his stomach, mumbled something and gnashed his teeth, but did not wake.

Mallory said, "Mama, your shirt's all unbuttoned."

Amelia flushed. "Oh. Sorry." Her fingers fumbled with the buttons. "Guess I got kind of hot last night."

"Yeah." Mallory looked at her levelly.

In the living room, Michael snored again on the couch. This morning, the beard was a real beard, wiry and luxuriant. In the middle of it, his mouth, with its red soft lips, hung open, and the breath rushed in and out with the windy noise of a vacuum-cleaner hose. His shirt was unbuttoned, to reveal a similar beard glinting on his chest. His legs sprawled; one foot still wore its sneaker. Amelia made coffee as silently as possible.

When it was ready, she took her cup downstairs and sat on the swing beneath the house. From where she sat, she could see the inlet pouring into the Sound, the soft wavelets running away into silver beneath the pearly sky. The water poured out, the wind poured in, warm as the milky coffee she was drinking. The coppery short hairs on her forehead scrunched in the humidity. From another inlet, closer to the bridge, a johnboat came puttering out, black on the pale water. When it was far out on the Sound, it stopped and rode the gentle swells, and Amelia saw, silhouetted, how the man in it raised his rod and cast. Closer in, a pelican she hadn't noticed dove like a dropped arrowhead and came bobbing up again, presumably gratified by the results of its effort. If, she thought, surrendering to gravity could be construed as effort.

It might have been any summer morning of her life. Over her head, her grandmother might have been sleeping on the old sofa, the TV on, static growling. In the room where Kurt slept on, her mother might have been stirring, buttoning her own soft shirt, preparing to face them all. Amelia might just have climbed from a hammock to come and watch the early water and the birds, to scan the Sound for dolphins. At any moment, the old Marnie B., the cheap fishing charter that went out hugging the island's perimeter, might sputter into view carrying her father, Mr. Emerson, Rick, and John. Left behind, a girl, she would stand on the dock and wave to them, certain that even over that great obscuring distance, they saw her and waved back. Often enough, her mother would stand beside her, waving, too. Shoulder to shoulder, the wind in their hair, gulls breast-stroking across their vision, they waved, two females who didn't get to go fishing. Maybe the fishermen saw them. Maybe they didn't. Her mother would take her hand. The next minute, Amelia might say or do something wrong, and her mother's comfortable mood would snap. But in that fleet moment, everything balanced on the silver rim of the morning, they could be happy together.

"Damn," said Amelia, wiping her face with the heel of her hand. "Damn it to hell. Just stop." But she didn't stop, not for a long time. Rocking the swing with her feet, holding her empty coffee mug, she let the tears pour down her face. The wind washed over her like more tears. She cried until surely every epitaph engraved on her mind had weathered away to nothing. But when at last she stopped crying, there they still were, clear and legible as ever, shining with rain in the sunlight.

She went to the dock, knelt, and scooped up water to wash her face. As she rose and turned, she saw a big man in a flowered shirt and baggy shorts picking his barefoot way over the seawall. He raised a hand in greeting.

"Recovered from your little dunk the other night?"

She smiled and spread her arms: there she was, whole and undrowned.

"Those dudes up?" He nodded at her house.

"They weren't when I came down here." Self-conscious now, Amelia smoothed down her hair and put on her social smile. "You all had a late night."

"Yep." As he stepped onto her dock, he put out a hand. "Rex. Down the way."

"I thought that was who you were. Did you catch a lot?"

"Some. More whites than specks. I got all those fish iced down in my big cooler over there. Y'all need to come take your share."

"I'll tell them," said Amelia, imagining herself at the deep fryer. They would have to buy a deep fryer, just to cook all those fish. It was not the kind of thing they did, but perhaps they were going to start.

"Dudes left their rods, too. Y'all staying through the weekend?"

"I'm not sure," Amelia said. "Our plans are kind of unsettled. But we're flexible."

Good Lord, where had that come from? They were not flexible. But why not, she thought in sudden solidarity with the others. If they were having a good time, why not stay longer? It was their house. It was their time. Why not?

"I'll remind them about the rods," she told Rex-down-the-way, "and the fish. Thanks for having them over. My little girl had a good time, too."

He grunted. "Bet she's a handful sometimes." Hastily he added, "I mean that in a good way. I like to see 'em with some sass."

"She's got that," Amelia said. "She trots it out to see what her daddy will do about it."

"Heh. Yeah." He looked at her. She wondered whether he wondered which of the men was the little girl's daddy, which one she was trotting it out for. Or whether he cared, one way or another. Or, she thought belatedly, whether she ought to worry about a man who liked to see 'em with some sass.

"Well, thanks for everything," she said to Rex. "I'll tell the guys."

Upstairs, she found them awake, at the kitchen island, hanging glumly over their cereal.

"Coffee's weak," said Michael with his mouth full. Kurt didn't contradict him.

Automatically Amelia said, "Sorry."

"Mal's in the shower. I told her to get packed. I'm leaving out of here in half an hour."

"What's the hurry?" Amelia said, startled.

"Just gotta get back."

"I'm packed, too," Kurt said. "Did you want to stop at the real-estate office on the way out?"

"Well, eventually," said Amelia, flustered. "There are some things I need to do before I'm ready to leave. Are you in that much of a hurry?"

"Well, I had a client text me a few minutes ago. He's having issues with his system, and there's not much I can do about it from here. I told him if he could hang on until tonight, I'd have the bugs worked out by morning. So I'd like to get going, sooner rather than later."

"I see." Amelia looked about her. There was the vacuuming still to be done, the bathroom to clean, the load of sheets and towels to wash. Maids would come eventually from the rental office, but she had wanted to finish things herself. Leave No Trace.

"Huh." Michael was watching her over his cereal. "She's got something on her mind, I can tell."

Kurt smiled a little wanly. "She always does."

Mallory came out of the bathroom, her hair hanging in wet waves over her face and ears. Whether she still had the earrings in, or whether she had repented of piercing them, Amelia couldn't tell and wouldn't ask, just then.

"Aren't you done eating?" said Mallory. "I want to get on the road."

"Michaela can just hold her little horses."

"*McKenna*, Dad. You know McKenna."

"Whatever. They all look the same to me, your little herd. They all have the same kind of name. How am I supposed to tell them apart?"

"But I can sleep over, right? If we get back in time?"

"Maybe."

"Because—"

"I said, Maybe. End of discussion." Michael ate another spoonful of cereal.

Kurt pushed back his stool and took his bowl to the sink. Then he turned to Michael. "Look," he said, "do you think you might have room for me to ride back with you?"

Michael raised his eyebrows and looked at Amelia. She raised her eyebrows at Kurt.

"I can tell Amelia has things she wants to do." He smiled at her, still a little wanly, though maybe he felt relieved, and happy to be relieved, of the imperative to help her do the things. Well, he had done a lot, more than she had asked or expected. Let him go, she thought. She would be all right.

Michael seemed to meditate a moment. Then he shrugged. "Yeah, sure. Why not? Mallory doesn't mind the back seat."

"Yes, I do," said Mallory, but nobody paid any attention.

Fifteen minutes later the car was packed, and Amelia stood in the driveway telling them all goodbye.

"I'll see you next Saturday," she said to Mallory, kissing the part in her hair, proffered to her. To Michael, a little awkwardly, she said, "I'll be talking to you."

With Kurt, too, she was awkward. Maybe it was just that they were all standing there together: herself, her current husband, her ex-husband, her child by that ex-husband. If they went on with each other for the rest of their lives—and why wouldn't they?—still the strangeness would persist, always, in currents of feeling that passed among them un-named. Psychologist Amelia, surveying the four of them as a case study in family dynamics, might have sought to name those currents. She might have said that in naming things, the mind found its health. But Person Amelia, standing in the driveway, a subject of nobody's study, thought it better, for now anyway, to leave the unspoken unspoken. Saying he'd call her later, Kurt kissed her chastely on the corner of her mouth. In the oleander, the mockingbird was singing again in raptures of longing. Michael touched Amelia's arm and got into the car.

It wasn't until they had driven away, and she had gone back upstairs again, that Amelia remembered that she had no phone. Nobody would be calling her. She would be calling nobody. "Well, crap," she said to the silent living room. Then she smiled.

The sun was up now, filling the high-ceilinged room, charging the freshly painted walls with a light all their own. Outside, the Sound was an endless ripple of light beneath the sky. In the oleander, the mockingbird paused to listen. Somewhere down the way, hidden in some other oleander, perhaps, another mockingbird was answering him. From the door she could see Rex, distant on his own dock, cleaning fish and tossing the guts to the frantic gulls. Pelicans rode the brown-green water at the foot of the dock, waiting for what he threw down to them.

She had forgotten about the rods. The dudes had not been told to get them, or their fish. Well, later she would go herself. She could put the rods away in the empty storage closet under the house. Eventually somebody would use them, or throw them out. If Rex wanted to keep all the fish, he could keep them. If he didn't, she would bring some back in ice, do *something* with them, she thought. It didn't much matter what. She would do what she wanted when she wanted, when she discovered what it was she wanted to do. Back and forth the two mockingbirds sang, call and response, desire answering desire. For a long time, at the open door, Amelia stood listening.

ACKNOWLEDGMENTS

Grateful acknowledgment is due the following journals, in whose pages these stories originally appeared:

The Agonist: "The Cool of the Evening," "Doing Without" (as "Mindfulness")

Dappled Things: "A Fire in the Hills," "In the Dark," "Not Less Than Everything"

Kindred: "The Beach House"

Relief Journal: "A Noise Like a Freight Train," "The Blackbird"

"The Cool of the Evening" appeared in 2022 as a limited-edition chapbook from Belle Point Press.

"The Blackbird" received the 2022 Editors' Choice Award in Fiction from *Relief: A Journal of Art and Faith.*

"A Fire in the Hills" received the 2020 J. F. Powers Award for Short Fiction from *Dappled Things* magazine.

"A Noise Like a Freight Train" received the 2017 Editors' Choice Award in Fiction from *Relief: A Journal of Art and Faith.*

My heartfelt thanks to Katy Carl, Mary Finnegan, and Janille Stephens for their editorial wisdom, and to Joshua Hren of Wiseblood Books, for making a home for these stories.

ABOUT THE AUTHOR

Sally Thomas's poetry, fiction, essays, and reviews have appeared over the last thirty years in such magazines as *The New Yorker*, *The New Republic*, *First Things*, *Plough Quarterly*, and *Public Discourse*, as well as many literary magazines. Thomas is the author of two poetry collections, *Motherland* (Able Muse Press 2020) and *Among the Living* (Able Muse Press 2024), and a novel, *Works of Mercy* (Wiseblood Books 2022). She is co-editor of the anthology *Christian Poetry in America Since 1940*, which received the 2023 *Christianity Today* Book Award in Culture and the Arts. Her fiction has received the J.F. Powers Prize from *Dappled Things* and two Editors' Choice awards from *Relief: A Journal of Art and Faith*. From 2022-2024 she served as associate poetry editor for the *New York Sun*; currently she is a regular contributor to the Substack newsletter *Poems Ancient and Modern*.

Printed in the USA
CPSIA information can be obtained
at www.ICGtesting.com
LVHW011223160824
788395LV00014B/293